Fina

John Palliser was born and educated in York. He read Modern Languages at Worcester College, Oxford, in the early 1960s. He then taught languages for eleven years in England, France and Germany. In the mid-1970s he qualified as an accountant and for most of his career worked in sports management, travelling extensively in Europe. Through his professional activities he acquired experience in buying, registering and operating business jet aircraft.

He has had a passion for all aspects of aeronautics since his teens. His entry into the world of business aviation at the end of his career finally gave him the job satisfaction which he was seeking. Without having ever become a professional pilot, he has nonetheless built a solid total of hours as a private pilot both in France and in the USA where he has obtained an FAA instrument rating. After having worked for many years in Monaco, he has now retired to Aigues-Mortes in the south of France. "Final Final" is his first published work.

Final Final

John Palliser

Goldenford Publishers Ltd
Guildford
www.goldenford.co.uk

First published in Great Britain in 2014 by
Goldenford Publishers Limited
The Old Post Office
130 Epsom Road Guildford
Surrey GU1 2PX
Tel: 01483 563307
Fax: 01483 829074
www.goldenford.co.uk

Cover design by Irene Black from photographs by the author

Printed and bound by CPI Antony Rowe, Eastbourne

ISBN-978-0-9559415-7-3

For Rosemarie
who has always encouraged me to fly in spite of the cost and
who has so often had to wait for me on the ground whilst I have
been up aloft.

CONTENTS

Prologue   ix

FICTION

The Sausage Shoot   3

Tin Goose down   19

The Comet which almost eliminated Hitler   27

To the bitter End   59

To die for the Emperor   69

Beyond the Pale   75

The fiery Tail of the Komet   84

Miles ahead   93

KIA, Vietnam, 15th May 1972   114

The Iceman cometh   122

A Type too many   131

Goodbye, Pop Buehle   149

NON-FICTION

The Orteig Trophy and the Oiseau Blanc   167

Amy, wonderful Amy   174

A Salute to Saint-Ex   179

The Tuskegee Airmen   184

The short Life of BSAA and its Avro Airliners   190

The Fall of the Flying Dutchman   201

The Mystery of the exploding Comets   207

George, were you denied twice?   216

Alas poor Yuri, too soon you fell   222

A French Nine Eleven   227

Scotty, you should have stayed on the ground
Steve, you should have been more careful   233

Errare humanum est   238

Epilogue – When it is time to go…   257

PROLOGUE

Setting up my turn to Final

According to the 'experts', Man has inhabited this planet of ours for no time at all. In their view, if the life of planet Earth is compressed within a 24-hour period, Man would only appear on the scene after 23 hours and 59 minutes. So, we are completely insignificant, which is also true when we are measured against the infinity of the Universe. However, we are articulate and capable of recording thought. My belief is that every human has a tale to tell but that probably at least 99.9% of mankind never had the opportunity or the talent or the wish to do so.

Man first "slipped the surly bonds of Earth" and defied gravity in 1786 when two French noblemen were launched on a platform at the base of a hot air balloon. This would have put Man within one second of midnight in the 24-hour period. Being transported by balloon caught on but the early aviators' progress was at the mercy of the prevailing winds and it was not until the beginning of the 20th Century, more than a hundred years later, that Man first had a say in where he wished to be transported by air, and initially that 'say' was extremely limited.

The Wright Brothers are credited with the first flight in a heavier-than-air machine (in other words, an aeroplane, airplane, plane, or aircraft, call it as you will) in December 1903. Flying has come a long way since then in just over 100 years. Pilots have come and gone. Flying heroes and heroines have come and gone. Passengers have come and gone. And yet those who have piloted the skies and those who have been carried aloft are still relatively few. Probably only about 5% of the total population of the Earth today has been able to defy gravity and look down upon the planet from a privileged position.

As a low-time pilot I have always enjoyed being able to exercise my privileges. I am able to do what most of my fellow humans have never been able to do. It has cost time, effort and money but it has been well worth it. I have seen the Earth below me and the skies around me as few have seen them and I am awed by the majesty of what I have seen. For most airline passengers today, flying is a huge bore. Airport departures and arrivals are no pleasure at all. I heartily concur with that. If one doesn't have an adjacent window and the weather does not cooperate, there is nothing to be seen. However, those with the window seats and having clear weather conditions usually do not bother to look outside and they miss the magic. How many have seen other airliners flying above or below them? How many have seen the shadow of the condensation trails on the clouds below? How many have seen the rainbow-coloured halo around the aircraft's shadow projected on the clouds below? How many have enjoyed the sheer beauty of crossing a mountain range or over-flying a well-known city? These gratuitous pleasures are there for the taking –and they are so often ignored.

We are all mortal. We have precious little time from birth to death. We should all endeavour to pass something on. We do not have to be a Homer, a Beethoven or an Einstein to do this. I have written and gathered together here some twenty-four stories, half being works of fiction and half dealing with real happenings. In each story a pilot or pilots or passengers meet their deaths in an aviation accident. This is my contribution. If it appeals to more than one person, my work has not been in vain.

FICTION

THE SAUSAGE SHOOT

The four S.E.5s crossed the enemy lines at 4,000 feet. The target was about a mile ahead. Shells from the German anti-aircraft guns were bursting around them. Timothy Forbes-Taylor was keeping a careful eye on the Major's plane off to his left. When the Major signalled that he was ready to commence his attack on the observation balloon, Tim would ease behind his plane ready to start his own run on the target. The adrenalin was flowing and he was determined to show that he could do his bit in the war against the Hun.

It was less than four months since Tim had left school with the prospect of a brilliant academic career before him.

One day in late June young Phipps, his fag, had poked his head around Tim's study door and had announced that the Headmaster wanted to see him. Tim went and knocked at the Head's door. It opened and Dr Knox appeared.

'Ah, Forbes-Taylor,' he said, 'come in and sit down. I have good news for you. You have been awarded a scholarship to Balliol. Hearty congratulations! You deserve it. Let us hope that this stupid war will soon be over and that you will be able to start your academic studies there. In the meantime you are going to serve your country. I believe that you have volunteered for the Royal Flying Corps. Is that correct?'

Tim acknowledged that this was so. He had chosen the R.F.C. because he did not want to be involved in trench warfare. His elder brother, George, had preceded him by two years and had gone into the Army only to be killed in a major offensive on the Somme one year previously. Tim was the only remaining son. His parents were Norfolk gentry who were an important element in the area. Tim knew that he was expected to carry on the tradition. His mother was French by birth and she had opened his mind to languages. Because of his mother, he had always been bilingual and through family contacts he had soon started to pick up German which was now rather a taboo matter as the Hun was the enemy. His only sister, Angela (in truth Angèle) adored him and they were very close.

Tim was not just an excellent all-round student but also a superb sportsman. However, there was something missing. He was not a 'team person'. Although he was a Prefect at his prestigious private school, he was not Head of School, nor even Head of House. Apparently he did not have the 'drive' to lead others, which was considered to be all important.

At school he had hated any sports which involved contact, and any form of suffering. He had opted out of rugby football and boxing but had won his colours in rowing and swimming where he could beat anybody. He also had won his colours in cricket, and was a superb fast bowler. He could demolish the batsmen of any other team but he could not rally a team around him. In short, he was the 'gentle giant'. Tim had grown to six feet two inches and had filled out because of his rowing and swimming.

Nobody at his school would have dared to challenge him to a show of strength because he could easily beat anyone but this was not his way. He had come through the 'school system' since prep school days and in the past had been abused and bullied along the way. Tim had particularly suffered in his early years at this school when he had been a fag to senior pupils. Now he was at the top, he did not abuse or bully anybody. Young Phipps had had the easiest life of any fag. He worshipped Tim.

At school he had already seen enough memorial services for Old Boys killed in action and he and his father had not yet got over the loss of George, the natural leader. He would miss his school life badly but time had moved on and he had to move on with it.

Tim's initial training was not the hellish experience that it was for many others. He had been in the school Officer Training

Corps and was used to being barked at. When it came to initial flight training he was outstanding. He had natural coordination. He quickly mastered the Avro 504 and was earmarked for advanced training as a scout pilot. He trained on the Sopwith Pup and soon became used to the idiosyncrasies of the rotary engine. One of his instructors who had seen combat on the Western Front had drilled it in to him. *The one which will get you is the one on your tail. Keep watching behind you. Keep your tail clear and you will survive.*

Now his training was over. He had mastered the vicious Sopwith Camel and he expected to go to war in that. He had a final week of leave at home.

'Tim, avenge George's death and kill as many Huns as you can,' his father had said.

His mother was in tears as he left. 'Just come home alive and healthy,' she added.

Angela broke down and said she would pray for him.

Everything happened so quickly that Tim could hardly follow the sequence. After his leave he was shipped to Calais and on to St-Omer where he was put in a "pilots' pool" ready to be sent to a front line squadron when ordered. After a few days of kicking his heels, he was put on a Crossley tender and was sent off to a combat unit 'somewhere near the front lines'. He had no idea where he was going. He had all his worldly goods with him, which did not amount to much, and he had just 40 hours of flight time in his log book.

In the middle of a fine early October afternoon he was dropped off by a large grass field. Where was he? The driver certainly knew where he was as he drew up beside a large canvas tent and after tooting his horn he was greeted by an R.F.C. officer who had to sign off for the receipt of a replacement pilot. Tim stepped to the ground and was greeted by the Adjutant who had signed for him.

'Lieutenant Forbes-Taylor, welcome to the Squadron. Let me show you to your quarters and then we can talk more freely.'

Tim followed the Adjutant into the big tent and they passed through the other side of it and made for a collection of smaller tents beyond it. They entered one and the Adj motioned to a bed.

'This will be yours. The previous occupant copped it yesterday. We have removed all his possessions. Make yourself at home. You share with Lieutenant Curtis. I shall come back in ten minutes.'

Tim sat down and started unpacking his kit. He could hear the occasional sound of aircraft engines being tested. He could also hear a distant rumbling noise like thunder which must have been the firing of big guns at the front.

True to his word the Adj was back in ten minutes.

'Now I shall take you to meet the Major and after that the other pilots,' he said.

Major Ferris was as small as Tim was tall but it was clear from the outset that he was a leader of men.

'So, Forbes-Taylor, your records show forty hours and you have even flown a Camel a couple of times and survived the experience. None of the latter will be of any use to you here. You will be flying the S.E.5. If you fly it properly you will be able to out-perform anything the Hun has. You will be in my flight. I shall introduce you to flying the S.E.5 at ten tomorrow morning. Meet me at my office. When you have unpacked, go out to the flight line and get a mechanic to show you one of our machines and become familiar with it. After that, meet your fellow pilots and get to know them. Dinner is at 7 p.m.'

That was it.

Tim went down to the flight line and got a mechanic to show him over one of the planes. He sat in the cockpit and had everything pointed out to him. He told the mechanic that he had only flown behind rotary engines for the last few hours.

'You will prefer this one with its Hispano engine, Sir. You won't have castor oil being flung over you all the time. The engine controls are much simpler. The only weak spot is the radiator. Get any damage to that and the engine will over-heat and seize up.'

Tim then wandered back and entered the second big tent next to the one he had already visited and which was clearly used for administration, briefings and the like. This second tent was the mess tent. One part was the dining area and the other part was a lounge with a bar in one corner. He entered and introduced himself. Those present got up and came over to meet him. There was a mixture of accents. Some were upper class like his but there were some which betrayed a more humble background and there were some which were clearly Empire ones.

Curtis's accent belonged to this last category. He was Australian.

'Blimey,' he said, 'you're a big fella and no mistake. What did you say your name was? Tim? Well you will be known to me as Tiny Tim. Just call me Dingo. That's what the others do.'

They all seemed to be friendly enough.

Before Grace was said at dinner, the Major reminded everybody that they would be stood down the next day except for the flight which would be at readiness with their planes in case any Hun pilots decided to sneak over and attack their airfield. As there was to be no dawn patrol the next day, most pilots let their hair down after dinner at the bar. The drink flowed and there was boisterous singing. Tim stood out because he did not drink anything alcoholic and just sat quietly taking it all in.

The next morning he reported to the Major at the appointed time. Ferris had a map spread out on his desk.

'Now, Forbes-Taylor, let me point out the features of our sector. We are here, some ten miles behind our front lines. Note this village here. We fly over it on the way out and we use it as a marker on the way back. This road runs from the village right up to the lines. On the enemy side of the lines, this little wood here marks the north-east limit of our usual activities. Down here is a small lake which marks the south-east limit. So we fight within this area. Our chaps regularly send out reconnaissance flights at first light to see what the Hun is up to. When it is our turn, we go out as a squadron to provide top cover. Usually the Hun is up there in strength waiting for us and then the action starts. You need to get the geography of our sector firmly in your mind so take a few minutes to study the map.'

Ferris left him to it and came back ten minutes later to take Tim across to the flight line. They entered a tent which was filled with lockers. They all had names on them.

'Here's yours', the Major said. 'Get your name put on the door. Corporal! Get some suitable flying clothing for the Lieutenant.'

When Tim was dressed for flying, the Major led him to an S.E.5 at the end of the line.

'This one is yours. Clamber in and make yourself comfortable'.

Ferris scrambled up beside him and made sure that Tim knew the cockpit layout. Tim, being meticulous, had got it all off pat.

'Now this morning, all you have to do is to fly off my starboard wing and follow me all the time. You lift off the ground when I lift off. You will note my rates of climb and descent. You will note the best approach and landing speeds. We shall cross the lines at 5,000 feet. Archie will be shooting at us but he is pretty ineffective at our height. We shall fly around our sector area. If I spot any Hun fighters I shall turn round immediately and we head for our lines fast. You do not want to get into a scrap on your first flight in a plane which is new to you.'

The major paused for a moment and then continued. 'Back on our side of the lines, when I waggle my wings and pull away from you I shall try to get on your tail. Do everything you can to stop me getting there. The S.E.5 is a great bus. It is less manoeuvrable than most of the Hun fighters but it is faster and stronger. Do not be afraid to throw it about. Keep the speed up in a combat situation and you can better most of the Hun pilots who will try to slow you down to their best manoeuvring speeds. Once I have got on your tail I shall then pull alongside and lead you home. That's it. Any questions?'

Tim had none as he was trying to digest everything.

A little later they were airborne and heading for the lines. Tim was managing to keep station quite well. When they reached the lines, he looked left and right in amazement. Stretching away to each horizon was an uneven line like a festering open wound. Then came a small strip of no-man's land which was completely devoid of any vegetation. Beyond it was the German front line. Running back from the front lines, the various communication trenches were clearly visible. The whole area well back from the front lines was a mass of craters and there was not a sign of human habitation in sight. Tim knew that this ugly open wound ran all the way from the coast of the North Sea in Belgium to the Swiss border. The war had been frozen by these front lines for three years. Massive military onslaughts which had cost the lives of thousands upon thousands of young men had gained at the most a few hundred yards. Down there men were living in appalling conditions under constant fire and those who were not killed were lucky if physical or mental ailments did not finish them off.

Tim kept an eye on the Major's plane whilst he mused on all this senseless carnage. What was that poem he had read recently? "The Leveller", that was it. How did it start?

Near Martinpuich that night of hell
Two men were struck by the same shell.

It went on to describe how the veteran of many campaigns died crying for his mother whereas the pale young recruit died cursing God. The real message was in the conclusion where in death all men are equal. How did it finish? The families of each man received the same letter.

He died a hero's death: and we
His comrades of 'A' Company
Deeply regret his death: we shall
All deeply miss so true a pal.

They were not troubled in the flight around their sector. Archie was indeed firing at them but the black shell-bursts never came near. Back over their own side of the lines, the Major waggled his wings and the duel was on. Tim tried all he knew to keep the Major in sight and not to let him get on his tail. He held him off for a couple of minutes but experience prevailed and the Major was finally sitting some fifty yards behind him. They then headed for home and landed.

'You did quite well, Forbes-Taylor.' He made a few more pertinent remarks and concluded by saying that Tim would fly off his wing and must try to stick to him like a leech when they went out on patrol. 'Stick close to me and you will learn a lot. In a dogfight if you go blundering off on your own, you will be an easy target until you have acquired some experience.'

The next morning, the reconnaissance R.E.8s, the Harry Tates of the unit which shared their field, would be out at first light looking to discover what units and equipment, if any, the enemy was bringing up behind its front lines. Tim's squadron would be flying top cover and there was bound to be a scrap. The Major had announced that they would be flying at 10,000 feet. Tim had never been up that high.

'Dress warmly, Tiny,' Dingo told him. 'It's bloody cold up there.'

All the pilots retired early. There was no carousing. Each man was wrapped up in his own thoughts. Tim found it difficult to sleep. He had too much on his mind.

Breakfast was at four the next morning. There was little in the way of conversation. Most men ate little and just drank coffee. There was a final briefing from the Major and then they all trudged across the field to their aircraft. It was still dark and very quiet. The pilots changed into their flying gear and their

10

mechanics, holding torches, made sure that each man was comfortably installed in his cockpit.

Then the noise of the R.E.8s starting up could be heard. They would be off first as they were much slower. With the first signs of light in the eastern sky, the R.E.8s began to take off. Then the signal was given for the S.E.5 pilots to start their engines. Tim's plane was parked next to the Major's so all he had to do was to follow him. Next to him on the other side were West and then Dingo. On the Major's signal, throttles were opened wide and 'A' flight began its take off roll. In the air, the squadron adopted a loose formation to minimise the risk of a collision. Tim kept a beady eye on the Major's plane.

They crossed the lines at 8,000 feet and still climbing. The ground below was becoming more and more visible. The bursts of Archie well below them indicated where the R.E.8s must be.

Two things kept running through Tim's mind like a mantra. He had been told that the average career of a scout pilot was about two weeks. Get through two weeks and the experience would come. The second thing was to make sure that no enemy aircraft got on his tail. He would not have the experience to shake it off.

Now the Major was waggling his wings. He had spotted enemy aircraft. Tim peered ahead into the growing light. He could see nothing. He just did not know where or how to look properly. The seconds ticked by. Suddenly the Major started to dive and the squadron followed. Tim could hear the crackle of machine gun fire above all the noise which his plane was generating. The Major was banking. Tim followed and now the sky seemed to be filled with planes in all sorts of attitudes and all sorts of angles. He lost sight of the Major. He kept stepping on his rudder and twisting his head round to make sure nobody was on his tail. Who was friend and who was foe in this scrap? He just could not tell. And suddenly he was alone. Where had they all gone? He could see one plane going down in flames. They had lost a lot of height in the short scrap. He banked round

11

and looked for other S.E.5s. He could see some planes ahead and they had to be from his squadron. He caught up with them and breathed a sigh of relief but he kept looking behind to make sure his tail was clear. The R.E.8s had also turned back and the S.E.5s were shepherding them home. The Huns had just run for it.

After landing, Tim found he was shaking and not because of the cold. He just could not stop the shivers.

His mechanic appeared beside him. 'Any luck, Sir?'

Tim shook his head but did not move. 'Just leave me be for a couple of minutes and I shall be alright.'

He could see the Major coming round to his cockpit. He had to move. Clumsily he got out.

'Well, Forbes-Taylor, what went wrong?'

'Sorry, Sir, I just lost you. It was all so sudden,' Tim stammered.

Some of the pilots were talking excitedly and using their hands to illustrate how they had flown. Some, like Tim, were silent and looked completely drained. At the de-briefing it was established that they had shot down five enemy planes and lost one of their own. O'Brien had gone down. He was a Canadian. Tim could scarcely remember what he looked like. The man had come all those thousands of miles to fight for the mother country and he would never return home.

There would be no early mission the next day, they were told. Unless the Hun fliers came looking for trouble, which they rarely did, they could all relax for twenty-four hours. Some of the younger pilots huddled together and started to discuss something which obviously pleased them greatly.

Dingo came over to Tim and said, 'Tiny, there will be a trip to the local whore-house after dinner tonight. The boys all know that you speak perfect French and that you don't drink. They want you to come along to keep Madame sweet, to settle the bill and to make sure that we all get back here in one piece.'

Tim did not like the idea but he had no reason to make

himself snooty and unpopular so he joined the group of ten who were driven to the brothel in St-André.

He was introduced to Madame, or rather he was pushed forward and had to introduce himself. His comrades disappeared with the girls of their choice and it was clear that they were fairly frequent clients. Madame was intrigued by Tim who spoke her language as well as any cultivated Frenchman and who remained perfectly in control of himself. She told Tim that they would have to fill the evening somehow so she brought out a bottle of vintage Burgundy. They sipped and talked. Madame could have been his mother. She was cultivated and gracious. Tim opened up to her. He told her he had been as scared as hell going into enemy territory.

Madame put a matronly arm around his broad shoulders. 'They are all as scared as hell,' she said. 'They just try to hide it in different ways like those here tonight. Everybody has a breaking point. During the day, I help out at the local hospital. I see our young boys who have survived the trenches but who will never be normal again. There are those who have lost limbs but the worst are those who have lost their minds. They have been pushed over the edge. Only the mentally tough survive. Don't ask me what their secret is. They probably do not know it themselves. You are intelligent. You will find a way, I am sure.'

The next thing he knew, Tim was making love to her. Both of them found a moment of absolute peace and tranquillity. Much later the party broke up. Tim had to calm down his charges who had drunk far too much, settle the bill and make sure that they all got back to base safely. For once he had been a leader of men, even if most of them were hardly aware of what was going on.

'I shall be back,' he had told Madame.

Her eyes were shining. 'Make it soon,' she said.

The next day most of the boys were not fit for anything. Not so in Tim's case. He went to see the Major. 'Sir, if there are no operations today, I should like to go up and fly in mock combat against one of the pilots in the flight on stand-by. Is that OK with you?'

'No, Forbes-Taylor, it is not OK with me. You will pit your skills against mine instead.'

On the way across the field Ferris gave Tim some good tips. They reached the flight line and changed into their flying gear.

'Now, said Ferris, 'this is what we are going to do. We climb up to 5,000 feet in line-abreast. We then turn out in opposite directions for one minute, then we reverse course and go for a head-on pass. You will aim off to keep me on your port side and I shall do the same. Once we have passed each other, we each try to outwit the other. Contest is over when one of us is on the tail of the other. We run the exercise three times and then return to land.'

On the first run, the Major was on Tim's tail in five minutes. On the second run, it took the Major eight minutes to get there. On the third run, after fifteen minutes, neither was in a winning position. The Major rocked his wings. It was time to land.

'Good show, Forbes-Taylor,' Ferris told Tim after they had shut down. 'I don't think I have to worry about you anymore.'

The next day the Squadron was up and crossing the lines again shortly after dawn. This time they were not escorting reconnaissance planes, they were trailing their coats, hoping to entice the Huns to come up and fight. Sure enough the Huns rose to the bait and a huge dogfight was engaged. This time Tim was not paranoid about any Hun on his tail. He stuck close to the Major. Twice he had targets and twice he opened fire. One of his targets had certainly taken hits and was emitting smoke but he would only be able to claim it as damaged. He had to keep his wits about him every second.

Suddenly, as on the previous occasion, the enemy just disappeared and the planes in his Squadron formed up and returned to base.

After landing Tim was shaking again but this time it was with jubilation. He had conquered his fear.

'Any luck, Sir?' his mechanic asked.

'Damaged one but he might have got back to his base,' Tim replied. The Squadron had done well: four definites and three possibles. They had not had any losses.

'Good show, chaps,' the Major had said. 'Now get yourselves some rest.

They had been at rest for about ninety minutes when they were all summoned to the admin tent.

The Major looked serious. 'Now listen, chaps. Regional HQ has told me that the Huns have sent up an observation balloon behind their lines to spot for their artillery. This isn't the first time we have had this and it won't be the last. However, there are reports of other balloons in adjacent sectors. It looks as if the Hun is training his fire today on the communications trenches leading to our front line. If they are doing this, it is to cut off our front line from our reserves. In short it would appear that the enemy is about to mount a major offensive. We have got to take out that bloody German sausage immediately. Other squadrons in the sectors near ours have the same orders. My plan is simple. I shall take my flight across the lines at 4,000 feet. That is the estimated height of the sausage. There is apparently a patrol of Hun scouts circling overhead at about 6,000 feet. Captain Ripley will lead the rest of the Squadron and will make sure that the Hun scouts do not interfere with my flight. Take off in thirty minutes. Captain Ripley, brief your men. I shall brief my flight. Any questions?'

There was a buzz of conversation about the room. Ripley gathered his boys together. Ferris spoke to his three. 'This is how we play it. We approach at the balloon's height. As soon as we are spotted, they will start to winch the balloon down. The observer will probably jump out. Apparently they all have parachutes. If the balloon gets down to 3,000 feet before we can attack, we can expect murderous fire from the ground. These balloon sites are very well protected but only up to about 3,000. If we have to go in lower, we do it. We just have to destroy that bloody sausage. We approach in line-astern. Try to keep about

15

200 yards behind each other. The order behind me is Forbes-Taylor, West and Curtis. When I break off, Forbes-Taylor will be in position to fire. When he breaks off, West will be ready. Even if they manage to haul the balloon to the ground, we have to destroy it. They cannot replace them very quickly. Now off we go.'

The Squadron was off the ground in record time. Tim had been with the unit less than a week and this was to be the fourth time he had crossed the lines. He was really geared up for this one. The adrenalin was flowing. It was the same feeling he had had before his sculling and swimming races at school. His head was clear. He knew exactly what he had to do.

They crossed the lines going flat out but the rest of the Squadron had taken off slightly before them to be able to deal with the enemy scouts circling above when the Major's flight arrived. Archie was doing his best to put them off and a few shells were busting quite close but they were not to be deterred.

Then they saw the sausage ahead of them. It was already lower than their altitude and was being hauled in. They saw the observer's parachute open after he had jumped out of his basket. Ferris waggled his wings and went into a shallow dive.

Tim could see the smoke coming from his guns. 'This one's for you, George,' Tim roared and as Ferris pulled away, he dived down and as the distance closed, he opened fire. He was hitting the sausage, there was no doubt about that. He could hear and feel ordnance smacking into his plane but he never flinched.

Suddenly the balloon burst into flames. Tim flew straight into the inferno, firing to the last.

Back at the field, West landed and parked next to the Major's plane. 'Sorry, Sir, but Forbes-Taylor copped it. He blew the balloon apart and was caught up in the inferno. At least it caused a lot of damage on the ground below.'

In his office, Ferris summoned the Adjutant.

'Sorry to hear about young Mr Forbes-Taylor, Sir. He was a

very gifted man,' said the Adj.

'For Christ's sake, Adj, do you think I don't know that,' the Major barked back – and then he calmed down. 'Sorry, Adj, I feel responsible. I have seen too many fine young men come and go.' There were tears in his eyes.

From a cupboard he pulled out a bottle of whisky and two glasses and poured a large slug into each glass. He pushed one glass towards the Adjutant.

'Here,' he said. 'It does help for a short time. We are losing our finest young men in this bloody awful war. It is the same for the French and it is the same for the Huns. When it is all over, our leaders will find they have no brilliant minds to replace theirs because they have all been killed for no good reason. That boy Forbes-Taylor would have been a real asset if he had survived it all but fate decided otherwise. Several more like him will come and most will die before they reach the age of twenty. What a bloody waste.'

A few more tears followed which Ferris quickly brushed away and then he pulled himself together. 'Now Adj, please draft a report for me to sign, in which I put forward Forbes-Taylor for a posthumous gallantry medal. You know the sort of words which are needed. Also please draft a nice letter to his parents for me to sign. They have lost both of their sons and life for them will never be the same.'

Ferris raised his glass. 'Cheerio, Adj, you're a good sort.' And with that the Major drained his glass in one gulp.

In a small tent, Dingo Curtis was sitting on his bed in despair. He stared at the empty bed next to his and he knew that he would be asked to pack up Tiny Tim's personal belongings. He had lost two 'room mates' in a week. How long would it be before his turn came round?

TAILPIECE

Robert Graves's magnificent poem was written in 1916 but I do not think that it would have been published in time for Tim to have read it. Graves served in the Trenches so he knew exactly what he was writing about. He was very severely injured in 1916 by enemy fire and was not expected to live. He finally died at the end of 1985 at the ripe old age of 90!

TIN GOOSE DOWN

Joe Lopez scratched his chin as he peered forward and shook his head. He did not like what he saw one little bit. The sky ahead was becoming darker, the cloud base was lowering and it looked particularly menacing. At the last stop on the line at Winslow he had been appraised that Albuquerque, the next stop, was in the clear and that thunderstorm activity had passed through, headed west.

As captain of the plane on a new, prestigious route, Joe's brief was to get the passengers to Clovis safely with the minimum of delay. If he thought conditions were bad enough to prevent continuing, he could stay on the ground, or, if in the air, turn back. The Company was risking its reputation on this new coast-to-coast service: Los Angeles to New York in 48 hours, thus taking one day less than the rail service. A lot of money was tied up in this venture and it just had to succeed. Therefore the pressure was on Joe to carry on regardless. If his passengers failed to meet the overnight rail connection at Clovis, he would be under investigation and if he did not have a good excuse he might be out of a job.

The flight had departed from Grand Central Air Terminal in Glendale shortly before 9 a.m. that morning. Five of the eleven passenger seats were occupied and the mail bags had been loaded aboard. Jake, the cabin attendant, in his immaculate uniform, had welcomed the passengers as they entered the cabin.

Joe sat up front with Ray Evans, a young co-pilot, with whom he had not flown before. It was late August 1929. Transcontinental Air Transport's coast-to-coast service was less than two months old. It was Joe's task to get his passengers to Clovis by 7 p.m. local time so that they could have dinner and then board the Santa Fe Railroad's overnight train to Wichita. The following day another company aircraft would fly the passengers to Columbus, Ohio, and from there the trip would end with another journey by rail to New York City. Joe and his crew would overnight in Clovis to pick up the passengers coming the other way from New York and deliver them to the Los Angeles area.

Joe had been flying for more than ten years. His parents, who spoke better Spanish than English, had established a successful fruit-growing business in California. Joe had been christened José. His elder brother was Ricardo, now just known as Rick, and it was the elder brother who would inherit and continue the family business.

Joe was born just before the turn of the century. When he had seen some of the first aircraft to fly in California, he knew that he had to become a pilot. His opportunity had come in 1917 when the United States entered the Great War. Joe persuaded his parents to let him enlist in the Army Air Service. He had been sent to Texas to learn to fly. He had natural aptitudes and was singled out for advanced training on single-seat scout aircraft. With his training completed, he was sent to New York where he embarked on an overloaded troop ship bound for France.

He would never forget the arrival at Le Havre. The date was November 11, 1918. When the ship docked, they were all told that the war was over. Joe was sent to a pilots' pool from which he would have been sent to an active unit if the war had continued. The military machine could not be stopped overnight. Personnel who had been on active duty were repatriated home first. Joe managed to scrounge a few flights in a SPAD XVII which he had hoped to fly in combat, but that was all. Then he was shipped back to New York, put on a train to his last base in Texas and there he was discharged. What was left of the Air Service was only interested in keeping its seasoned pilots.

It had been difficult for Joe to find work as a pilot immediately after that. He had finally managed to secure a stable job with Earl Daugherty at Long Beach for a few years, instructing, giving pleasure flights, and taking part in air shows, and then he flew mail throughout the state of California. He learnt a lot from that. Flying an old and weary Liberty-engined de Havilland DH.4 with the mail sack in the cockpit in front of him, he had survived his share of engine failures and bad weather experiences. He could sense that he would not survive much longer in that environment and towards the end of 1927 he had managed to become one of the small but growing band of airline pilots.

Pilot certification in the States only began in that year so Joe received one of the first licences to be issued. Moving from the old and frail DH.4 to the all-metal Ford Trimotor with accommodation for up to twelve passengers had been a big step. Now, for the first time in his flying career, Joe was protected from the elements as he and his co-pilot (a novelty for him to have an extra pair of hands) sat in an enclosed cockpit. They had three engines for extra safety and this tough old bird could just about maintain altitude at low level on one engine. Flying the big Trimotor required plenty of brute strength. It was nice and stable when established in straight flight but it needed a Superman to get it to turn and it responded very slowly to control inputs.

Now, because of the paucity of licensed airline pilots and among those few, those who could cope with a multi-engined aircraft, Joe had become a captain with Transcontinental Air Transport just before the new coast-to-coast service had begun. Joe had heard that the services of Charles Lindbergh had been secured to establish new routes and in the middle of 1929 he had been summoned to the President's office to be introduced to the famous "Lone Eagle".

When Joe had entered President Keys' office, he had no idea why he had been called. In the office, standing next to Mr Keys

21

was a tall, slim gentleman who could not have been mistaken for anybody else, given all the media attention which he had received over the last two years.

'Captain Lopez, may I introduce you to Major Lindbergh, who, as you know, is assisting us with expanding our network. Major Lindbergh has planned some new routes for us and he would like to see at first-hand how our Trimotor will perform over those routes. He has no Trimotor experience and needs a capable pilot to assist him. This is where you come in.'

Joe flew with the Lone Eagle all the way from Glendale to Clovis and back. The two got on well together. Lindbergh was a man of few words but was quite friendly.

'Take the left seat, Major,' Joe had said.

The answer was, 'The left seat is yours. You are in command. By the way, just call me Slim – and may I call you Joe?'

They shared the flying. There was no question about Lindbergh's piloting skills but he was prepared to do all the menial tasks as well. After the trip, Lindbergh shook Joe's hand warmly and said that he hoped they would meet up again.

The inaugural east-bound flight with passengers was planned for July 8th, one day after the inaugural flight from the East Coast. It had been publicised by the company that Lindbergh would be captain on that flight. There was lots of media attention. Joe was informed that Slim had personally requested his presence in the cockpit, so Joe took part in the inaugural flight well away from all the publicity but he did not mind this one little bit. After the flight and before the Lone Eagle was whisked away for the official celebrations, he had shaken hands with Joe, thanked him for all his assistance and added that he would look him up the next time he was in the LA area.

Now the service had become routine for Joe. There were four legs to fly to get from Glendale to Clovis which worked out to about nine hours of flight time. The intermediate ground stops at Kingman, Winslow and Albuquerque were scheduled to last twenty minutes each. The route crossed the Rockies but was planned to follow railway tracks along valleys as far as possible. There were no aids to navigation available to the pilots so they had to try to remain in visual contact with the ground. On-board radio had not yet arrived so the pilots could expect no assistance from the ground. The cockpit of the Trimotor was noisy to say the least. The central engine was grinding away just in front of the pilots and the propellers of the two wing-mounted engines were in line with the pilots who were therefore assailed by noise from the front and on both sides. Ear plugs became standard issue for the pilots as well as for the passengers and the only way the pilots could communicate when the engines were running was by sign language or scribbled messages.

On the ground between flight legs whilst mail was being loaded or unloaded, whilst the plane was being serviced and whilst the passengers stretched their legs, slaked their thirst and used the toilets, Joe would get the latest weather and any other pertinent information from the next point of arrival and he would brief his co-pilot on what to expect. Joe made sure that whoever sat in the right seat got his share of the flying and the take-offs and landings and he also made sure that his co-pilot knew which features to identify on the ground as they flew along. 'Two pairs of eyes are better than one,' he would always say.

Joe frequently wondered why passengers would pay a lot of extra money just to get to New York in two days instead of three. The Trimotor was as noisy in the main cabin as in the cockpit. The smell of gasoline and hot oil was not good for queasy stomachs, the whole contraption rattled and vibrated and the usual turbulence over the mountains just added to the discomfort. Added to this, any passenger could only take 30 pounds in weight of personal baggage on board. Why should anybody want to put up with all these hardships when there was much more comfort to be had on a train? Who wanted to save just one day in any case? Joe had come to the conclusion that most of his passengers simply wanted the adventure. There were those who loved the flying. On the other hand, there were those who got off the aircraft at Clovis looking deathly pale and ill and who vowed never to go near a plane again.

On the ground, when taxiing, the Trimotor was an ungainly beast. Somebody had remarked that it looked like a goose waddling along and the airliner had come to be known as the Tin Goose. As for Transcontinental Air Transport, somebody who presumably had not enjoyed the experience had taken the initial letters of the Company and had branded the airline as "Take a Train". It was up to people like Joe to convince others that travelling by air was the way ahead.

After Joe had picked up the weather information at Winslow, he had taken Ray aside.

'I don't like the sound of the weather report from Albuquerque,' he said. 'There is an area of low pressure coming our way. It is hot and humid today and this will degrade our performance. Also I expect we will run into some pretty nasty stuff. The terrain ahead is rising and I expect the cloud base to be dropping. We have to stay in the clear so we know where we are. I shall fly this leg as I have more experience. Keep your eyes peeled so we stay away from any terrain on your side. If I think we can't get through we shall turn back as long as the clouds haven't closed in behind us. If that happens, I shall land somewhere where we can find a level piece of ground and sit it out. Above all we must stay out of the clouds. I am not just thinking of your neck and mine but we are responsible for our passengers. Any questions?'

Ray had none but he looked concerned.

They departed Winslow on time. A ground mechanic had wound up each of the three inertial starters in turn and Joe had managed to get each engine started, which was not always easy when they were hot. Thank goodness the co-pilot did not have to perform the winding of the inertial starters chore. He and his captain were perspiring freely in any case in spite of the opened side windows and their shirts were sticking to their backs.

They had only been airborne for a little more than half an hour when Joe spotted the nasty weather ahead. He nudged Ray and pointed forwards. By sign language he asked Ray to leave his seat and pass through the cabin to make sure that each passenger had his seat belt securely fastened. Jake was also advised to remain seated and not to serve any more coffee.

Flashes of lightning were now visible in the dark mass ahead. The plane was starting to bump its way through increasing turbulence. For Joe it now became a trial of strength trying to keep on track. Should he turn around and head back to Winslow? He kept deferring the decision, not wanting to be later accused of being chicken.

As they got closer to the dark mass ahead, Joe sensed that he could see a gradual lightening in the colour of the sky between the cloud mass and the ground. It offered some hope. There would be little altitude to spare between the base of the boiling cumulo-nimbus clouds and the ground below but it suggested a way out. Joe went for the gap.

They reached the point where the gap was at its narrowest and then the hailstones hit them. My God! They were the size of golf balls! Then a huge fist from above pressed them down towards the ground. Joe's mouth dropped open in disbelief. The altimeter was unwinding fast. He had added full power and was desperately trying to climb but they were still going down. The airspeed was right but the speed over the ground had shot up and they were also being pushed sideways towards the mountain slopes on the edge of the valley. They needed a miracle and didn't have one.

Joe opened his mouth again to scream but no sound came out. He had no time to think of Ray or anybody else. The plane slammed into the ground at high speed and a high rate of descent. It broke up immediately. The ensuing fireball consumed the eight people on board.

TAILPIECE

This story was built around real events.

TAT did operate the advertised 48 hours coast-to-coast service. Charles Lindbergh did fly the first eastbound service from LA to Clovis. TAT was shortly to become Transcontinental & Western and then a little later Trans World Airlines. For many years its aircraft carried the inscription "The Lindbergh Line". Clement Keys was the founder of the original airline.

Disaster struck the new service on September 3rd 1929 when the Trimotor from Albuquerque to Winslow, bringing passengers from the east, crashed on the slopes of Mount Taylor in bad weather. It took three days before the wreckage was found.

In spite of the inauspicious beginnings, this service prospered and by 1930 the overnight rail journey was replaced by a night flight, starting the first true coast-to-coast airline service.

What terminated the flight described above was an encounter with a microburst, an intense downdraft below a cumulo-nimbus cloud. Such downdrafts can exceed 6,000 feet per minute. Even today's airliners cannot out-climb such a downward push. At least two jetliners have been destroyed when encountering a microburst on a final approach. The Tin Goose never had a chance.

Earl S Daugherty is worthy of a mention. He is no figment of my imagination. He was one of the aeronautical pioneers in California who helped to promote aviation by setting up a flying school and giving pleasure flights. He was killed in 1928 when his aircraft disintegrated in flight. For several decades the Douglas Company built its airliners at Long Beach Airport. Not many people today know that this airport was originally named Daugherty Field and even fewer will know why it was so named. *Sic transit gloria mundi*. We should never forget our aviation heritage.

THE COMET WHICH ALMOST ELIMINATED HITLER

Flight Lieutenant Tony Bradshaw undid his seat harness and eased himself out of the cockpit. He stepped down onto the wing walkway and jumped to the ground. It was Monday 28th November 1938 and just after four o'clock in the afternoon. Tony had been at the Royal Aircraft Establishment at Farnborough for a little over one year. He had just turned 26 and had been in the Air Force since he had left school eight years previously. All he had ever wanted to do as far back as he could remember was to fly. His father, one of the wealthiest and most influential businessmen in the City, had wanted him to go through university first but he could see that his son's mind was set on flying and he did not stand in his way.

Tony had done exceptionally well since he had joined up. He went through flight training with his skills rated as exceptional. He was posted to fighters and he had been a member of one of the formation teams which had performed tied-together aerobatics at the Hendon displays. Popular and outgoing, he was also keenly interested in the how and the why of flying. He could very easily have had his own squadron by now but last year one of his superiors had remarked that with his skills and knowledge he would be a great asset as a Service test pilot. Tony knew that he would get no promotion with this posting but the nature of the job really appealed to him. He loved every day of test flying as he flew in all the types operated by the Air Force and he had to fly test profiles which were not in the book as the boffins were always trying out new ideas. His test reports were classics. Nobody could analyse test flights as he could. Twice he had had to bail out of a stricken aircraft but this did not shake his nerve at all – for him it was just part of the job.

27

As Tony turned to walk to his office he caught sight of his CO standing with a man in civilian clothing. Even from this distance, the man looked familiar and it was clear that the two men were waiting for him. As he got closer to them, he recognised the 'civvie' as being one of the most powerful members of the Cabinet. Politics was not a subject which greatly interested him but his Dad knew most of the prominent politicians and Tony had met this one at his parents' home on more than one occasion.

'Good flight, Tony?' asked his CO, but before Tony could answer, his boss went on. 'I didn't know that you had friends in such high places but His Lordship particularly wanted to see you before you go off duty. Leave writing your report until later. Now I shall let you have your talk. Good day, Sir.'

The CO shook hands with the Minister and set off for his office.

'Sir, would you like to come to my office?' Tony asked.

'No,' his guest replied, 'let's just walk along the pathway here. I don't want anyone to hear what I am about to tell you.'

Tony was mystified by this introduction but he fell into step with the Minister.

'Tony, in spite of all your flying, I think you have a pretty good idea about what is happening in Germany.'

'Yes, Sir. In spite of the Prime Minister telling us all at the end of September that he had won peace for our time, I am sure that we shall be at war with Germany before too long.'

'That will certainly come,' the Minister replied, 'but I am thinking about what is happening inside the country right now. Do you know about *Kristallnacht*?'

This had happened less than three weeks before. It was the night of the burning of the synagogues, the ransacking of Jewish shops and the internment of many Jewish males in special camps. Tony knew about this because although his father was not Jewish, his mother was. Tony's father had been introduced to Rachel in Berlin in 1910 and had fallen madly in love with

28

her. Rachel and her younger sister Sarah were the daughters of a prominent German industrialist. The sisters had always remained close and during his schooldays Tony had frequently visited Berlin with his parents. Sarah and her husband had also visited Tony's family in London on several occasions. Sarah and Rachel's father had seriously considered leaving Germany after the Nuremberg Laws had been enacted but his factories were a major asset for the Nazis and he and his family had been spared the humiliations which most Jews had had to suffer. Tony had spoken to his mother just a few days previously. She was very worried about what was happening. Her sister and her husband would surely not be treated as kindly as her parents were.

'Yes,' Tony replied, 'Mother has always made me aware of what it means to be Jewish and she has educated me well about what is happening to the Jews in Germany.'

'That will make my errand much easier,' said the Minister. 'You probably did not know that I am Jewish myself. I do not flaunt it openly but I care very much for my people. I am in touch with many prominent Jews around the world and we are all agreed on one thing. This madman Hitler has to be stopped. I am here with one specific request. We want you to eliminate Hitler.'

Tony stopped walking. He took a deep breath. He could hardly believe what he was hearing.

The Minister continued. 'I shall tell you briefly of a plan which my contacts have created. We wanted to put it into effect this summer but a suitable occasion never presented itself. Now it is clear after recent events that those Jews living in Germany who cannot get out will be eliminated. Drastic times call for drastic measures. We know that Hitler and some of his senior cronies will be in Kiel on Thursday of next week for the launching of Germany's first aircraft carrier. We have had a specialist team working on the assassination project for some time. It cannot be done from within Germany because security is too tight. The only way is to deliver a bomb from the air. We need a highly skilled pilot, somebody as skilled as you. We also need an aircraft. We know that you own a de Havilland Comet racer which is fast and which has a nice long range. We know that you have flown it in air races with much success. So we have found the means to deliver the bomb.'

The Minister paused. He knew that Tony was having difficulty taking all of this in. 'I am naturally, as a servant of His Majesty's Government, not involved in this matter. My friends have asked me to speak to you. They will offer you whatever you want.'

'Excuse me, Sir. Have I got this right? Your friends want me to carry out a political assassination? This has to be carried out in ten days' time and I can name any price I want?'

'Exactly,' replied the Minister. 'We shall understand if you do not accept. It will not be held against you. Your skills are being put to good use here and they will probably be in greater demand in the near future. However, this is possibly our only chance and we can find nobody more suitable to execute it.'

Tony let out a nervous laugh. 'What if I asked for a million pounds?'

'That would not be a problem,' the Minister replied. 'Clearly I did not come here expecting an instant decision. The reason for me being here is to assure you that this is not a hoax. My presence is that guarantee. What we want you to do is to sleep on the request. You will not be seeing me again on this matter. I told your CO that I had come with a message from your mother. Our security has to be kept absolutely tight. If on reflection you do not want to be involved, you do not need to do anything except to forget this conversation. On the other hand, if you think you can assist us, please be outside the main gate at four tomorrow afternoon in civilian clothes. I have told your CO that you may need to take some leave for family matters and that you may have an errand tomorrow afternoon. Your CO will not schedule you for any flight duties tomorrow afternoon unless you tell him your errand was not necessary.'

The Minister cleared his throat and glanced around before continuing. 'If, as I said, you are willing to assist, after leaving the main gate, turn right and proceed up the road. After half a mile on the left side of the road there is a little lay-by. You will find a red MG parked there. Its owner will have the bonnet open and he will be fussing over the engine. Approach him and say, *I have brought the part you need, Lionel.* He will reply, *Thank you, Jacob, but I need something else as well.* Then the two of you will go for a little drive. Lionel will wait in the lay-by until 5 p.m. If you do not turn up, he will know that you do not wish to participate.'

Tony was absolutely riveted to the spot. He just could not take all of this in.

He felt the Minister's hand on his arm. 'Tony, I cannot tell you what to do. It is difficult enough for me to ask you to do it. You alone can decide. I do not know the details of the plan. I do not know what the chances of success are. All I know is that you are used to taking calculated risks. Oh, one final word, your parents do not know about my visit and I know that I can count on you not to say anything about it. Now, I must get back to London.'

With that, His Lordship turned on his heel and walked towards a shiny black chauffeur-driven limousine parked some distance away.

Bloody hell! thought Tony, Bloody hell!

He slept very little that night as he kept turning the matter over in his mind. One side of his mind told him that he was being asked to become a hired assassin. The other side of his mind told him that the fate of the Jews in Germany was not going to be stopped by any diplomatic pressure and that somebody had to help them. If the plan succeeded, would the persecution stop with Hitler removed? Would it avert a war? How could he commit himself to something like this without knowing exactly what he had to do? Lionel, whoever he was, would probably fill him in more, but if he didn't like what he

31

heard, could he still back out? Those involved in the plot were running out of time. If he declined, could they find somebody competent in time and also a suitable aircraft?

His mind turned to his beautiful de Havilland Comet racer, an aircraft specifically designed to win the 1934 London to Melbourne air race. His aircraft was not one of the three which had participated in the race but had been built for a British motor racing driver who had managed to kill himself on the circuit. Tony's father had offered to buy it for his son, which was very generous of him. The aircraft was in absolutely pristine condition. It was finished in dark racing green overall with a white fuselage flash, white registration letters and a black 12 racing number in a white circle on the fin. Tony had flown the Comet in a few races and had taken it abroad. He was allowed to keep it hangared at Farnborough and he was always ready to give rides to fellow pilots. His CO particularly liked flying in it. It could cruise at 220 miles per hour and had an awesome range but it was very tricky at low speeds and was only for experienced pilots. How on earth could this beautiful machine carry a bomb and even if it could, how could the bomb be delivered accurately?

Tony finally fell asleep. He still awoke at six as usual and as soon as he opened his eyes, he made his decision. He would do it. He was in any case in a risky job and getting the chop was always a possibility. The whole technical side of this mission was already intriguing him and finally, and perhaps most importantly, he would do it for his mother and her family.

At nine o'clock, dressed in his uniform, he knocked on the CO's door. Inside, he came to attention and saluted. 'I believe, Sir, that my visitor of yesterday told you I had some family problem to attend to. Is it okay if I take the afternoon free and perhaps take next week as leave?'

'Tony, I'm sorry to hear there is a problem and I hope it will soon be sorted. Of course you can take that time. I am sure it is owing to you in any case. If there is anything I can do to help, just ask. I know that you are up to speed on all your programmes. I suggest that this morning you start preparing for the next tests. Will you be up to flying tomorrow? You are looking a bit taut.'

'I'll be fine, Sir. The flying will take my mind off things.'

That afternoon Tony turned up at the lay-by within the time frame. Lionel was there pretending to tinker with the engine of the MG. The password phrases were exchanged. 'Hop in,' Lionel said as he closed the bonnet. He eased himself into the driver's seat and then extended a hand.

'Welcome aboard, Jacob,' he said. 'We are so relieved. We thought you would turn us down. Now we do not have far to go but just relax until we are there. Then we can talk.'

Ten minutes later Lionel pulled up in the grounds of a fairly substantial private house. It was by no means a country seat but it exuded prosperity. The front door opened as the two men approached it.

'Thank you, Robertson', said Lionel, 'just check carefully that we were not followed. It all looked clear to me but I am not in your league.'

Lionel beckoned Tony into a comfortable lounge and waved him towards an even more comfortable chair.

'Code names, I'm afraid. My name is no more Lionel than yours is Jacob, but we have to be careful. The Nazis have their spy network even here. We trust nobody apart from the vetted few. His Lordship vouched for you. By the way, he is "Abraham". In his secret life he pulls all the strings. Whisky? Don't worry, I shall not get you drunk and Robertson will drive you back. I just want you to be relaxed. By the way, I know your father very well but we two have not met before. I can see why he is so proud of you.'

Robertson appeared carrying a tray with glasses, a bottle of scotch and a siphon of soda. Drinks were served. Lionel smiled. 'Dear boy, this is not my house but Robertson is my man. A good friend of mine lent me this place for a few days. He asked no questions as he is one of ours. I shall be looking after the British end of this operation. I remain here until it is over and we hope that the outcome will be successful. I can only tell you of how you are to get into position for the - how shall we put it - delivery. I am not allowed to know more and that is probably a good thing. If the mission is a success, I shall then deal with the consequences here. Now I shall tell you what I know. Please stop me at any time if you have any questions. There are certainly some blanks to be filled in.'

Lionel took a sip of Scotch before continuing. 'We know you have just over 3,000 flight hours. We have a copy of your log book. Don't ask me how we got it. We have many more devoted agents than the Nazis have. We know you have certain girlfriends – we have all their telephone numbers. But we know you are not engaged. We know how many flight hours your Comet has done. We know that it is maintained by Sergeants Farebrother and Wilkins. We know that they are excellent mechanics and that your aircraft is in perfect condition. We also know that you have a slight worry about the vision in your left eye – the result of one of your two bail-outs.'

Tony let out a whistle. 'Jesus Christ, you know more about me than the Air Force does.'

'That is our job. We need all the intelligence which we can get. Now, let me tell you what I can. Abraham has already told you that our target will be in Kiel on Thursday 8th December for the launching of the aircraft carrier *Graf Zeppelin*. Hitler is scheduled to deliver a speech to the assembled crowd at eleven local time and then launch the ship at eleven-thirty. The attack has to be delivered within this half hour. We have a private airfield available just south of Malmö in Sweden. My main task is to get you there and, if everything goes to plan, to get you back from there. Any questions so far?'

'So far, so good,' said Tony.

'Now the first thing to plan for is your departure from Farnborough,' said Lionel. 'We know you are going to take a week's leave, so your CO will not be bothered about your absence, but what about the missing Comet?'

'I have the answer,' said Tony. 'My parents have a place in Scotland near Gleneagles. My paternal grandmother has been taken ill there. She has been asking for me. This is the truth. I am going up there for a few days. Nobody will check on that.'

'Okay, we can fine-tune that story,' said Lionel. 'However, now comes the tricky bit. You are used to flying the Comet with a navigator in the rear seat. I have to get you to Malmö without a convenient navigator in the back. You also have to fly out on Sunday so that you will have three days there to be fully briefed and for your aircraft to be prepared. I am not a pilot but I have spoken to several who are, just to test the water, you understand, without giving anything away. We do not know what the weather is going to be like. We know you have no on-board navigation equipment. We know that you have no radio. What we do know is that you have plenty of range. Listen to what I propose but chip in if you want to.'

'I'm listening,' Tony said from the depths of his comfortable chair.

'You take off and head north as if bound for Scotland. Just north of London, you turn north-east and head for the East Anglian coast. You can select your own over-water departure point. Then you can head virtually due east until you sight the Dutch coast. From then on, no matter how bad the weather is, you can keep low and follow the coast. Ideally we should like to keep you offshore all the way around Denmark so that your presence is not noted by anybody. Then after passing the northernmost tip of Jutland, you turn south and head for Malmö. What I need from you is a time calculation from leaving Farnborough until you arrive overhead Malmö. We could no doubt do this ourselves but this is your mission and we would rather it came from you. We do not wish to put you under any unnecessary pressure. What do you think?'

Tony thought for a minute. 'Well,' he said, 'You seem to have a pretty good handle on this. I can do some calculations tomorrow and let you have them.'

'Fine,' said Lionel. 'We shall meet on Thursday evening and then I can pass on an estimated time of arrival to our people in Sweden. We are in touch with them by coded radio messages every day. When you leave tonight, I shall have the greatest pleasure of informing them that the plan is on.'

'I shall obviously need a map to be able to locate my destination airfield.'

'You will have this on Thursday. Be in the Three Crowns in Market Square at 8 p.m. on Thursday evening. I am sure that you know it. Robertson will appear. Just follow him out and he will bring you to me.'

'Okay. I have enough going through my mind to keep me awake for ever. I shall be in the Three Crowns on time. Just two things. First: how do I get in touch if anything crops up unexpectedly from my side and vice-versa how do you contact me if you need to do so urgently?'

'Easy.' Lionel smiled. 'If I need you, Farebrother will come and see you about a maintenance issue. If you need me, just go to Farebrother and ask him to check the magnetos on the Comet. Either way I will see you within the hour, but this is a last resort.'

'The last thing,' said Tony, 'is that I do not want a penny out of this. There are enough Jewish children out there being deprived of their rights. My million is for them and they deserve it. I have never had to worry about money. It is time that I thought of the less fortunate for a change.'

Lionel seized his hand. 'Jacob, we need more like you. Pray to God that you will succeed.'

Robertson drove Tony back to the airfield and dropped him off outside the main gate. Tony kept himself busy with his test duties for the next two days to take his mind off things. He was in the Three Crowns at the appointed hour on Thursday evening and noticed Robertson sitting in a corner. Robertson got up and made for the door. Tony followed him. A few minutes later he was in the comfortable lounge of the house which Lionel was using as his base.

'So, Jacob, everybody in the team is delighted. Are you able to give me a time for your arrival on Sunday?'

'I estimate to be overhead Malmö at 3 p.m. as long as I don't have any headwinds.'

'I shall pass that on,' said Lionel. 'I take it that you have all the maps you need to be able to get you there? What you need from me is to know how to get to the private airfield. Firstly, here is a map of the Malmö area. The site of the airfield is marked with a cross. You will see that it is fifteen miles to the south-east of the town. The second sheet here is a plan of the airfield showing height above sea level, length of runways and the usual stuff which you need to know. Note the hangar in the lower right corner.' He pointed at the plan. 'When you arrive over the field you will see that white marker boards will have been set out to indicate the runway in use as it is just a grass field. There is a white T by the hangar which will show you the wind direction. Do one pass along the runway line at low level and then look towards the hangar. You should see a group of people standing there. One of them will flash a green signal from an Aldis lamp and you will be cleared to land. After landing, taxi towards the hangar. Stop short of it where there is a small concrete apron. One man will come forward to meet you. This will be Saul, the project leader. He will simply ask you, *Jacob, what news do you bring?* All you have to do is to give him this envelope which you should keep in a pocket in your flight suit, and reply, *I bring you greetings from Lionel.* That is all there is to it.'

'Well, that's simple enough,' said Tony.

'I hope that I shall be able to see you again when all of this is over,' Lionel said. 'Please accept this from me and wear it around your neck for luck. It is a Davidstern. It may give you the extra protection you will need.'

Then it was time for Robertson to drive Tony back to his base.

Sunday morning soon came round. The Comet had been wheeled out of the hangar and was ready to go. Tony had looked at the weather synoptic charts for the UK but also for the whole area of the North Sea and the Baltic. There were no significant weather features. He might run into some low coastal stratus off Jutland but he could easily cope with that. The previous evening he had called his parents to tell them that he was off on a test assignment for the whole of the following week and that he would not be able to call them again until the following weekend. He had also called his grandmother to tell her he would be coming up to see her on Sunday but he also had asked her not to inform his parents as he might have other duties. He secured his small suitcase on the rear seat as he would be flying alone. Sergeant Farebrother was on hand to swing the propellers but before he moved round to the front of the wing, he said 'Hope you'll find your Gran okay, Sir.'

There's more in you than meets the eye, my lad, Tony thought. You know exactly what's going on.

Tony switched the magnetos on for the left engine first and called 'Contact!' Farebrother swung the prop and the engine fired. They repeated this procedure for the right engine. Farebrother pulled the chocks away from the mainwheels, Tony closed the hinged canopy and started to taxi to the duty runway. Farebrother flung him a salute, Tony waved back and he was on his way. Not having a radio, Tony waited for a green light from the tower before lining up on the runway and off he went. One of the annoying features of the Comet was that the pilot had to turn a large wheel on his right 33 revolutions before the mainwheels were retracted and this would have to be done again before landing.

Once the Comet was well to the north of London, Tony turned north-east to make for the coast. He was in for a long flight but that did not bother him at all. It turned out to be free of any incidents and some hours later, just a little before three in the afternoon, he had passed over Malmö and was looking for the private airfield. He found it easily enough and set up for landing as Lionel had advised him. He saw the green signal light being beamed at him and he brought the Comet in for a smooth landing. He taxied to the small concrete apron and shut down.

Sure enough one man stepped forward to meet him. Tony clambered out of the cockpit and jumped to the ground. The pre-arranged greetings were exchanged and Saul led Tony towards the hangar.

'Jacob, your Comet will feel quite at home in our hangar. Just look what we have inside.'

Tony could see a de Havilland Moth two-seater and a de Havilland Dragon Rapide ten-seat transport. Tony had run tests on both of these types at Farnborough. These two aircraft occupied the left side of the hangar, the right side had been cleared for the Comet which was now being pushed inside.

'Just get your things from the aircraft and come with me,' said Saul. 'The other men know exactly what they have to do and we should leave them to it. The hangar is effectively under guard all the time so they will not be disturbed. There is a telephone line between the hangar and the house to which I am now taking you.'

Tony was driven about half a mile to a large house which was fairly well concealed by a belt of trees. A man was standing at the top of the steps leading to the double front doors. 'Jacob, may I introduce you to Moshe. This is his house and we are his guests.'

'Welcome, Jacob, I hope that you had a good flight and are not too tired,' Moshe said in perfect English. 'I am not one of the team for this operation but I provide the facilities. My business activities prevent me from taking a more active part.'

'What Moshe is not telling you is that he is probably the biggest entrepreneur in Sweden. He runs factories, mines and many other activities. We are on his country estate. We approached Moshe with a list of what we needed and he provided everything.'

'I am just glad to be of some help,' said Moshe. 'Now if you will excuse me, gentlemen, I have some work to do. Saul knows where everything is and he will look after you. We shall meet again at dinner time.'

'Firstly, Jacob, let me get one of the servants to show you to your room so that you can freshen up,' said Saul. 'Take your time and then come and find me in the lounge.'

When Tony came back downstairs and found Saul, the latter waved him to a comfortable seat. 'Let me get you a drink. Scotch and soda?'

'That will be fine.'

'Now,' Saul began, 'I don't want to overburden you with information straight off. You should relax for the rest of today. My team needs two days to have everything prepared for the mission so their work will be finished by Tuesday night but we have built in an extra day just in case it is needed. I shall give you a full briefing tomorrow morning. I have maps and documents for you to examine. When you have the full picture, you will need to study the maps and the documents until you have memorised everything. On Wednesday morning you will meet Ulf who is Moshe's personal pilot. Ulf flies him on most of his business trips both in Sweden and abroad. That is why the Dragon Rapide is based here. The Moth is just for fun flying. Moshe likes to be taken up for local flights for relaxation. Ulf is also teaching him to fly.'

'That's nice,' Tony said as he sipped at his drink.

'On Wednesday morning Ulf will fly you in the Dragon Rapide over most of the course which we have worked out. In this way you will see what lies before you instead of having to fly it unprepared, so to speak, on Thursday. Ulf will not fly you into Kiel Bay. The Germans would not approve of this at all as you can imagine. After this reconnaissance flight, we shall see how well you have assimilated what you have to do. We shall all be there to see you off on Thursday morning and we shall all be waiting for your return. We cannot know what our chances of success are. However, we must grasp this opportunity. We may not get another chance to rid the world of this madman.'

Tony was able to spend a pleasant evening with Saul and Moshe. There was an excellent dinner. They made small talk on many subjects but avoided anything connected with what lay before them. Tony had the impression that Moshe knew his father but this would not have been surprising. Both men were highly cultured and it was clear that both travelled a great deal. Tony did his best to keep up with them. He had had a good education but eight years of life in the Air Force was not conducive to widening one's horizons outside of military matters.

At the end of the evening Saul said to Tony, 'Now Jacob, get a good night's rest. Breakfast is at eight in the dining room. I shall be there. At nine, I shall start your briefing.'

Tony did not sleep well. He had given his commitment and was thoroughly wrapped up in this operation. Many questions formed in his mind but he felt sure that everything had been planned very carefully and he was equally sure that Saul would be able to provide most of the answers. Certain things could not be predicted, for example, what if Hitler was ill and could not attend? What if the ship was not ready to be launched? What if the Nazis had got wind of something? Tony knew that there were such people as double-agents. What if Abraham's or Saul's network had been infiltrated and the Nazis knew about this plot?

Puzzling over these questions, he finally fell asleep.

The next morning he was having breakfast with Saul. He heard the sound of aircraft engines and looked quizzically at Saul.

'It's Moshe. Ulf is flying him to Hamburg today. Don't worry. Moshe hates all the Nazis but he has to do business with them as he produces the best ball-bearings in the world. The Nazis sometimes talk to him a little too much and he has often come back with useful information. He was the first to know that Hitler was scheduled to be in Kiel on Thursday. He contacted me and said: *Saul, it has to be this time.* Now, when we have finished breakfast we shall go to his office and I shall start my briefing.'

In Moshe's office there was a huge desk. Saul went to a safe in a corner of the room and twirled the dials to unlock it. He had already taken the precaution of locking the door on the inside and the window blinds had been drawn.

'We can never be too careful,' Saul said. 'Moshe employs a house staff of ten who for the most part live locally and who might be tempted to talk. We can trust Moshe, my team at the airfield and Ulf absolutely but that is as far as it goes.'

He extracted a file from the safe, placed it on the desk and switched on a powerful desk-top lamp. 'Now this morning, Jacob, we will just concentrate on how you get to the target. The rest will follow in due course.'

First Saul drew out an aeronautical chart and unfolded it. 'This is how you get to Kiel. We asked Ulf to select a route which would keep you away from the land so that your flight will not be picked up. We know that you are familiar with very low-altitude flight. Once you have left the Swedish coast, which is only a few miles to the south of us, we want you to stay at 100 feet above the surface and maintain 220 miles per hour. The big question is: can you do that?'

Tony replied, 'It all depends on the distance to be covered. Flying low over water for a long time can tempt one to fly progressively lower until there is a fatal impact. I know that your airfield is fifteen feet above sea level. I would set my altimeter to read plus fifteen feet. This reading would be good for about half an hour. It would be nice if I knew what the pressure setting is at Kiel just before my take-off from here and if the pressure there is rising or falling.'

'We can monitor the German shipping forecasts on the radio to get you that information.'

'Now,' Tony said, 'having looked at my charts back at Farnborough, I could see that the distance from Malmö to Kiel is not all that great. There may be no pressure change at all so that once my altimeter shows me to be at 100 feet above the surface, I shall be able to rely on that reading for the rest of the flight.'

'That's good,' Saul said. 'From here you only have 160 statute miles to fly to reach the critical part of the mission. But how about the speed?'

'The Comet can cruise comfortably at 220 mph even at low level, provided that I am not carrying anything external which would slow me down. Getting to the critical part of the mission would take about 45 minutes flight time and I would consume only about fifteen gallons of fuel in that time.'

'That's even better. That's exactly what I wanted to hear.'

Saul and Tony looked at the chart which lay before them. It showed the whole route marked by a thick grease pencil with various numbers written adjacent to it. 'Ulf produced this based upon a cruise speed of 220 miles per hour. It shows the magnetic heading to steer for each leg and the time for each leg. Ulf has already flown this route stopping just short of the entrance to the Kieler Förde. Beyond this point, he would probably have sparked off a diplomatic incident. In this envelope you will find photographs which Ulf took en route. These photos will help you to identify various headlands, lighthouses, etc. which you should see on the way. This afternoon I want you to study the map and the photographs until you have everything committed to memory. Naturally if you are not happy about anything we shall discuss it to find the best solution. As I have already told you, Ulf will give you a dry run over the course on Wednesday morning.'

Saul paused for a minute. Tony had no immediate questions, so the former continued. 'Now we come to the most difficult part of the mission which we cannot rehearse beforehand. You

43

are probably bursting to know how you can deliver a bomb at low altitude on a very small target. We have worked all this out. Please be patient until tomorrow afternoon and then I shall explain the weapon to you. You can be absolutely certain of one thing. If you can get your Comet at the correct altitude and speed and at the right spot, your bomb will do the job. We have tested everything. The system works. We also know that if nothing interferes with your final run-in to the target, you are capable of delivering our parcel perfectly to Mr Hitler. Unfortunately we cannot know what precautions have been put in place to protect the ceremonial area. We can be sure that there will be some sort of exclusion zone and it would be wrong of us not to alert you to any possible threats. We shall deal with this later.'

Saul put the map and photographs back in their folder but he left the folder on the desk. 'When I have finished this morning's briefing, please start to study these and prepare any questions which you may have.'

He returned to the safe and produced another folder which he kept closed in front of him. 'Do you know anything about an Australian businessman by the name of Sidney Cotton?'

'Yes, I have heard of him but we have never met. He has produced a high-altitude flight suit called the Sidcot suit which scored high marks at Farnborough. I believe that he keeps a private aircraft somewhere in the London area and that he frequently flies on business to Germany.'

'Let me add to your knowledge,' said Saul. 'Mr Cotton is very friendly with many Germans in high places. He flies to Germany and gives them free flights in his Lockheed Electra which is normally based at Heston. He is very much appreciated in Germany. He offers his guests flights over their home towns and keeps them supplied with canapés and drinks as they fly along. He will circle over the places his guests want to see several times to make them happy. Unknown to his guests, in the belly of his aircraft three cameras are clicking away taking photographs of Germany's secret installations. Sidney returns home and hands his films over to the Air Ministry. They are absolutely delighted. His under-cover work is invaluable.' Saul pulled a photograph from the file. 'Now, what do you make of that?'

The photo was a vertical view of an aircraft carrier in a shipyard. It was crystal clear and showed great detail. On the right of the aircraft carrier was another large vessel under construction.

Before Tony could answer, Saul continued, 'This is the *Graf Zeppelin* as Sidney Cotton saw it only ten days ago. Do not ask me how we got this photo and the others which I am about to show you because I shall not answer.'

Saul produced more photos of the carrier taken from more oblique angles as the aircraft was flying towards it or away from it.

'With the help of these photos,' he continued, 'we know exactly where the ship is in the Deutsche Werke shipbuilding yards. We have superimposed the position of the ship on this map of the southern end of the Kieler Förde. Now, we know exactly where the ship is and we also know where the VIP tribune is being constructed. It is to be seen here 50 yards in front of the bows. It is from here that Hitler will make his speech.'

Saul drew another document out of the folder. 'Now please look at this detailed chart of the whole of the Kieler Förde. You will see that it is long and narrow. At the northern end which opens out into the Kieler Bucht, there are two lighthouses which serve to guide ships into the narrow channel. There are photographs of these in the file. We are counting on you on Thursday morning to locate these two lighthouses and to enter the Förde halfway between them. Keep to the middle of the channel and maintain 100 feet of altitude and 220 miles per hour. It will take you only just over two minutes to reach the position of the *Graf Zeppelin* but you will see it before that as it dominates everything else. As you see, the ship will be on your left at an angle of about 45° to your flight path.'

'Very impressive.' said Tony. 'You seem to have thought of everything.'

'The tricky part of the flying comes right at the end but as long as you keep to your speed, you will do fine. Make your turn to the left so that you are aligned precisely with the centre line of the flight deck. Keep that heading and stay on that centre line. Fly as low as you possibly can down the deck. That is all you need to know today. I am now going to leave you to see how my boys are getting on in the hangar. I shall come back and collect you for lunch. Then, this afternoon you can study all of this material and we can discuss any questions this evening.'

Tony gave Saul an admiring glance. 'If you have paid the same attention to your weapon, I am sure it will work.'

Tony spent the rest of the day studying the profile of the mission. He had lunch with Saul and in the evening he had dinner with him. Saul was an excellent person to work with. He cut through all the peripheral material and concentrated Tony on what mattered. However, he was very human and made sure that Tony had answers to all his questions. They had dinner and then played cards for an hour. 'That's enough for today,' said Saul. 'Breakfast at eight tomorrow and then we continue at nine in the office.'

The next morning Saul quizzed Tony on his route and on his approach to the target. Tony had everything off pat.

'I can see why you are so highly rated at Farnborough,' Saul said. 'You have memorised everything perfectly. I cannot tell you everything about the bomb until you see it, which will be this afternoon, but I can better prepare you for what is to come. By late spring this year, we already had the weapon but we did not know how or when to deliver it. Then Abraham informed us that you would be the best person to do the job and that your Comet would be the ideal aircraft to use. Moshe decided to hold an international fly-in here in May. He invited many of his business contacts and some well-known display pilots. The event was a great success. We had some thirty aircraft here from many European countries, including Germany, Italy, France, Switzerland, Belgium, Holland and not forgetting Britain.'

Saul paused for a moment. 'We invited Blake and Turner to attend with their Comet. As soon as they knew that all their expenses would be paid and that they would carry off the main prize, they were only too pleased to attend. We all had a magnificent weekend. Pilots always mix well together. They were giving rides in their respective machines and enjoyed slapping each other on the back. In the evening Moshe made sure that there was plenty to drink and that there were plenty of pretty girls to stoke the party spirit. Blake and Turner's Comet was in the hangar.

'Whilst the carousing was going on, my team examined the rear cockpit area in great detail so that they could devise a sort of bomb bay, if you will, which will fit exactly into your aircraft. This should relieve you of one thing. You will not be carrying any bombs out in the airflow which would degrade the Comet's performance. This special construction is being fitted in your aircraft now and you will see the result this afternoon. You will also see your weapon, as I have already said.

'Before you see the result of our preparations this afternoon, I need to talk about timing but not all of this will become clear until we are in the hangar. As you know, you will be going in to your target very low down and at high speed. You need to know exactly when you have to release the weapon to achieve the result which we want. When you line up to fly over the deck of the carrier from the stern, you will not be able to see the target because it will be hidden by the bows of the ship. You will be bombing blind. Two moments are absolutely critical to this operation. The first is when you are four seconds from the stern of the ship. The second is when you reach the forward end of the flight deck. I shall not explain now why these two

47

moments are so vital but I want to prepare you for this afternoon.'

'But at that low level and that speed, my bomb will just bounce off the target, and continue its path until it explodes some distance away, possibly underneath me.'

Saul smiled. 'We have thought of all of this and we have solved that issue. You will just have to be patient and wait until this afternoon. Now I have got to go and see how my team is getting on in the hangar. I think they have almost finished everything. We shall have lunch at twelve. In the meantime, I have arranged for Jens to give you a bicycle tour of the estate. He speaks good English and he is waiting outside the front door with two bicycles. I shall introduce you. After that I shall see you at twelve.'

After lunch Tony was left to his own devices as Saul was busy with his team in the hangar. At one point he heard the sound of aircraft engines and assumed that the Dragon Rapide was returning. At 3:30 Saul came back to the house to collect him. 'My team has finished its work on the Comet. I shall drive you over there and everything else will be revealed to you.'

The hangar doors, which slid sideways, were closed. 'Just an extra precaution,' Saul said. He rapped on one of the heavy metal doors in a manner which was obviously a code. One side slid open just enough to admit the two men. Saul spoke in Swedish to his men. They picked up their tools and equipment and left.

'They are free until tomorrow when they will put the final pieces in place,' said Saul. 'We have one man standing guard outside now and my men will work a guard rota until you take off on Thursday.'

The inside of the hangar was bathed in bright light. The first thing which Tony noticed was that the tail of the Comet had been jacked up so that the aircraft was in a flying attitude. The second thing which he noticed was that the registration markings, the white fuselage cheat line and the racing number in its white circle on the fin had all been painted over in the same shade of green as the rest of the aircraft.

'This will make your aircraft less conspicuous,' said Saul. 'Even if it is seen at close range, probably nobody will be able to identify it, so that if you are successful, we hope that the attack can never be traced to you. Also, viewed from above, your aircraft should blend pretty well with the colour of the sea.'

There was a ladder in place to give access to the cockpit. Saul motioned Tony to climb it and to take his seat in the front portion of the cockpit. As Tony climbed in, he noticed that the rear seat and the controls had been removed and that the rear portion of the cockpit was now occupied by a sort of box structure which fitted the space perfectly.

Saul had followed Tony up the ladder and standing on a rung, he said to Tony, 'We have done three things to the front portion of the cockpit. I shall explain these one at a time. If you look down to your left and behind you, you will see a sort of handle emerging from the front of the box. It is in the shape of a parachute opening ring, which I believe you call a D-ring. Please give it a good pull. It will not break anything.'

Tony did this, the handle came forward and then moved back again.

'Now please come down and we shall have a look underneath your aircraft.'

The two men descended. Tony noticed that two flaps had opened in the bottom of the fuselage below where the second seat had been.

'These are the bomb doors,' said Saul. 'One pull on the left handle to open them and one pull on the same handle to close them.'

A thick mat had been placed on the floor under the opening. 'Now let us look inside your bomb bay.'

Tony looked up and whistled. 'Two bombs eh?'

'Yes,' replied Saul. 'We had considered using just one bomb but a second bomb gave us an extra level of comfort. Now I want you to notice that the nose cones of these two bombs are missing. They were pulled off when the bomb doors opened. At the front end of each bomb you will see a little propeller. I shall explain its purpose to you shortly.'

'I also notice some packaging around the tail of each bomb,' said Tony.

'Well spotted,' said Saul. 'I shall explain that shortly as well. Now please climb up into your cockpit again and when you are sitting down, look down to your right and behind. You will see another handle which is identical to the one on the left. Just give it a sharp pull and then come back down and join me here.'

Tony did as he was asked. When he pulled the handle, he heard a dull thud. Then he scrambled back down the ladder and joined Saul. He could see that he had released the bombs which were now lying on the thick mat.

'So,' said Saul, 'left handle to open the bomb doors, right handle to release the bombs. So far, so good. Moshe did a brilliant piece of work with these bombs. One of his factories produced them. As he makes all sorts of stuff for various governments he told his staff that these bombs were ordered by the Swedish Air Force under an experimental contract.

'I believe that you have done quite a few bombing trials, Jacob? What are the main problems which you encountered?'

'Well, if I am flying low, as I shall be on this mission, the main problem is judging the right moment to release the bombs. For this sort of bombing delayed action fuses are needed so that the bombs do not go off when the aircraft is still in the blast zone. Then the bombs may bounce, miss the target and explode behind it in the air. Also many of our bombs turn out to be duds and fail to go off.'

Saul nodded and said, 'We studied all of these issues and my team came up with some very smart answers. May I draw your attention to the little propeller on the front of the bomb? When you opened the bomb doors, the protective caps were removed. The little propeller would then begin to spin in the airstream. After ten seconds exactly they will have driven the percussion caps up against the charges and the bombs will explode. We have tested this thoroughly and it works as planned every time. Next, you had already observed the packaging at the tail of the bomb. Note that it is now slightly detached from the bomb and is also attached to a thin cord which runs up inside the bomb bay. Now observe what happens.' Saul picked up one of the bombs with ease. 'This bomb is inert – it does not have any charge so it is very light. Fully loaded it weighs 30 kilos, or about 66 pounds. The two bombs combined weigh less than your usual navigator.'

Saul walked away from the aircraft carrying the bomb and after he had walked a few steps, the packaging had become a miniature parachute.

'This solves the problem of the bomb skipping over or skipping through the target before it explodes. When the bombs are released in flight, the cord pulls out the parachute. This immediately slows down the forward trajectory of the bomb and in two seconds it is falling vertically. If the bomb is released at a pre-determined altitude and at a predetermined speed and at a predetermined distance from the target, it cannot miss. Furthermore these bombs have very thin cases, they are packed with a mixture of high explosive and shrapnel. They are designed to do the maximum damage to soft targets like people. These bombs will eliminate everybody standing on the platform with Hitler and many other people in close proximity. I have no remorse over this. All those present at the launch of the *Graf Zeppelin* have gone along with Hitler's racist policies and they do not deserve any sympathy. I am sorry, but I was getting slightly carried away.'

'Now, there is one further thing which I must show you', Saul continued. 'Please return to your seat in the cockpit.'

Saul followed Tony up the ladder and stood on it by the side of the cockpit. 'Now if you look to each side of the central windscreen support, you will see that one of my men has placed a small short black line at the base of the Perspex on each side. This is to help you with the timing. When you have made your final turn to line up with the fore-and-aft line along the centre of the carrier's flight deck, you must precisely hold that heading. The ship will appear to grow in size as you approach it, as you would expect.

'When the rear edges of the flight deck appear to hit those two small black lines you will be four seconds from the rear of the flight deck if you are at 220 miles per hour. At that instant, you pull the left handle and the bomb doors open. This will take one second. The little propellers begin to spin. Three seconds later you are over the rear end of the flight deck. This deck is 794 feet long. It will take you four seconds to fly down it. Pull the right handle just before you reach the front end of the flight deck. By that time, the propellers have been spinning for six seconds. The bombs will be slowed down to drop vertically two seconds after release and they will explode two seconds later. As I have told you, you will never see the special platform built for Hitler and his cronies but by the time the bombs explode, you will be a full deck length away from the ship and out of harm's way.'

'My God, you really have thought of everything,' said Tony in absolute awe. 'All I have to do is fly accurately and get my timings right.'

'Remember that nothing in life is certain,' said Saul. 'There are bound to be fighter aircraft patrolling around to protect the area. We are hoping that they will not see you flying low above the Kieler Förde. Now, let us turn to more pleasant matters. It will soon be time for dinner. Moshe is back and he will entertain us with some of his stories.'

Wednesday morning was scheduled for the dry run with Ulf, who had been dying to get to know Jacob but he had strict orders not to be too familiar. When the two were introduced by Saul, Tony had the feeling that Ulf knew far more than he gave away.

'My poor Rapide only cruises at 130 miles per hour,' said Ulf, 'so we shall need nearly two and a half hours to fly out to just short of the Kieler Förde and to return. Hop in to the front passenger seat on the right and I shall join you up front.'

Tony already knew that the pilot sat on his own up front in a Rapide. Tony had his charts and photographs with him, but how would he communicate with Ulf during the flight? The answer was apparent when Tony wriggled into his seat. There was a voice/listening tube next to his seat. This reminded Tony of the old Gosport tube used over many years in RAF training. If either person on the end of the tube wished to communicate, he blew down the tube. This produced a whistle at the other end. The recipient would place the end of the tube to his ear and listen to the message. When the other party wanted to reply, he blew down the tube and then took his turn to speak into it.

When Ulf was installed in the pilot's seat, he turned round to Tony with a grin and said, 'The boss wanted this system so he could speak to me in flight. The old Gosport system is not finished yet.'

Off they went. Tony immediately sensed that Ulf was a skilled pilot. They flew parallel to the coast east of the shores of the Danish islands of Sjaelland and Lolland and then the German island of Fehmarn. Tony was studying the maps and his photographs. It was clear that Ulf had everything committed to memory. His comments were always to the point and were most helpful. They got to within five miles of the entrance to the Kieler Förde.

'This is where we turn around,' said Ulf, 'otherwise we shall have the Messerschmitts checking us out.'

At the end of the flight Tony thanked Ulf for his input. 'You are better qualified than simply being a chauffeur for Moshe,' he risked.

'Don't worry about my employment,' Ulf replied. 'I may not be in your league but in your Service I would already have received several medals for what I have done.'

At lunch Tony complimented Ulf on his flying qualities to Saul and told him that he wanted to spend some time alone in the Comet cockpit, briefing himself with his maps and photos and making sure that he could grab the two D-rings and pull them without having to think about it.

Saul gave him a free rein. 'My team will not interfere,' he said. 'They will not be loading the live bombs until early on Thursday morning.'

The final pre-mission evening came round. Moshe had invited all Saul's team and Ulf to be present. Some of the team had no English but there was always a willing interpreter. Saul was absolutely bubbling away. 'The latest news is that apart from Hitler we shall have fat Herrmann (Goering), Admiral Raeder, Keitel, Bormann and Dietrich on the platform as well. What a coup if we eliminate all of them!'

Spirits were high but Tony drank very little and answered only in monosyllables. The others knew only too well that he was running the mission through his mind again and again.

Tony was there for breakfast at eight the next morning. Only Saul was present. 'Your aircraft is bombed up. You only have fuel in the main tank as your need is minimal. We have made sure that you have enough for the flight out and back plus a one hour reserve. The forecast is good. Here is what the German shipping forecast has to say.' He passed the sheet to Tony. 'Ulf thinks this is as good as what we could expect. No low cloud at all. A sheet of overcast at about 5,000 feet and only light winds. Maybe the gods are on our side.'

Tony made no comment as he read the forecast. He was finding it difficult to swallow any food. All he wanted to do was to get on with the mission and to perform successfully. 'Take off is at 10:30,' added Saul. 'Your aircraft will be ready at the beginning of the duty runway. You board at 10:15. We shall all be there to see you off. With the timing you should be releasing your bombs at 11:15, right in the middle of Hitler's speech. Jacob, you have given us hope. You have shown us what it is to be a man. You know as well as we do that the odds are against you but you have not wavered.' Saul had tears in his eyes.

Tony cleared his throat and replied, 'Saul, even if I fail, one day the world will be free of this madman. There will still be escapees from this horrible persecution. It is better to finish the persecution now but if it does not work, look forward to the future.'

Neither man wanted to say any more but they shook hands.

At ten o'clock Tony started his pre-flight walk-around. He meticulously checked everything as usual. Then he swung himself into the cockpit. The engines were started, the chocks were removed. Tony closed the canopy and taxied forward to turn on to the grass runway. He waved to Moshe, Saul and his team and to Ulf and then he eased the throttles forward and was on his way.

The flight went absolutely as planned as far as Ulf had taken him. After turning the north-west corner of Fehmarn, Tony went to the required heading to bring him to the entrance of the Kieler Förde. A few minutes later he saw the two lighthouses guarding the entrance and he aimed to enter the inlet right in the middle. He glanced forward and upward and noticed a few specks in the sky circling around over the entrance. I knew the Luftwaffe would be around, he thought. If the Führer is in town, he has to be protected. Those boys must have been circling around for at least half an hour. Let's hope that they are low on fuel.

Tony looked at his watch. It was 11:13 precisely as he shot into the Kieler Förde at 100 feet. Right on time and two minutes to the target.

He was now concentrating very hard on the run-up. Out of the corner of his eye he saw a dark shape draw up off his left wingtip. Blast! It was a Messerschmitt 109. The pilot was motioning to him by hand signals to turn left and to follow him. No way! thought Tony. At the same time another Messerschmitt 109 appeared off his right wingtip. Okay, thought Tony, I am boxed in but until they start shooting I am pressing on. Only 90 seconds to go.

The pilot on his right was also indicating that Tony had to turn left. How long would they sit there and do nothing? Not long was the answer. Suddenly the two fighters turned outwards in a climbing turn. All I can do now, thought Tony, is to start weaving to put them off their aim. Perhaps they are lousy shots.

Tony thought wrong. The leader of the pair was a veteran of the Legion Condor in the Spanish Civil War. He knew it would be difficult to hit a weaving aircraft from the rear so he stayed out on the left and above the Comet's altitude until he could come swooping down to time his attack when the Comet started to swing to the left.

The leader timed it to perfection. He was flying a new 109E which was fitted with a very destructive cannon as well as machine guns. His opening burst smashed into the Comet which exploded in a ball of fire. Death was instantaneous. The attacker's aircraft was caught in the blast and fell in pieces into the water. Tony had been just four miles from the target.

Back in Sweden, Moshe, Saul and his team and Ulf were listening to Hitler's speech on Reichssender Berlin. When Tony's aircraft exploded, they all heard a dull thump in the background to the broadcast. Hitler paused for a second or two and then continued his haranguing.

'We've failed,' Saul said and he mumbled a quick prayer. They continued to listen until Hitler's speech was over and the commentator had described the launching of the *Graf Zeppelin*.

Saul and Moshe had lunch together. It was a time for reflection. 'We sent young Jacob to his death,' said Moshe. 'We should not have done that.'

'Just remember,' said Saul, 'that Jacob volunteered for this mission. He felt that he had to do something for our people. He told me that he owed it to his mother. She is Jewish, but you probably do not know that.'

Moshe actually smiled in spite of his grief. 'Now here is something you don't know. I have known Jacob's father for years. I have known his mother's parents for years. In fact I have a meeting with Jacob's paternal grandfather next week. Of course, I shall say nothing. My network may not be as technically organised as yours but it probably reaches out further. We have people in place who will bring out from Germany as many of our faith as possible. In the end we shall prevail.' He paused and looked at his companion before continuing, 'And another thing. Ulf pleaded with me to fly the Comet mission. He sensed that Jacob would not make it and he would rather have taken his place. I told Ulf that he could not handle the Comet without a proper training course but much more importantly, I need his services for the future. He is friendly with many German pilots and the information which he brings back is invaluable.'

Back in Britain, Tony's paternal grandmother became worried when Tony did not show up in Scotland as promised. She contacted the local police. Tony's CO was informed. Some sort of a search was made but nothing was found as nobody really knew where to look. Tony had disappeared and his CO had to break the news to his parents. What actually happened was known only to very few people and it remained that way.

TAILPIECE

Many years ago, and probably more years ago than I would like to think, I read the flying memoirs of a former test pilot at Farnborough. He had access to a de Havilland Comet which was owned by the Air Ministry. This was the very machine which had won the London to Melbourne air race in 1934. The author made many record-breaking flights in this aircraft. In the early summer of 1938 he was approached by a well-known public figure and was asked if he would be willing to drop a bomb on Hitler. The fee of one million pounds was suggested by the author as a joke. Finally, the author decided that he could not become a paid assassin. There is no reason to doubt the truth of this story. I have simply taken it further.

The aircraft carrier *Graf Zeppelin* was launched at Kiel on December 8th 1938. Hitler and his cronies listed above were present. Hitler had no time for the Navy apart from its submarine operations. Kiel was a major centre for submarine construction. "Fat Hermann" as head of the Luftwaffe resented any interference in the running of "his" Luftwaffe. This is just as well. The *Graf Zeppelin* was never allowed to enter service. The aircraft types earmarked for it were never flown. The ship remained in dock until the end of the war. When the Soviets found it, they used it for target practice. It was stumbled upon on the Baltic sea bed by a team drilling for oil off the Polish coast in 2006. It has been positively identified. The keel was laid down for a sister ship but it never proceeded further than that.

The Sidney Cotton episode is genuine. He was a larger-than-life showman who had several wives and several failed businesses. However, when his services were sorely needed, he responded to the call. He set up the Royal Air Force's Photographic Reconnaissance Unit. He should never be forgotten for his contribution.

Finally we have to be thankful for Hitler's irrational choices and for Goering's pompous stupidity, otherwise the world as we know it might be quite a different place today. After all, the Reich was supposed to last for a thousand years.

TO THE BITTER END

The squadron was in the process of packing up at Poix to move further west to Crécy-en-Ponthieu as the German advance was getting uncomfortably close. Most of the ground equipment was already loaded aboard trucks. There were only three Blenheims left out of the original complement of twenty-five which were still airworthy. Those which could not be flown out had been soused in gasoline and were burning away. The crews of the airworthy aircraft were about to depart for Crécy when the Commanding Officer summoned them. It was the afternoon of 16th May 1940.

Jabbing at a point on the map, he said, 'Look, chaps, there is the spearhead of a German motorised column right here. It has to be stopped and we are the only unit with any available aircraft to do it. If we can hold them up for just a few hours, our ground reinforcements have a good chance of getting there to counter them. If Jerry is not stopped by us, he will be through our last defences. Your aircraft are being bombed up now. Flight Lieutenant Lewis, as senior pilot, you will lead. After you have bombed, make straight for Crécy. We shall all have moved out from here by then. Good luck.'

The observers marked the point of attack on their maps. Lewis gave the other two crews a quick briefing and then they all hurried to their machines. A few minutes later they were on their way for another one-sided mission.

Pilot Officer Alan Acres was finding it difficult to take all of this in. He, like the other eight airmen on this mission, had barely had any rest in the last six days. He felt that it was a miracle that he was still alive and functioning. At the age of 19 he had suddenly grown old and had seen enough of war to last him for the rest of his days.

He had finished his time at his local grammar school in the summer of 1938. He had done well. He had several career choices open to him. It was the time of the Munich crisis and many thought that war with Germany was about to break out. Alan had decided that he would volunteer to join the Air Force. He saw himself becoming a Spitfire or a Hurricane fighter pilot. His training had lasted for a little more than a year. He had accumulated 250 flight hours. He was disappointed that he was not singled out to fly fighters but at least he had been chosen to fly the Blenheim, the RAF's high-speed bomber, which was regarded as the fastest light bomber in the world.

War with Germany had been declared by Britain and France on September 3rd 1939 when Alan was coming to the end of his Blenheim conversion course. After a few days' leave he received his posting to one of the Blenheim Mark IV units which had been sent to France as part of the Advanced Air Striking Force. The Mark IV was a big improvement over the initial Mark I. On his arrival at Poix he had expected to be in action immediately but after Germany's rapid conquest of Poland, nothing happened. The 'phoney war' set in with neither side wishing to provoke the other.

The French had full confidence in the Maginot Line which ran along their border with Germany. It would stop the Germans in their tracks, they boasted. So, for more than seven months after the arrival of the Advanced Air Striking Force in France, an uneasy peace held sway. There was plenty of flying training but there were strict orders that no aircraft should penetrate enemy air space.

Alan was assigned Sergeant Maydown as his observer and Corporal Chance as his wireless operator/air gunner. Both of these men were much older than he was and had far more experience of the Blenheim and life in the RAF. However, he was the officer and he was in command. He decided it was politic to be tactful and to welcome their comments and advice. This method clearly worked and as a crew they got on well together which was definitely not the case with some of the other crews.

They soon got used to finding their way about northern France. They had plenty of bombing practice and from this they learnt that it was extremely difficult to hit their targets and that many of their bombs failed to explode. Still, life was pleasant enough and Alan was able to try out his schoolboy French on some of the local inhabitants. Alan had visited all the airfields used by the RAF in northern France and he had been particularly interested in Crécy. He recalled from his history lessons at school that it was here in 1346, under Edward the Black Prince, that the English had resoundingly beaten the French in the Hundred Years War.

The winter of 1939-1940 was the most severe on record for many years in northern France and the ground crews faced an almost impossible task trying to keep their aircraft in a flyable condition. They all hoped that the Germans were having the same problems.

The war had moved up a gear in April 1940 when the Germans had invaded Denmark and Norway. British air and ground forces clashed for the first time with German forces in Norway but the unreal peace in France continued. Prior to that, there had only been the naval encounter between the German pocket battleship *Admiral Graf Spee* and the Royal Navy off the coast of South America.

Suddenly that unreal peace came to an end on May 10th when the Germans launched Operation Yellow. In a daring airborne assault, German troops attacked the key Belgian fort of Eben Emael at first light. It fell early in the afternoon leaving the way through Belgium open. On the following day, German aircraft attacked allied airfields in northern France. The Germans had an attack force of over 2,700 combat aircraft for the campaign against a total of 800 combat aircraft supplied by the British and French.

Alan's squadron, like the others, was called upon to attack

enemy positions and to bomb bridges to prevent the enemy crossing them. It was an impossible task against such huge odds. At least Alan was flying a relatively fast aircraft. Those British pilots flying the slow, underpowered, single-engined Fairey Battle bombers were just shot out of the sky. The inadequacies of the Blenheim were soon revealed. It lacked proper armour protection of vital parts. Its defensive armament of one Vickers gun of First World War vintage in the rear turret was woefully inadequate. The bomb capacity was too small. The outer wing fuel tanks were not of a self-sealing type.

Alan did not have time to be frightened. Everything happened much too quickly. The first operational sortie was undertaken by the whole squadron. They were to attack a bridge on the Albert Canal. The enemy ground fire was intense. There were also enemy aircraft about. Somehow Alan's aircraft managed to drop its bombs but the observer was unable to verify if the target had been hit. Five of their aircraft failed to return to Poix at the end of the raid. The squadron was left with twenty aircraft including the spares which had not participated in the raid. They flew a second attack later that first day. Two further aircraft failed to return.

On the following day, early in the morning, Poix airfield was hit by low-flying German bombers for the first time. Fortunately the Blenheims had been well dispersed around the perimeter of the airfield and none were lost although two hangars, several ground transports and some of the buildings were destroyed.

This attack delayed the mounting of their first strike of the day and following that, a second strike was flown. More aircraft were lost to withering German ground fire. Alan's own aircraft was hit but the damage was not serious.

The mood was sombre in the mess that evening. Empty places at dinner were conspicuous. The CO told them about what had happened to one of their sister squadrons that morning. The whole squadron of Blenheims at another airfield was lined up wing-tip to wing-tip, fully fuelled and ready to start a raid. Suddenly a unit of German Dornier bombers appeared at very low level with the clear intention of bombing the airfield. Unfortunately for the British, their aircraft were lined up precisely in the path of the attacking Germans. The Dorniers made two bombing runs and destroyed every single Blenheim. The whole squadron had been wiped out in five minutes.

The allied attacks on bridges and troop concentrations continued on the 12th and then there was something of a lull on the 13th. Whenever a bridge was knocked out, the Germans quickly replaced it with a pontoon bridge which was immediately protected by lethal anti-aircraft guns. The 14th was another desperate day. Alan flew two more missions and more squadron aircraft were lost. It was on this day that the Germans bombed Rotterdam and crossed the river Meuse at Sedan. The Maginot Line had proved to be completely useless. The Germans had simply by-passed it to the north. Spearheading German units were now moving rapidly towards the French Channel coast. Two more missions were flown on 15th May and more aircraft were lost. Alan's squadron was now down to seven serviceable aircraft. The decision was taken to abandon Poix and to move further west to Crécy the next day.

Now Alan and his crew were on their way on their tenth mission in six days in company with the two remaining Blenheims. They were supposed to have an escort of Hurricanes but the fighters never showed up. The target was easy enough to find. On approaching it, the three aircraft slipped into a line-astern formation with Flight Lieutenant Lewis in the lead and Alan bringing up the rear. They could see the black puffs of bursting flak ahead of them and they knew they would be in for a rough ride. At least there didn't appear to be any enemy aircraft in the vicinity.

Flight Lieutenant Lewis's aircraft was hit before it could drop its bombs and it went down in flames. The second aircraft managed to drop its bombs and was then hit. It caught fire but at least two of the crew managed to get out as two parachutes could be seen.

Alan's observer released their bombs. Alan immediately started a diving turn to get out of the way of the enemy fire. They took some hits but they appeared to have got away with it. When well away from the target, Alan checked all his instruments carefully. The engines were running fine. They were losing hydraulic power which meant that they might have to land without flaps and with the undercarriage up. One of the outer wing tanks had been holed and fuel was streaming out of it but there was enough fuel in the other tanks to get them to Crécy. The crew started to relax. They had been very lucky.

Pilot Officer Rodney Phillips-Turner was flying his Hurricane back towards Abbeville. He had been part of a section of six which had been briefed to cover the attack of the three Blenheims.

On their way to the target area they had been bounced by a section of four Messerschmitt 109s which were out looking for targets of opportunity. A fierce dog fight had developed. At least three of the Hurricanes had gone down. Phillips-Turner had damaged one 109 but he would only be able to claim it as a probable as he had his hands full trying to save his own skin. Suddenly the dog fight was over and the sky was clear. Phillips-Turner set course for home. Was he the only British survivor of this encounter? Even his aircraft had taken some hits. He could see bullet holes in one wing and his engine was starting to run a little roughly. He was hoping to make it back to base but at least now he was over friendly territory and if the worst came to the worst, he could bail out.

Suddenly Phillips-Turner spotted a twin-engined aircraft ahead and below him, flying in the same direction. Was it friend or foe? Phillips-Turner still had some ammunition left if he needed it. In the last few days he had shot down a Messerschmitt 110 and had damaged two German bombers. He knew that the remnants of his squadron were about to fly back to England so this might be his last chance to finish off another Jerry.

In the Blenheim, Chance, manning the turret and searching the sky behind him, called on the intercom, 'Fighter behind us, Sir, at about a mile and somewhat higher. Looks like a Hurricane but I can't be sure from this range.'

'Fire off the colours of the day, Chance, in case it's one of ours,' Alan replied. The crew knew that more than one Blenheim had been shot down in error by its own side. Chance fired the correct sequence of cartridges from the Very pistol.

Phillips-Turner in the Hurricane swore. 'Bloody Junkers 88 and it's shooting at me. I'll nail the bastard.'

The Hurricane swooped down on its target which soon came within range. The eight Browning machine guns roared away. The pilot kept his thumb on the firing button until the Blenheim blew up in a ball of fire. Phillips-Turner pulled out of the way but was so close that oil from the stricken bomber covered his windscreen. Pieces of wreckage smacked into the Hurricane which went out of control. Phillips-Turner tried to slide open his cockpit canopy so that he could bail out but it was jammed. He desperately fought with the controls but the Hurricane flicked onto its back and dived into the ground just a hundred yards from where what was left of the Blenheim came down. Four priceless airmen had been killed because of a stupid case of misidentification.

Just over a year previously Alan Acres and Rodney Phillips-Turner had been on the same initial training course at the Elementary and Reserve Flying Training School at Tollerton, near Nottingham. They had known each other but were not friends. Alan was serious and was an introvert. Rodney was a dare-devil extrovert and came from a public school background. He already had his own sports car.

In Alan's training records was to be found the remark: 'Serious, methodical and reliable. Will make a first-rate bomber pilot.'

Rodney's training records contained the comment: 'A complete dare-devil and practical joker. If he can curb his impulsiveness and accept discipline, could become an outstanding fighter pilot – if he does not kill himself in the meantime.'

TAILPIECE

The Battle of France is often overlooked as it was a humiliating defeat. France was ill prepared to defend itself and just caved in. Britain lost too many aircraft, but more importantly, too many valuable airmen. When Air Chief Marshal Dowding blew the whistle to stop sending aircraft and airmen on suicide missions to France, it was almost too late. When the Battle of Britain started at the end of July 1940 it became clear that supplying replacement aircraft would not be a problem but that supplying replacement pilots would be another matter. Too many British pilots were thrust into the Battle of Britain lacking any combat experience. Too many who had the necessary experience were already dead or captured. The inexperienced new boys became 'easy meat'. What effectively saved Britain was that narrow strip of water between France and England.

Sadly, 'The Few' who 'won' the Battle of Britain have had all the glory. Those who perished trying to stop the German advance into France, and who fought against much greater odds, have been forgotten. The Alan Acres of this world deserve our appreciation for what they tried to do.

Since man first fought against man there have been examples of 'friendly fire'. This euphemism means killing one's own forces by mistake. In the heat of the moment this is quite easy to do. When air combat began in the First World War, aircraft flew at such a sedate speed that there was usually enough time for a pilot to distinguish friend from foe. By 1940, aircraft were flying much faster and because of camouflage schemes in use, there was little time for a pilot to distinguish between friend and foe.

Fighter aircraft could be closing at a speed of 600 miles per hour. A dot in the distance could become friend or foe in no time. In addition, aircraft recognition was not seriously taught in 1940. During the first two years of the war, RAF pilots on many occasions reported having been in combat with the German Heinkel He 113 fighter aircraft. This was a type which the Germans never put into service but which was displayed in various propaganda photographs. The ruse worked. Later in the war, the British resorted to painting black and white stripes under the wings of their fighter aircraft to prevent over-zealous British gunners from firing on them. These stripes later adorned the wings and fuselages of all allied combat aircraft from D-Day until peace in 1945.

I have followed the facts of May 1940 as closely as possible in my story. During the Battle of France there were at least four incidents of Hurricanes attacking Blenheims in error and there had been other such incidents before this. Indeed, one fighter pilot had shot down a Blenheim after a crew member on the bomber had fired off the correct colours of the day. When the fighter pilot in question was interrogated over his 'stupidity', he replied that he had mistaken the coloured pyrotechnics for fire aimed at him!

The incident of the Blenheim squadron, which was completely annihilated on 11th May by a flight of Dornier 17s, is also factual. The unfortunate squadron was Number 114 based at Vaux. The airfield defence was so inadequate that one of the attacking Dorniers carried out a leisurely third circuit of the airfield to photograph the burning aircraft. The cine film of this was displayed throughout Germany. Who gave the stupid order to have all the squadron aircraft lined up wing-tip to wing-tip? Presumably he was demoted, but the damage was done.

The collapse of France was so swift that Hitler was able to parade himself in Paris on 23rd June 1940 in complete safety. That he then failed to invade Britain must count as a huge slap in the face for him. The start of the long road to the final defeat of the Third Reich began with the Austrian Corporal's completely irrational decision to take on Soviet Russia in May 1941. With hindsight we must be grateful for his unshakeable belief in his own military genius which was, thankfully, quite unrealistic.

TO DIE FOR THE EMPEROR

As Flight Petty Officer Takashe Sasebo emerged on the flight deck of the aircraft carrier *Soryu*, darkness was still complete. The ship had turned into the wind and was working up to its maximum speed to launch the first aircraft. The only objects visible were the lights of the deck party at the rear of the flight deck as they prepared one Mitsubishi Zero-Sen for departure. This aircraft would fly a combat air patrol above the carrier to prevent any enemy attacks during the entire mission. Sasebo could feel the whole ship vibrating beneath his feet. It was also pitching and rolling quite heavily. They were in the worst of the weather conditions which they had encountered since leaving Japan fourteen days earlier.

Now the first traces of grey light were appearing on the horizon as the fighter roared down the flight deck and climbed away. All that Sasebo could see of it were the small bluish flames coming from the engine exhausts. At the rear end of the flight deck, eighteen Nakajima B5N2 aircraft were already in position. Some were carrying torpedoes and some were carrying bombs. At 05:55 local time, the sound of engines starting up could just be heard above the roaring of the wind and the waves crashing against the carrier. It was 01:25 in Tokyo on Monday December 8th 1941. The Japanese Navy always adhered to Tokyo time and Japan was also one day ahead.

The light was now increasing and Sasebo could make out the shapes of the aircraft. He looked at the bridge and saw the Air Operations Officer raise his white flag. The first attack aircraft started its take-off roll along the wooden deck which was streaming with water and pitching heavily. Sasebo joined his comrades in waving and shouting encouragement although the flight crews would hear nothing over the roar of their engines.

Every twenty seconds an aircraft started to roll and in six minutes they were all airborne. Now the lifts from the hangars brought up nine Zero-Sen fighters and very quickly they too were on their way.

Apart from the *Soryu*, five other aircraft carriers were in the attack force. These were the *Kaga* and *Akagi* of the First Carrier Air Division, the *Hiryu* which, like the *Soryu*, belonged to the Second Carrier Air Division, and the *Shokaku* and *Zuikaku* of the Fifth Carrier Division. These carriers were supported by two battleships, two heavy cruisers, one light cruiser, nine destroyers and seven fleet oilers. All the ships had been refuelled the previous day.

Sasebo knew fully well what a risk this strike operation constituted. Not only was most of Japan's carrier fleet involved but just over 400 aircraft were also being risked. Sasebo was one of the rookie pilots on this operation. He came from a family with a naval tradition. His father was an officer on a battleship and might even be on the same operation. The Flight Petty Officer had graduated from the Naval Academy and had only finished his flight training one year earlier. His training grades were excellent and he was earmarked for the Zero-Sen fighter which he had been flying since then. The aircrews on this operation were nearly all veterans with over 600 hours flight time. Sasebo did not qualify on the basis of flight hours but he was considered good enough to participate in the operation.

By 06:20 local time, the first strike force of 189 aircraft drawn from the six carriers had formed up over the task force and set course for the island of Oahu, 200 miles to the south. It was estimated that they would start their attack against the Pearl Harbor facility some 90 minutes later.

In the meantime there was no respite for the ground crews on the carriers. As soon as the Zero-Sens were on their way, eighteen Aichi D3A dive bombers were brought up from the hangars. Their crews boarded them, the carrier turned into the wind once more and worked up to its maximum speed. At 07:15

local time, the launch of the second wave began. Young Sasebo waved and shouted as each aircraft roared past him but he now had to think of his own launch. With the Aichis climbing away and circling to join the second attack group, a further nine Zero-Sens were brought up from the hangars below. One of these was Sasebo's own aircraft.

Before the pilots scrambled aboard, his flight leader said to him in his rough voice, 'Young Sasebo, just stick close to me and you will be alright'.

Sasebo had a tremendous respect for his flight leader who had fought in the Manchuria campaign. The latter was a tough old salt who was constantly berating his pilots but he looked after them all and only wanted to bring them up to his own high standards.

Now they were all strapped in with their engines running. Sasebo was trying to fight the wave of fright which was welling up deep inside him. Now his leader opened up his throttle and started to move. Twenty seconds later Sasebo advanced his throttle and was on his way. He was now too busy to be afraid. His hands and feet were only there to control his aircraft and his mind was focussed on carrying out a successful mission.

Tucked in behind his leader's wing, he climbed up to rendez-vous with the other elements of the second strike force. There were 171 aircraft in this second wave and they were soon on their way headed due south. The Nakajimas from the other carriers were flying in the lead at 9,000 feet followed by the Aichis at 11,000 feet. The Zero-Sens were bringing up the rear at 14,000 feet and they were having to weave to stay behind the slower attack aircraft ahead of them. There was pretty solid cloud cover below them but the meteorological officers had indicated that it should be relatively clear over the island. All crews had their radios turned on and set to the channel for the raid but they were all under strict instructions to maintain radio silence.

Soon after the second wave was on its way, the pilots heard

71

the leader of the first wave announce, 'To, To, To', which was the signal to attack, and four minutes later they heard the second message, 'Tora, Tora, Tora', which meant that the first attack had been successful.

The second wave started its attack at 08:54 local time. Sasebo's element of Zero-Sens had been briefed to attack Hickam Field. They went in low and made several passes, shooting up parked aircraft, hangars and other buildings, until they had expended all of their ammunition. The ground defences were putting up a formidable curtain of fire and on the last run, Sasebo had felt a couple of bumps but nothing critical appeared to have been hit.

Now it was time to head for home. The fighters were the last to leave the target area as the bombers had only had to make one attack each. As the Zero-Sens climbed away and set course for the north, they slowly gathered into a loose formation, following their leader who was homing on to the carrier group by radio compass. One fighter drew fairly close to Sasebo's aircraft and a voice crackled in his earphones, '115, you have smoke coming from your engine. Check your oil temperature and pressure.'

The readings on the gauges looked quite normal. However, Sasebo started to review his options. There was still about an hour's flight time to reach the carrier. If his engine packed up during that time, he would be finished. The carrier crews would have their hands full recovering aircraft and once they had finished this, they would head for Japan as fast as they could. Nobody would come looking for him and trying to find him would in any case be like trying to find the proverbial needle in a haystack.

He anxiously watched his engine gauges. Now the oil pressure was starting to fall and the temperature was starting to climb. There was only one thing for it. He would return to Pearl Harbor and crash on a target of opportunity. This was what would be expected of him – to die for the Emperor. The military had been running Japan for the last ten years and all youngsters had been conditioned to die in battle causing the most damage.

Sasebo peeled out of formation and reversed his direction. He needed about ten minutes to be back over the island. He wanted as much altitude as possible and he needed to cool his engine as much as he could. He reduced power and opened the engine cooling gills. He willed his aircraft on, not knowing how much oil he had left. The coastline was already visible on the horizon but his oil pressure had fallen to zero and suddenly his engine seized. Tears of frustration filled his eyes. He would not make it. He now had to glide down to land on the heaving ocean below. His situation was hopeless. If he survived the landing and managed to get out of the cockpit, he had no dinghy to keep him afloat and nobody would find him. It would be better to get it over quickly. He pushed the stick forward and went into a vertical dive to make sure that the collision with the water would prove fatal. His very first combat mission was to be his last.

TAILPIECE

The Pearl Harbor strike force had to assume that war with the USA had been declared before the target was hit. Due to unaccountable delays the Japanese ambassador in Washington did not deliver the declaration in time.

The Japanese plan was to neutralise United States naval power in the Pacific. There was, however no aircraft carrier group in Pearl Harbor on the day of the strike. It had left two days earlier. The destruction caused by the Japanese bombers on 'Battleship Row' was considerable but not decisive. The Japanese failed to attack oil storage tanks and workshops which would have produced much more crippling results.

What the Japanese did achieve was to awaken a slumbering giant. They knew that in the long term they could not compete with America's industrial might and the truth of this came home to them much sooner than expected. Just six months later, four of the six aircraft carriers which had taken part in the Pearl Harbor attack were sent to the bottom at the Battle of Midway. Not only were the carriers lost but also their air groups and many highly skilled pilots.

The military code of sacrifice was not a myth. Admiral Yamamoto, who had masterminded the Pearl Harbor attack, flew into a rage when he learnt that one Japanese airman who had been shot down on the mission had actually allowed himself to be taken prisoner. The leader of the Zero-Sens in the second strike wave was hit in his fuel tanks over the target and deliberately dived into a target of opportunity on the ground. This was expected of him.

The appearance of the Zero-Sen fighter came as a nasty shock to the Allies. For several months it proved to be superior in combat to any fighters which opposed it. Only when an example was recovered intact and tested by the Americans were its limitations discovered. In order to achieve such an outstanding performance on a relatively low powered engine everything had been sacrificed to lightness. There was no armour protection and no self-sealing fuel tanks. In consequence it caught fire easily and could take very little battle damage without breaking up.

BEYOND THE PALE

Pilot Officer Harry Williams gradually came round and as his eyes opened, he realized that everything was not as it should have been. He remembered that there had been a massive explosion which had rocked his Lancaster and that Willie Jones in the tail turret had just announced over the intercom that he had 'hit one of the bastards'. Apart from that, everything was pretty vague, apart from the acute pain in his back, which was now gone.

What was happening? He was in the clouds and it was daylight. A few seconds ago – or so it had seemed – the night was dark and they were over Germany on their way to bomb Berlin. The flak was deadly as usual and they knew that there were German night fighters about. It was shortly after midnight on March 15th 1944 and they were in the middle of the bomber stream. He had seen a couple of other bombers going down in flames. Ahead, Harry could see the glow of the fires caused by the first bombs to be dropped on the German capital. He and his crew were on their 26th mission. Just four more to go, and they would be rested. They had been through enough missions to know what 'total war' was all about. They knew that only one in six aircrew members completed a tour of 30 operations but they had to believe that they would get through it. He had a good crew, a mix of colonials and Brits, and in the air they were an efficient unit, although they did not always see eye-to-eye on the ground.

Why was it light outside? Harry looked at his watch. It showed 12:05. That wasn't right because the light outside showed that it was either early or late in the day. But how long had he been unconscious and where were they? There was no doubt that they had been seriously hit but the plane seemed to

75

be functioning normally. The instruments were reading properly. He looked over his right shoulder to ask Bob Drew, his Canadian flight engineer, to fill him in, but Bob's position was vacant. Squinting forward and to the right, he could see nobody in the nose compartment. He pressed the intercom button on his yoke. 'Skipper to crew, check in'. He could not hear his own voice in his earphones. Was the intercom system dead? In any case there was no answer.

He looked at his instruments and was horrified. The Lanc was at 3,000 feet and descending at 500 feet per minute. This would not do. Harry pulled back on the yoke but it would not move. He tried increasing the power but the throttles would not move. He started to panic. He appeared to be all alone and about to dig a big hole in the ground. His heading was 270° and this was certainly not the way to Berlin.

In spite of his predicament, Harry came to accept the situation. Suddenly it was if he was on the outside looking in – just as if he was watching a filmed version. There was a crackle in his earphones and a familiar voice said, 'E - Edward, cleared to land on runway 27 – do not acknowledge'. Where the hell was runway 27 in relation to his position and how was he so near to his base? He could not move the controls and in less than six minutes he would crash. However, he felt strangely calm and detached and decided to let events take their course.

As the aircraft descended through 1,000 feet, Harry could glimpse through the broken cloud base signs of the land below and at 500 feet he could pick up familiar cues leading to runway 27 but the clag reached further down and he could still see nothing straight ahead. This will be interesting, he thought, in his new detached way. Suddenly the low clouds parted and there was the familiar runway smack ahead. The nose came up, the throttles eased back, the elevator trim wheel rotated, the propellers went to fine pitch, the mixture went to rich, the undercarriage rumbled down and the flaps were lowered. Harry had done nothing but took all this information in automatically.

The aircraft was perfectly set up for landing. Harry gave up wondering who was in charge. Clearly he was not and he sensed that he had been relieved of all his decision processes.

The aircraft touched down beautifully and slowed to a walking pace. On the right, Harry could see some Lancasters and Halifaxes parked near the tower. What were the Halifaxes doing there? There were none based in his area. Also the tower did not look very familiar. A car glided out in front of the aircraft to guide it to its parking spot. Harry still could not move any of the controls but the Lanc followed the car to a concrete pan and proceeded to shut itself down. There was no familiar ground crew standing around, waiting to secure the aircraft and then service it, but there was one solitary figure which emerged from the car and this looked like Doug Middleton, the Squadron Intelligence Officer.

Harry unclipped his seat harness and before evacuating the now silent bomber, he went forward and back to make sure that there were no crew members aboard. As he had guessed, there were none. But if they had bailed out after the aircraft was hit, escape hatches would have been left open. All such hatches were closed and there were no signs of any battle damage. Harry opened the rear fuselage door and jumped to the ground.

'Welcome home, Harry', said Doug. 'Your worries are over. Jump in and I will drive you to your de-brief'. Harry jumped into the car but noticed that Doug no longer looked like the Doug he knew and that he had lost his Midlands accent.

The car bumped across the grass field. It was headed away from the squadron's admin block. Low cloud and mist were swirling around making it difficult to see much at any one moment. Why were they crossing the airfield? There was nothing on the southern side. Suddenly the strands of mist parted and Harry could make out some parked aircraft with a low building behind them. Harry blinked and looked again. These aircraft were Messerschmitt 110 and Junkers 88 night fighters! He had been tricked. He had been lured into a trap by the Germans and now he was being taken prisoner. However, he felt no emotion. It was as if he didn't care what was going to happen.

They got out of the car at the entrance to the low building. There was a guard on duty. He was certainly wearing a German steel helmet. The door opened and a Luftwaffe officer came out. Doug and the German saluted each other and Doug handed over a piece of paper. The German officer examined it and beckoned to the two men to follow him into the building. They walked along a central corridor with various doors on each side but none of the doors was numbered and there were no name plaques on any of them. Come to think of it, there were no door handles visible. The German pushed open a door and all three men entered.

In the middle of the room was a table. On the near side was an empty chair but on the other side was an airman in his flying clothing. Harry knew that the man must be a Luftwaffe pilot as he displayed an Iron Cross on a ribbon above the partly opened zip at the top of his leather flying jacket. The pilot made as if to stand up but the German officer motioned him to remain seated. Doug asked Harry to take the other chair. Doug and the German officer who had brought them to the room exchanged glances and nodded at each other. 'You have half an hour to talk and then we shall be back to collect you', Doug said. The two left the room.

For a few moments both pilots examined each other across the table. The German pilot was tall and looked no more than 20. He was fair-haired and had a scar on one side of his face. He looked as if he had just come through a traumatic experience.

What do I do next? Harry thought. All I should do as a prisoner is give my name, rank and number.

It was the German pilot who broke the ice. 'My name is Helmut, how do you do', he said in perfect accent-free English, and extended a hand across the table. The men shook hands but Harry could not feel the other man's hand.

Harry gave his name and asked how Helmut spoke such perfect English. 'I have no English', Helmut replied, 'apart from the bit I learnt at school. But how do you speak such excellent German?' Harry had no German at all except 'Danke schön, auf Wiedersehen', and 'guten Morgen' and he admitted as much. The strange thing was that they could understand each other perfectly.

'I would gladly offer you a cigarette,' said Helmut, 'but I do not have any.'

'That's OK', Harry replied, 'but I don't feel the need for one'.

'Were you up in that big mess last night?' Helmut asked.

'Oh, you mean the Berlin raid', Harry said. 'Yes I was, but some bastard nailed us from behind and I have no idea what happened after that.' Was he talking too much? Was he giving away information which might help the enemy? The room was probably bugged in any case.

'Relax,' said Helmut. 'I thought I was back at my base but apparently I am not, I don't have a clue where I am and, quite honestly, it does not bother me. I feel fine and all the stress of the past few months has left me. But you look pretty awful. Are you OK?'

Harry replied that he was also feeling fine but he admitted to himself that he didn't know what in hell was going on.

'I was up there last night as well,' said Helmut, 'doing my bit for the Reich. After the Eastern Front, anything was going to be a picnic. Anyway, we were guided into the bomber stream and there were so many fat cats about that our job was easy. I have shot down several this year but it is no pleasure. We have been ordered to defend the Fatherland until we cop it. It is a question of killing or being killed and we are losing the war. My last recollection was coming up underneath a Lancaster in its blind spot. I was slightly to one side and could see the code letters SP-E on the fuselage. I raised the nose to fire and as I opened up, the Lanc's tail gunner opened up on me. I think I got him but his rear gunner got me. My aircraft was on fire and we had to get out fast but the hood was jammed. The next thing I knew was that it was daylight and coming out of the base of the murk I could see my home field right ahead. The fire was out and the plane seemed to be flying itself. My crewmember was not responding and I appeared to be on my own. I got down and was put in this room to be debriefed.'

'Christ!' said Harry. 'SP-E, that was me. My tail gunner reported he had nailed one just before the big explosion. So it was you that got us'.

'And that's why we are sitting together now' replied Helmut. 'One side, either yours or mine, wants to know what really happened. I'm truly sorry that I shot you out of the skies but that was what I was supposed to do.' 'What the Hell,' said Harry. 'We were up there to bomb all of you into submission so that this crazy war can be brought to an end.'

The ice was broken. Both men began to talk as if they had been friends for a long time.

Harry revealed that he was just twenty years of age and that he had been born in Rugeley in the British Midlands. His father had served in the trenches in the Great War and reckoned that he had been lucky to survive. He was now a bank manager in his home town. When the call-up came, Harry had decided that he wanted to fly. He was selected for aircrew training and had been shipped off to Canada for his elementary and basic training. He had liked all of that but it wasn't so much fun when he returned to Britain and its austerity conditions and was taught to fly the Lancaster. He thought he would never make it through the OCU course but he was finally posted to an operational squadron and had a crew assigned to him.

Then the serious business started. Everybody on the squadron knew that the chances of surviving a tour were slim. The defences over Germany were becoming stronger all the time. Flying missions turned boys into old men in no time. The tension ratcheted up and the only way to relieve it seemed to be getting drunk after each mission. Harry had had enough of this but he would not admit to anybody that he was scared, and he would keep on going until that final mission was flown and then hope to have a quieter life instructing.

Helmut told Harry that he was also twenty. He was born and raised in Hamburg. He had always wanted to fly and as soon as he could, he joined the Luftwaffe. His piloting skills were assessed as excellent and he was posted to a unit flying the Messerschmitt 109. He had hoped that he would see action over France against the RAF but his unit was in Russia. He had shot down several Russian aircraft as they had nothing at the time which could compete with his Messerschmitt and he had been awarded the Iron Cross but one day his luck ran out. He was hit by ground fire and was badly injured in the ensuing forced landing. After a lengthy period in hospital he was passed as fit to fly again as the Fatherland was in desperate need of experienced pilots but he was not up to single-seat fighters anymore and was trained to fly the Messerschmitt 110 as a night fighter pilot. He had been doing well at this until last night's incident.

'Look', said Helmut, 'I know that we are going to lose this bloody awful war. Nobody dares to speak of defeat because we are living in a police state. It was madness of Hitler to take on Russia and once the USA entered the war, it was clear to me that we could never hope to win.'

'I think you're right,' said Harry, 'but there's still a long way to go. I know that we have an army fighting its way up Italy right now. There has been talk of the Americans and us opening a second front in Europe but I don't know when that will happen. Anyway, it looks as if we are out of it until it's all over.'

'Lots of my people are particularly bitter about the way you Brits are bombing our cities,' said Helmut. 'They say that it is inhuman. However, I accept that my side started it first. I was too young to serve at the time but there were questionable bombing raids from our side on Warsaw and Rotterdam although it was stated that these were only against strategic

81

military targets. Well, Hitler then ordered indiscriminate bombing of London and there was no justification for that. As I said, I'm from Hamburg and as you know, your bombers devastated it last summer, I was in Russia at the time but my family was there. They were lucky. The only bad news which I have had is that my elder brother was in the 6th Army at Stalingrad and we do not know if he is dead or in captivity.'

'War is a bastard,' said Harry. 'I don't like what we are doing one bit but Hitler and his clique somehow have to be eliminated. What do you, as a German, think of what Hitler has done to the Jews?'

'Well, like most Germans, I sensed that it was all wrong but if you spoke out as some did, you would just disappear. I paid lip-service to the Nazis. I was in the Hitler Youth because if you did not join, it would be noted down in the records. I can understand why a lot of Germans of my parents' generation supported Hitler. The conditions laid down in the Versailles peace treaty of 1919 were too crippling for Germany and the following years of poverty were the ideal breeding ground for the rise of the Nazis. *'Ein Volk, ein Reich, ein Führer.'* Helmut laughed. 'Just look where it has got us.'

They talked some more about the war, their families and their aspirations. Given the right circumstances, they could have become good friends.

However, several minutes later, the door was pushed open and Doug and the Luftwaffe officer entered the room. This time it was the Luftwaffe officer who spoke, and once again Harry was amazed that he could understand everything. 'All right, gentlemen, your time is up. Please follow me.'

As Helmut stood up and started to move, Harry could see that the German pilot had a terrible limp which must have been due to his crash in Russia.

The two pilots followed their 'minders' back along the corridor. A guard saluted them and opened the front door. When they stepped outside it was already very dark and Harry could not see Helmut and the Luftwaffe officer. Turning around, he could not see the building they had just left. He could only just sense Doug's presence.

'The transition is over', Doug's voice said, but he seemed to be speaking from within Harry. 'Your mind, your soul, or your spirit, whatever you like to call it, is now free from your body. Anything which is physical no longer exists. You will never need to move, to breathe, to eat or sleep or perform any other human functions again. We always try to make the transition as painless as possible. You do not know me but I am your mentor. I was tasked to bring you out of what you knew as 'life' and to help you on your way.'

The voice continued. 'From now on you live within your mind. You will be able to contact anybody you knew in your former life just by thinking of them. Conversely, people who knew you and who are still on Earth will be able to contact you just by thinking of you, although they will not be aware of it. Your mind is indestructible and eternal, whether it is dominated by good or evil thoughts. It should be your aim to improve your mind through interaction with other minds. It seems to me that you are on the right track. If you have any questions or problems, just think of me and I shall be there to advise you. Good luck!'

Harry absorbed all of this without any emotion. He had been liberated.

THE FIERY TAIL OF THE KOMET

The Kommandant had all five pilots standing to attention.

'Gentlemen', he said, 'the Fatherland needs volunteers for a special project. You are my most experienced pilots. We are losing too many men attacking the streams of American bombers over our homeland. We have a radical new weapon which may defeat them but it is still in the experimental stage and highly dangerous. It requires the best pilots who know how to shoot down the B-17s. I shall be sorry to lose any of you, but we must put the defence of the Reich first. If you volunteer, I shall be losing my best men, but if you decline I shall not hold it against you. I cannot tell you any more. You are free to decide.'

Leutnant Erich Bachmann risked a glance at the other four standing in line. He had proved his worth. Too young to be involved in the first four years of the war, he had been trained to fly the Focke-Wulf Fw 190 fighter in a homeland defence unit. It was clear to him that the war was no longer going Germany's way. Many German cities were being reduced to rubble by the British night bombing offensive. Industrial targets were being hit hard by the American bombers by day. It had been held that the US Army Air Corps would abandon its daylight bombing offensive because of the considerable losses incurred, but their resources were bottomless and the huge daylight raids continued and in increased strength.

Bachmann had taken part in several new ideas. His Gruppe had been used to drop time-fused bombs on the serried ranks of the attacking Flying Fortress bomber stream. This idea achieved very little. The next idea had been to attack the B-17s from behind in a line-abreast formation. This had been abandoned when American P-51 fighters began to accompany the bombers into German airspace and could pounce on the German pilots before they could do any real damage. Now the only effective method of attack was to adopt a line-abreast formation well ahead of the advancing bomber stream and to hit them head-on before the American fighters could intervene. The Fw 190s with their cannon armament could open fire before the B-17 gunners with their shorter-range machine guns could respond and the bombers were particularly vulnerable to head-on attacks. The problem for the Fw 190 pilot was to keep his nerve. The two opposing forces were closing at speeds in excess of 500 miles per hour. From the time the B-17s came within cannon fire range, there were only a couple of seconds available for cannon to be fired before the attackers had to break off to avoid colliding with the enemy. This was extremely wearing on the nerves, and Bachmann, in spite of his successes, was starting to develop the dreaded 'twitch'.

Bachmann's mind told him that he was not going to survive much longer in this environment. He stepped forward – and so did his four colleagues. They were given their posting orders immediately. They had just time to garner all their meagre belongings and then they were on their way.

'What do you make of all of this, Erich?' his friend Bernd Paulsen asked him. A few days previously on returning from a mission, Bernd had been scared to death as a fighter had swept past him at an amazing speed. It had no propellers but Bernd had breathed more freely when he had noticed that the aircraft carried Luftwaffe markings. Thank God it's one of ours, he had thought. There were plenty of rumours about secret weapons but the State's security lid was kept very tightly in place.

Erich was dropped off at an airfield in middle Germany. He had two of his former fellow pilots with him. They were not told where they were. Security was obviously very tight.

There were SS soldiers on gate duty which was not a very encouraging sign but the pilots' papers were in order and they were allowed to enter. They were taken immediately to the Kommandant's office. The man wore the Iron Cross, First Class, about his neck. He did not waste time with pleasantries. They had to report at 06.00 the next morning at Hangar A.

The following morning Erich was lined up with nine other pilots inside Hangar A.

The Kommandant came limping in. Erich had not noticed the limp the previous day as his new CO had not had to move. 'At ease, gentlemen. I am Major Haudegen. You have all volunteered for special duties and I am grateful for your love of the Fatherland. Here you will be trained to fly an aircraft which will eliminate the enemy's entire daylight bomber offensive. It is a wonderful weapon but it is entirely unforgiving. My broken back is a witness to that. You have all signed an oath of secrecy. Please note the security guards at the doors. They are trained to shoot before asking any questions. Please do not provoke them. The Fatherland needs your special skills.'

Haudegen motioned to an object in the middle of the hangar which was under wraps. 'Kapitän Plötz, remove the wraps.'

What followed was a complete surprise. Plötz beckoned the men forward. In front of them sat a diminutive flying machine. The short fuselage was shaped like a bullet. The wings were swept back. There was no conventional tailplane. There was no undercarriage. There was no propeller! The pilots looked at this creation in absolute awe.Haudegen positioned himself in front of the tiny aircraft.'This will be your first briefing. In two weeks' time, you have to be able to fly this thing. If it does not kill you, you will master it because you are all exceptional pilots. You have noted that there is no propeller. That little thing on the nose only turns to power the electrics. Gentlemen, this is the world's first rocket interceptor. It is the Komet. It has taken years to develop because it was only given low priority. In 1941, when many of you were still at school, the prototype aircraft became the first aircraft in the world to exceed 1,000 kilometres per hour *in level flight.* That is 250 kilometres per hour faster than our Messerschmitt which established the world's official speed record in 1939.

Haudegen paused for all of this to sink in and then continued. 'However, the forward speed is not important. Your rocket motor will take you from the ground to 12,000 meters, which is your ceiling, in just over 3 minutes. Your motor will run for a maximum of 8 minutes – then you have to glide back to base. Aerodynamically this aircraft is superb at operational speeds and even as a glider it is outstanding but its approach speed is way above what you are used to and if you do not land directly into wind, you can kiss goodbye to life. The fuels required for the rocket motor are extremely volatile. They have to be handled with the utmost care. Here is a little demonstration.'

The Major drew the group's attention to a man standing near a bench. He was dressed in full protective clothing like a military fire-fighter. 'Gentlemen, you have two fuels which we call C-Stoff and T-Stoff. The technician before you will pick up one drop of each fuel on the two glass rods which he is holding and will then let the two drops come into contact with each other.'

The result was a violet explosion.

'Now that was just an argument between two drops. You do not need much imagination to know what will happen if there is any major intermingling of the fuels outside of the rocket motor. We have had fully fuelled aircraft sitting on the flight line which for no reason just blew up. Kapitän Plötz is responsible for your training programme and it only remains for me to wish you 'Hals und Beinbruch''. This was the traditional German macabre Good Luck wish – 'break your neck and your legs'.

The next day, the training started and the course had been compressed as much as possible because of the urgency of the situation. First, Erich and his colleagues had to become glider pilots. If they were ever going to make it back to base after a mission, they would need to do this without an engine to help them. For a few days they were towed aloft behind Messerschmitt Me 110s in sporting gliders. They were cast off at different altitudes and in different locations until they were capable of making it back to base without landing in some farmer's meadow, cornfield or potato patch. They were all very good pilots and they all made the grade. The next phase was similar but the gliders had several feet of their wingspan removed so that they descended much faster and their landing speed was greater.

Then came the introduction to the Komet. Because of the very short duration of the proposed missions, it went without saying that each pilot had to master all the switches and instrumentation so that he could handle everything without thinking. The aircraft had two powerful cannon and the latest gyro gunsight. There was a radio fitted for communications with ground control. The pilot had a parachute but it was deemed that his chances of bailing out were pretty slim as the airflow would keep him firmly pressed in his seat once he had jettisoned the canopy. The worst feature was that there was no pressurisation and no cockpit heating. The ears and stomach would suffer agony with the rapid fall in pressure on the way up. The same would happen in reverse on the way down. The only consolation was that a mission would not last more than fifteen to twenty minutes so there would be little risk of frostbite.

For an introduction to the Komet's flight characteristics, Erich sat in an aircraft without any fuel aboard and was towed aloft by a Messerschmitt Me 110. The aircraft took off on a dolly which had to be released after leaving the ground. If this was done too quickly, the dolly could bounce back off the ground and damage the aircraft. Plötz had drummed it in to all of them that prior to landing, when the landing skid was extended, it had to be put in the neutral position, otherwise the landing roll would be extremely rough. Several pilots who forgot this developed a severe case of the 'Komet back' which removed them from flying status. Erich found that the little Komet was a joy to fly as a glider. It picked up speed very quickly in a dive.

Care had to be taken not to exceed the limits. At red-line speed, the nose tucked under and a graveyard spiral would follow.

Then the day came for Erich's one and only powered flight before being released for combat duties. His only fear was of the aircraft exploding on him. He could cope with all the rest. It was known that slave labour was being used in the production of all war material and that quality control was not what it should be. Erich had seen two Komets blow up since he had been there. One exploded when being fuelled and the second one had exploded on landing.

Erich's aircraft had a shield painted on the nose depicting Baron Münchhausen's mythical ride on a cannon-ball. This was very appropriate, he thought. His aircraft had already been fuelled when he clambered aboard and the ground crew manoeuvred it into wind.

His instructions were simple: climb up to 10,000 metres, report on reaching that altitude, cut the motor, jettison all remaining fuel, check all gliding parameters on the way down, call when on final approach and then land. The radio would only be switched on when the little propeller on the nose had spun up, so take-off would be authorised by a green light signal from the tower. Otherwise, turning on the radio on the ground would only drain the batteries. The rocket motor had no throttle – it either ran at full power or not at all. Erich threw the switch to fire up the engine. The kick in his back was unexpected in spite of all he had been told. The little aircraft leapt ahead like a greyhound from the starting gate. In no time he was at take-off speed. He eased back on the stick and dropped the dolly. He pulled back further and started to climb like a bat out of hell. This was incredible. There was no vibration and hardly any noise reached him from the screaming motor behind him. He cleared the pressure in his ear-drums as he soared upwards. In no time at all he was at 10,000 metres.

'Base from Baron One at ten,' he announced and he cut the motor. He had not been fully fuelled for this flight so there was not much remaining fuel to dump.

The sky was clear so he did not need a steer from ground control to get home. He put the aircraft through its paces on the way down and was absolutely exhilarated. The only thing which he had not done was to fire his two cannon. They were not armed for this flight and in any case, he had done firing practice on the ground. He calculated the correct moment to turn in for his landing approach.

'Base from Baron One – final.' He extended the skid and made sure the lever was in neutral. The Komet touched down beautifully and ran straight and true until one wingtip slowly lowered to touch the ground and the aircraft came to rest.

Kapitän Plötz appeared as Erich opened the canopy. 'Well, Bachmann, how was it?'

'Magic', Erich replied. 'Get enough Komets and we shall sweep the Americans from the skies.'

Two days later, Erich was at readiness for his first operational flight. He sat on the grass by his fully fuelled aircraft. Because of the state of aircraft availability only three machines were ready to go. At 10.00 in the morning, radar had picked up a large raid coming in over the Dutch coast. It remained to be seen where it was headed. If it was to continue south towards Frankfurt, they would be in business. The Komet with its very limited endurance could only operate within about 50 miles from base. As time went by, it was clear the raid was headed in their direction. The three Komet pilots went to cockpit readiness. They were lined up 100 yards apart so that there would be no danger of collision on take-off. It was still relatively peaceful but they had seen Messerschmitt 109s and Focke-Wulf 190s heading north in considerable numbers to meet the attackers which were still beyond visual range. Finally they could hear the sound of anti-aircraft fire and the three pilots were instructed to scramble.

Once aloft with their radios functioning, they were given vectors to intercept the bombers. This was hardly necessary as they could all see the approaching armada. Erich checked his gunsight and was ready for business. He was soaring up ideally positioned for an attack from below on the lead group. He would bring one B-17 down on his first pass, soar above the box and dive down to pick off a second one. He would continue until he ran out of fuel or ammunition. He was now closing incredibly fast from below. One fat B-17 was squarely in his sights. Erich pressed the gun button. Each gun fired two shells and then jammed. He screamed in frustration. By now he was above the formation and he turned to dive back down. His guns were still blocked. There were red-tailed P-51s about. They were only a minor nuisance as they could not match his speed. Erich tried all he knew to clear his guns as he soared upwards and plunged downwards but to no avail. Then his motor quit and he had to get back to base. One P-51 tried to get on his tail but even as a glider, the Komet easily out-distanced the enemy fighter.

Erich hit the switches to vent all the remaining fuel before he came in to land. A small quantity was still registering on the gauges but these were not particularly reliable. He was bathed in perspiration and was extremely angry but he did not forget his flying skills. He set up a nice approach and lowered the skid. Instead of making a nice soft landing, the Komet bounced on a ridge. He had forgotten to put the lever into neutral. Erich had no time to react. The remaining fuel in the pipes ignited and blew aircraft and pilot apart as if they had never existed.

TAILPIECE

The Messerschmitt Me 163 Komet was years ahead of its time. Messerschmitt actually had no part in it apart from the fact that his facility produced it. The whole concept failed to achieve any real results because of Adolf Hitler's stubbornness. As far as he was concerned, any project of merit which could not be in service within one year was of no use. The war would be over by then. Furthermore, he was only interested in offensive weapons. With hindsight we all know how wrong the arrogant little Austrian corporal was. The Germans never produced a strategic long-range bomber. The Komet and the Me 262 jet fighter could have been in service at least two years earlier. The Germans were the only nation to have some mastery of rocket technology. In 1945 their rocket scientists were poached by the Russians and the Americans. Because of the German know-how, both rivals were able to develop powerful rockets for space research.

The Me 163 programme was a classic example of 'too little, too late' and the blame has to be laid at Adolf Hitler's door. Thank goodness that he was blinded by his belief in his genius and that those around him slavishly obeyed him. Nearly 400 operational examples of the Komet were produced. Many were lost in accidents because they were breaking new ground – but this should have been sorted out two years previously. The Komets only brought down ten American bombers, with two others claimed as probable. They could have caused much greater damage if their potential had been noted much earlier. Fortunately Hermann Goering, head of the Luftwaffe, did not have the intelligence or the technical knowledge to back the right horses. The prototype of an improved version, the Me 263, which flew just before the final curtain call, had a pressurised cockpit, retractable undercarriage, greater endurance, greater climb performance and a rocket motor whose thrust could be controlled by the pilot. It would have been an awesome weapon but by the time it flew Germany was in ruins and the game was up.

MILES AHEAD

Flight Lieutenant Peter Bardsey regarded himself as being a very fortunate young man. He could not have wished for a better job. For just over a year he had been a member of the Experimental Flying Unit at the Royal Aircraft Establishment, Farnborough. He had flown two operational tours on fighters during the war and had acquitted himself well. He had shot down several enemy aircraft and was known to be able to get more out of his own aircraft than any of his colleagues could get out of theirs. Because of his natural flying aptitude and his interest in all technical matters, he had been posted to Farnborough in March 1945 as an experimental test pilot.

He was one of the few RAF pilots to have flown a captured example of the Messerschmitt Me 262 jet fighter. He had built up an impressive number of hours test flying the British Meteor and Vampire jet fighters. He was familiar with all the British high-performance propeller-driven fighters and had pushed them all to their limits.

It was now early May 1946 and the war in Europe had been over for just one year. Peter still had the best part of a year to run on his current posting and he hoped that at the end of it he would be allowed to continue with his experimental work. He was looking forward to his next challenging assignment, whatever that might be.

He had been running some low-speed handling tests on the new Meteor Mark IV that morning and after changing out of his flying clothing he had been tracked down by the Commanding Officer's secretary. 'The CO wants to see you in his office at 1500 this afternoon. Can you make it?'

'Sure,' replied Peter. 'Have you any idea what it's about?'

The answer was a negative. Peter wasn't expecting anything

unpleasant and he hoped that it would be good news.

Just before the appointed time, Peter turned up at the secretary's office. He was surprised to see Flight Lieutenant Alex Long there as well. Right on the hour they were ushered in to the CO's office. Both men came to attention and saluted. The CO quickly put them at ease. It was then that Peter noticed Lieutenant Eric Brown sitting to the right of the desk. Brown was a Navy man and was one of the experimental pilots in their unit. 'Winkle', as Brown was known to his friends, was a very accomplished test pilot and who, because of his fluent German had been able to test-fly most of the German military aircraft used in the war and he was known to have dived a Spitfire, which had been specially modified, to the unheard-of speed of 86% of the speed of sound.

'Gentlemen,' the CO began, 'we have a new project, or rather an old one has been revived. Winkle here was the designated pilot for that project until it folded. He now has so many carrier-landing trials to perform that he is going to be hard-pushed to do them all. He wanted this new project badly but Winkle is nothing if not a realist and he knows that his first duty is to satisfy the needs of his Navy. So the new project needs a new lead pilot and, because of the risks involved, it will require a back-up pilot as well. Winkle and I think that you are the two for the job. Peter, with your greater experience, as lead pilot and Alex as back-up. This project is going into completely unknown territory. It will be dangerous work. However, if the project succeeds, your names will go down in history and our country will receive an enormous moral boost. You do not have to accept this assignment. If you decline, there will be no bad mark on your records and no setback in your service careers. If you accept, Winkle will give you an initial briefing here and now. If you want time to consider, just let me know.'

Peter spoke up immediately. 'I know you haven't said as much, Sir, but I think you are referring to the M.52 project. Even if it isn't, please count me in. Our testing work is inherently dangerous in any case. Flying can be unforgiving even in the safest aircraft. I am certainly ready for a new challenge.'

Alex chimed in. 'Please count me in too, Sir. I endorse what Peter has said.'

'I was pretty sure that you chaps would agree,' said the CO. 'Now listen carefully to what Winkle has to say. He knows far more about this project than I do. You may have questions at the end and if so, Winkle and I shall do our best to answer them.'

Winkle stood up and drew back a piece of cloth which had been covering a board. On the board was pinned a three-view drawing of an experimental aircraft. 'Peter, you were right in your guess. Yes, it is the Miles M.52 and here she is in her latest form.'

Winkle reminded them how the project had been cancelled in February of that year. Sir Ben Lockspeiser, scientific adviser to the new Labour government, had decided that the project was just too risky and the Ministry of Supply then stopped the funding. The first prototype was over 80% complete at the time. The cancellation raised a huge outcry in the aircraft industry and among many prominent scientists. Now, as if by a miracle, the government had relented and the project was on again.

Winkle then went on to describe the Genesis of the project. 'Back in 1943, it was decided that we really needed to develop some flight technology which would be superior to the latest developments in Germany. A specification was drawn up around a research aircraft which would be able to reach a thousand miles per hour in level flight and which would be able to reach an altitude of 36,000 feet in a minute and a half after take-off. Those goals are still far from attainable even today. You chaps know that at best you can get about half that speed at altitude in a Meteor and that you need about fifteen minutes to reach that altitude. I can let you into a little secret about how this impossible specification came about. The translator who was working on the German documentation about their latest projects made the fundamental error of translating a level speed of 1,000 kilometres per hour as miles per hour. When the error was discovered, the thought was to be bold and to try for the impossible in any case.

'Miles Aircraft obtained the contract. You chaps know that most of their stuff is pretty low-performance but they have some very clever brains in their design team. They came up with a design very similar to the one which you see on this board. The wings are the thinnest ever designed. They have been tried out at low speeds. A pair was fitted to one of their little Falcon cabin monoplanes. Look at the tail assembly and note that there is no rudder on the fin and no elevators on the tailplane. The design team concluded that conventional control surfaces would not work at high speeds. The result was to make the fin and tailplane pivot to provide the control needed. The tailplane has also been tested on the same Falcon. I have flown this aircraft. It is called the Gillette Falcon because the wings are like razor blades. At low speeds, all the flying surfaces are perfectly well-behaved.

'The nose section is shaped like a pointed bullet. The cockpit is extremely small. The pilot is almost lying on his back so as to keep the fuselage diameter at the front end as small as possible. Part of the reason why I was chosen for this project is because I am small. Part of the reason why you two have been selected is for the same reason. Anybody over five feet eight just will not fit into that cockpit.

'The original M.52 was to have had a turbojet engine. It would have received air from an annular intake just behind the cockpit. The engine would also have had a system of thrust augmentation. Such a system has already been tried on a Meteor back in 1944. When the axe fell in February, the first prototype was about a month away from its first flight, provided that the engine would have been ready on time. There were serious doubts about the engine being able to do the job. From the experts I have spoken to they seem to have no real doubts about the ability of the airframe.

'After the cancellation, a few boffins under the direction of Professor Coles, who had been working on rocket propulsion after studying the engine used in the German Komet interceptor, came to the conclusion that a rocket motor would have been a much better solution for the M.52. A rocket motor has been devised which is more powerful than the Walter unit in the Komet and which is also far more reliable. As you may know, I was not allowed to test the Komet in powered flight because of the risk of the volatile fuels blowing the aircraft apart.

'Now the project has been resuscitated. The aircraft has become the M.52R with the 'R' indicating 'rocket powered'. Miles Aircraft have done a great job incorporating all the changes. It is confidently expected that flight testing may begin in as little as two months' time. My only regret is that I won't be there to fly it. And now let me hand you over to our Commanding Officer.'

'Thank you for that presentation, Winkle,' said the CO. 'Any questions at this stage, chaps?'

There were none.

'Now I can add some more information relevant to the new revised project. The rocket motor takes up far less space than the planned turbojet and weighs less. In consequence more fuel can be carried which is just as well because the rocket gets through fuel in no time at all. There are four chambers to the rocket motor. They can be fired individually and shut down individually or they can all be fired together. With all chambers running, there is enough fuel for about five minutes. That is clearly a major issue. The solution is that the M.52R will be carried aloft slung under the bomb bay of a Lancaster. Two Lancaster bombers are being modified now for their role as launch platforms. The M.52R will weigh about 8,000 pounds fully loaded which is far less than some of the bomb loads the Lancaster used to carry on missions during the war. When the rocket fuel is exhausted, the M.52R will have to glide down to land, which will not be easy. There will be a chase aircraft accompanying each flight. You will fly the chase plane on most occasions, Alex, but we shall make sure that you get some rocket flights as well.

'Another important point is that this project is highly secret. I know that you chaps won't talk about it outside of the team but others may. The Americans already have a lot of our research material and more was released when the project was first cancelled. We don't want the Americans or anybody else knowing what we are up to. We want to be first. For this reason we shall not run the project from Farnborough where it would be all too conspicuous. We want it as far away from prying eyes as possible. Winkle will have heard of Machrihanish but I doubt if it means anything to you chaps. It lies on the Mull of Kintyre in Scotland. It was until two months ago a Royal Naval Air Station. It is about to have one of the longest runways in the country laid there just for this project. The runway length will be all of 10,000 feet. The M.52R will touch down at 170 miles per hour so it will need plenty of runway. We expect a typical mission profile to be something like this. The Lancaster will take off with the M.52R slung under its belly. The pilot, for safety reasons, will not enter the rocket plane until altitude is reached. The Lancaster will head out over the Irish Sea climbing up to 20,000 feet. It will then drop its baby. The pilot will fly his mission as planned. We shall start with a series of glide flights with no fuel on board but water ballast to replace it. When we are satisfied with the unpowered performance, we shall start with powered flights and start building up the performance in increments. The higher the M.52R can fly, the lesser is the air resistance so the performance will increase. When we are well into the programme, part of the rocket fuel will be used to get the plane up to about 40,000 feet and then a level high-performance run can be carried out. Then will come the long glide back to base.

'The M.52R will never be too far from base not to be able to return for a glide landing. Ground observation posts will be established on the axis of the new runway. Two posts equipped with kine theodolite apparatus will be established five miles apart on the extended runway centreline. From their data the speed attained on high speed runs will be measured. We also have radar to keep the aircraft on the desired path.

'One thing which Winkle omitted and which I should not forget is abandoning ship. You both know that you have virtually no chance of being able to bail out successfully from a Meteor or a Vampire if things go badly wrong. There is a seat being designed which will catapult the pilot from a high-speed aircraft in an emergency but that equipment is some time away. Miles have come up with the neat solution that the whole of the pilot's capsule can be blown away from the main airframe by explosive bolts in an emergency. When the nose capsule has slowed down, the pilot can get out and open his parachute. Whether this system will work at high speeds, we do not know. Maybe this is why the government first cancelled the project, conveniently overlooking the point that at the high speeds you are already used to, you have no chance of escaping from a disaster in any case. I think that this message has been delivered loud and clear and perhaps this is why the programme has had a reprieve. So, there it is chaps. Tomorrow, if weather permits, the Anson will fly you down to Woodley to meet the Miles people and the boffins. Winkle will go with you to make the necessary introductions. If the weather closes in, you will all go by road. After all, it is not far from here. At this point, I wish you good luck, but I know that from the pilotage angle the project is in good hands.'

The CO produced a bottle of whisky and poured out four shots. Winkle raised his glass and said, 'Well, Peter and Alex, as the Germans say – *Hals und Beinbruch* – which is to wish you good luck. Jerry has a macabre sense of humour as the saying literally means *break your neck and your legs*. I'm sure that it won't happen to you.'

The next morning they flew down to Woodley, just outside Reading, which is where Miles Aircraft had its factory and airfield. Winkle made all the introductions which were necessary. The three were taken into a remote hangar which was under very tight security. Inside was a full-size mock-up of the M.52R. They were accompanied by the design team and by Professor Coles. The chief designer pointed out the salient features of the aircraft. Peter and Alex tried the pilot's capsule for size. Each of them could just wriggle into it and reckoned that they could still get in with full flying gear. The controls looked conventional enough as did the instrument panel. The one innovation on the panel was a machmeter which neither of the pilots had seen before. This instrument did not show airspeed but rather the relationship between the speed of the aircraft and the speed of sound. It was calibrated in terms of Mach. The pilots knew that Mach 1 is the actual speed of sound. It is 760 miles per hour at sea level and 660 miles per hour at 36,000 feet on a 'standard' day where temperature and atmospheric pressure are 'average' but they had not previously seen an instrument which could show this. Both of them knew that when an aircraft flew faster than seven to eight tenths the speed of sound, the air would start to compress and start to behave like a liquid and that so-called shockwaves would start to form on the wing, separating high from low pressure. These shockwaves, as they increased in intensity, would move across the wing leading to instability. It was predicted that once an aircraft reached the local speed of sound, the shockwaves would go and that flying would become smooth again. Would this happen? This is what the whole project was about.

Professor Coles gave a short lecture on the rocket motor which was being bench-tested at present and which was performing satisfactorily. The pilots were told that the fuel was a mixture of liquid oxygen and water/methanol. These fuels were quite volatile but less so than the fuels which the Germans had used in the Messerschmitt Komet and which had caused so many of these aircraft to blow up. Professor Coles pointed out that the power of the rocket motor could not be adjusted. It either ran at full power or not at all. The only control available to the pilot was to be able to switch individual chambers on or off.

After lunch, Peter and Alex were introduced to the Miles company's chief test pilot. He showed them over the Gillette Falcon.

'We have another aircraft being converted', he explained. 'Both of you will get some low-speed handling experience on these two aircraft. We thought long and hard about how to give you some training for the glide back to base in the M.52R when the rocket fuel has been exhausted. Winkle told us what he had heard about how the Komet pilots were initially trained and we decided to copy the idea. We scrounged a couple of Slingsby gliders which had been used in radar tests. We have clipped the wings and added some ballast to them so they will glide and land much faster. They will not approach the 220 miles per hour glide speed of the rocket plane but the training will be useful, particularly since there will be no engine in front of you and you will have the sort of forward visibility which you will experience in the M.52R. These gliders will be towed aloft by one of our Martinet target towing aircraft. We reckon that if you are cast off at 5,000 feet above the airfield, you will get plenty of experience of what gliding is about.

'From next Monday you will both be here for two weeks flying the Falcons and the gliders and becoming familiar with the cockpit layout of the M.52R. Believe me, you will both be very busy. At the end of that period the first prototype should be ready and it will be transported to the location where you will test it. Security is so tight that even I am not allowed to know where that will be.'

The next two weeks went by in a flash and both pilots were working hard from dawn to dusk. They were kitted out with all the gear which they would be wearing on the experimental flights and they had to practise over and over again getting into that small capsule and getting out of it as quickly as they could and being able to run through the check lists from memory, manipulate the controls and all the switches and read all the instrumentation until all functions were quite automatic. In addition they were flying the Gillette Falcons and the specially modified gliders.

By late May the initial training was over. Peter and Alex had cleared their desks at Farnborough. They each had a brand new Meteor, specially cleaned up and highly polished, to ferry up to Machrihanish. These aircraft would serve as the chase planes for the test flights. The CO was there to see them off. 'Winkle says he is sorry that he can't be here but he is already doing some carrier trials off Arran. He says he will look you up as his Navy base is quite near to where you will be. Anyway, Chaps, all the best of luck and we look forward to some really stunning performances.'

Although the Navy flying units had already temporarily moved out of Machrihanish, the base was a hive of activity. The huge east-west runway had just been completed. Military transport aircraft were coming and going bringing in personnel and equipment for the experiments. A high security accommodation block had been set aside for the entire team. It was permanently guarded and ID had to be shown at all times. The flight test hangar was also permanently guarded.

When Peter and Alex had unpacked their possessions, they were taken over to the flight test hangar to be shown the first prototype. It was being fussed over by a team of Royal Aircraft Establishment engineers and mechanics. There were also a few hand-picked Miles mechanics there who had been seconded to the project. The ground staff for this project numbered more than a hundred individuals.

The M.52R had been left unpainted and devoid of any identification marks. In the large hangar it appeared to be so small and insignificant. It would even appear to be small next to a Spitfire, which was among the smallest of the famous fighters of the war, but it exuded an air of belonging very much to the future. Nobody had ever seen a completed aircraft looking quite like this.

On the following day, the pilots were introduced to the two Lancaster crews whose job would be to haul the rocket plane aloft and to release it at altitude. The crews were, as expected, Royal Aircraft Establishment personnel. Peter knew one of the two pilots as he had flown with him back at Farnborough. This was the number one crew pilot, Flight Lieutenant 'Taffy' Jones. Taffy had flown the Lancaster operationally in the war and knew his aircraft better than anybody else. He gave Peter and Alex a guided tour.

'You will note,' he said, 'that the bomb bay doors have gone and that the opening has been widened to take your rocket plane. Tomorrow we proceed with the first mating between my aircraft and the M.52R. It has all been thoroughly worked out and it should be a piece of cake. The only other external modification which you will notice is the lengthened tailwheel leg. This was done so that there will be sufficient clearance between the M.52R and the ground when the rocket plane is attached. Come inside and I will show you more.'

'I shall only have two crewmembers with me on the tests,' Taffy explained. 'I have my flight engineer and young Dobson, who has been trained to help you get into that nose capsule when we are in flight. That could be quite a tricky operation. You have this platform here which can be moved into position next to the capsule. Dobson will help you in. When you are fully settled, he will advise me over the intercom. When you give him the thumbs up, he will tell me that you are ready to be dropped. I shall then put the aircraft into a shallow dive. We need to drop you at 220 miles per hour to give you a good margin over your stall speed. I have been told that this is your best glide speed. Is this correct?'

Peter confirmed that this was so. Taffy continued, 'By the way, our ASI is calibrated in miles per hour. Is yours the same?'

Peter joked, 'I shall be flying a Miles product, so naturally my ASI is in miles per hour. Only the chase Meteor has an ASI calibrated in knots and we don't need to worry about that.'

Taffy resumed, 'When we are at the correct speed, I shall tell young Dobson we are ready and he will give you a thumbs up and release the shackles permitting you to fall clear. You will already be on the master frequency on your radio to link you with the chase plane, the tower, and the boffins on the ground. I shall be on a different frequency with the tower and after I have dropped you, I keep well out of your way and allow you to complete your mission and land. I shall then let the chase plane land and when you are both clear of the runway I shall make my landing approach. That's it. We are all up to speed and raring to go. We are sure that you are as well.'

In the afternoon there was a general briefing for the entire team. It was led by Squadron Leader Ray Parkinson who had been appointed as project manager.

'Gentlemen,' he began, 'I think that the only reason why I have been appointed to this exalted position is that I have done a good stint of test flying and that I also have a degree in aeronautical engineering. I am supposed to be good at managing people as well but you will be the judge of that. I am not alone at the pinnacle of this project as I am in daily contact with the CO of Experimental Flying at Farnborough, the manufacturers of the M.52R and the aerodynamics and rocket boffins. I shall be setting the flight test schedule but I want you all to know that nothing is written in stone. We are one big team. Our strength comes from the combined knowledge and skill of each of you individually. We all want to see this project succeed. It marks the single biggest step in aviation for a long time. We are here to show the world that Britain can still lead the way. Please note each of you that my door is always open. If you have any positive suggestions, or any complaints, please come and see me.'

After that, Parkinson, introduced all the main participants to the assembly. As a concluding remark, he added, 'Please get to know each other. The better we work together, the greater is our chance of success.'

The briefing went down very well. It had had the desired effect of motivating everybody.

Peter and Alex were then taken up on a series of flights in the two Lancasters to get them accustomed to the airspace in which they would be operating and to get to know all the local landmarks.

Lying prone in the bomb aimer's position in the nose, they had a superb view looking down and Taffy and the other pilot helped them with identifying the salient features. Both project pilots had a daily briefing with Ray Parkinson. They were on first name terms. Parkinson had a special knack of not only pushing everyone to the limit but of putting them at their ease at the same time. No wonder that he had been chosen to manage the project. There had been some complaints about the food, for example. After a few days a completely new catering team was in place and there were no more complaints. One mechanic had been found to be inefficient and uncooperative. He was removed and replaced within 24 hours.

Peter and Alex had been told that the flight schedule would always be subject to the weather. Clear skies and almost nil wind conditions were needed for these flights and as everybody knew, British weather was fickle and changeable. The west coast of Scotland was certainly remote enough but it attracted some of the most severe weather in the British Isles. They all knew that often they would be ready to go but would be put on hold until the meteorological criteria were met. They had a long runway which lined up nicely with the prevailing south-west winds but the M.52R had a very narrow-track undercarriage and would be

105

quite tricky in anything more than a light crosswind when it came in to land. Every day when conditions looked good enough for a test flight, a Mosquito from the Meteorological Flight would fly up and down the course at the selected altitude checking out the actual conditions up aloft. Based on those findings, the meteorologists would then decide if the flight was on or not.

The beginning of June had come and gone. The team had been on stand-by for three days waiting for suitable conditions and now the met experts had announced a clear window from 1000 to 1600. The M.52R was already in position under Taffy's Lancaster. It had been fuelled with water to simulate the rocket fuel weight. All Peter had to do was to cast off at altitude and glide down for a landing, gradually venting the water as he went. It should be a non-event but nobody knew how the little aircraft would glide. Paper calculations were one thing, actual performance was another.

Peter felt calm enough. He had already convinced himself that the real testing would only come when he started to ignite the rockets. He shook hands with Alex before he took off in the chase plane and then he boarded the Lancaster. Dobson had made sure that everything was in place for his special charge. The Lancaster took off and seemed to take an age to reach 20,000 feet. Above 10,000 feet Peter was plugged in to the aircraft's main oxygen supply. When he squirmed into the capsule, Dobson would pass him a portable supply which he would clip into a holder. The test flights at altitude would never require a lot of oxygen as they would be so brief. The rocket plane's batteries were fully charged so that Peter could run the cockpit pressurisation, dump the water and have enough electrical supply for the other needs, including lowering the landing gear.

When he was comfortably settled and strapped in tightly, he gave Dobson the thumbs up. Taffy put the Lancaster into a shallow dive. Dobson returned the thumbs up and counted with the fingers of one hand five, four, three, two, one, and then he released the shackles. The M.52R initially dropped like a stone. Peter aimed for the correct nose-down attitude to hit 220 miles per hour indicated air speed. He had been dropped on the extended centre line of the runway. He would land on 29, facing almost south-west. Therefore he would execute a turn when over the west end of the runway and fly downwind keeping the runway in view and judging his turn in to the final approach. He could see Alex's Meteor off his left wingtip. It was an easy ride for him as the Meteor was just mushing along nose-high.

Peter released the water at the scheduled times. The plane handled beautifully and had no vices as a glider. Opposite the beginning of runway 29, he dropped the landing gear and ran through his pre-landing checks. His approach was fine and he judged his height nicely. He had no flaps to help him and he could add no power if he got too low but his experience paid off. He rounded out at 170 miles per hour precisely and touched down in the first hundred yards of the enormous runway.

He let the aircraft run and slow down of its own accord before turning off. Ambulance and fire engine had been chasing him along the parallel taxiway just for practice. There was also a heavy duty tractor equipped with a tow-bar ready to take him back to the hangar. The de-briefing was minimal as everything had gone better than expected.

Peter then performed another five glide tests, pushing the envelope on each one. He had explored the effectiveness of the ailerons and the moveable tail surfaces. He had carried out a stall and recovery, had done some steep turns and had dived to a speed of Mach 0.7. The little plane had behaved itself perfectly. The way was now clear for powered flights. Before this, Alex was given the experience of one glide flight. Peter had insisted on this.

'Look, Ray,' he had told his boss, 'if anything happens to me, Alex will have to take over. He has to be ready to step in at any stage.'

Parkinson could only agree.

The transition to the powered flights also went very smoothly. Peter had absolute faith in Professor Coles and in his rocket motor. It did not make him nervous to see men in asbestos fire-fighting suits putting highly volatile liquids into the plane and seeing the frost form on the aircraft's skin near the fuel tanks due to the extremely low temperature of the liquid oxygen.

On the first test just one rocket barrel was fired. The aircraft suddenly leaped ahead. The supine position helped Peter to absorb this huge kick in the pants. The aircraft hit Mach 0.8 and Peter went into a gentle climb which stabilised at Mach 0.85 on just one rocket cylinder. Peter was now almost certainly flying faster than anyone before, except in a power dive. Peter reached 36,000 feet before the rocket quit. He had not been carrying a full load of fuel. The glide back to base took longer because of the altitude achieved. On the ground, the observers confirmed Mach 0.85.

The series of powered trials continued with more rocket power being gradually used. Peter reached Mach 0.97 on powered flight number seven and he could feel some turbulence and a tendency to yaw and roll but it was nothing he could not cope with. At the de-briefing, Peter and Ray mutually agreed that on the next run, the so-called 'sound barrier' would be up for grabs.

The big day came in mid-July 1946. Weather conditions were perfect. The test routines had been finely tuned and everybody was on their toes. The drop had been fine. Alex's chase plane was in position and Peter fired one barrel, then a second and then a third in succession. The M.52R shot up to 40,000 feet and Peter levelled out for a run along the course. The machmeter seemed to stick at 0.98 but suddenly all vibration stopped and the needle flicked beyond 1.00. He was flying faster than sound and he still had one rocket barrel in reserve. The aircraft was handling beautifully. He noted Mach 1.05 on the scale before the motor quit and then it was time to descend and land. There was chatter all over the radio frequency. Apparently a large sonic bang – the first in history – had resonated over the airfield. Windows had been rattled. Tower told everybody to shut up as they had aircraft to recover but it was clear that everyone was in party mood.

When Peter cleared the runway this time there was a gaggle of cars to greet him. There was an official photographer and an official newsreel cameraman present. Pictures were taken as Peter eased himself out of the cramped cockpit capsule to be greeted by an exuberant Ray Parkinson.

The whole team was assembled outside the hangar when the aircraft was towed in. Peter had hitched a ride on the tractor. Everybody wanted to congratulate him. The official speed recorded had been Mach 1.045.

Ray raised his voice above the hubbub. 'Party for everybody at 2000 in the Mess tonight. Everything will be on the house. Now just finish your tasks for the day and let Peter have some peace and quiet.'

When the two were alone, Ray added: 'Now get out of your flight gear, have a shower, write up your notes and come to my office just before 1800. Alex will be there as well.'

Peter turned up at five minutes to the hour. 'How are we going to keep the lid on this, Ray? Somebody is going to let the cat out of the bag.'

Ray just smiled and turned on the radio. After a couple of minutes of music, a male voice said, 'This is the Home Service and the World Service of The BBC. Here is the latest news read to you by Arthur Greenaway. Earlier this afternoon a British aircraft became the first aircraft in history to exceed the speed of sound in flight. This performance was achieved in level flight and the aircraft has the potential to fly even faster. This achievement has been confirmed by official observers from the Royal Aeronautical Society and from the Fédération Aéronautique Internationale.'

Ray turned off the radio. 'You see, the cat is already out of the bag. The Americans will be furious but they can do nothing about it. The whole of Britain will be celebrating this and in these hard times, most people need something to cheer them up.'

Ray fetched out a bottle of champagne from behind his desk, popped the cork and poured three glasses. 'Now, let's drink to all those who made this possible. Peter, you flew it and I know that you and Alex have worked bloody hard, but let us not forget all those who made it possible from the Miles design team to Professor Coles, not forgetting the government minister who had the guts to get the project reinstated.'

The party that night was a wonderful occasion. Everybody let his hair down. Winkle turned up in the middle of it in his naval uniform only to be sprayed with champagne.

When he got together with Ray, Peter and Alex, Ray, who was already starting to slur his speech, said to his two pilots, 'I bet you don't know that Winkle here landed a Meteor on an aircraft carrier last month.'

'Bloody hell!' said Peter. 'If you did that, Winkle, that's a darned sight more difficult than crashing through the sound barrier.'

The next day should have been back to normal but there were too many fuzzy heads for serious work and messages of congratulation just poured in. They were all routed via Farnborough as the facility at Machrihanish was completely unknown to the outside world.

Peter took Alex aside. 'I have agreed with Ray that if I can work the M.52R up to Mach 1.2 without any problems, you should have your supersonic run. You have put in all the work that I have and you deserve to have the opportunity.'

The programme continued and Peter pushed to Mach 1.2 without any problems. Alex did his Mach 1 run but it did not generate any euphoria. Only one person can be first.

August had now arrived and Peter had gone past Mach 1.3. On his last flight, at about Mach 1.33 the aircraft started to yaw and pitch so Peter cut the rocket motor and glided back to base. He discussed the problem with Ray and the aerodynamicists. The aircraft looked fine on inspection. There were several high-level discussions and the conclusion was that a little more lateral stability was needed. The second prototype was almost ready for delivery and it was decided to fit a small ventral fin under the rear fuselage. There would be no flights above Mach 1.3 until the new aircraft had been tested.

Peter was sent down to Woodley to look at the second aircraft. Apart from the new ventral fin, this aircraft incorporated some minor modifications resulting from recommendations made by the test team. During Peter's absence, Ray briefed Alex for a run up to Mach 1.3.

'Do not exceed this speed,' Ray warned him. 'You have read Peter's report and the conclusions of the boffins. We have another pilot coming in to fly chase for you.'

On August 20th 1946 Alex was launched from the Lancaster at 25,000 feet. He fired up his rockets and was approaching Mach 1.3 when he came to the beginning of the timed stretch. Curiosity got the better of him. He fired the fourth barrel which had never been done before. The aircraft started to wallow and porpoise. Alex knew he should cut at least one barrel and slow down but he thought he was sufficiently in control.

A few seconds later the tower heard the transmission, 'I'm losing it.' And then there was silence.

The chase pilot also heard the transmission and looking up and ahead he could see the white vapour trail from the rocket, which had been as straight as a die, start to wriggle and then he had seen a violent explosion. Both he and the tower called the pilot but there was no answer. Alex and the M.52R were gone. He had pushed it just too far. Perhaps he had become tired of being second string.

When Peter heard the news at Woodley, he was devastated. He and Alex had become close friends. He believed that Alex had been too heavy on the controls trying to stop the wallowing and that he had introduced oscillations which caused the aircraft to break up. The wreckage recovered from the sea clearly confirmed what the chase pilot had seen, a catastrophic structural failure and an explosion as the remaining fuel escaped from its tanks.

Peter quickly got on the phone to Ray. He told him that aircraft number two would be ready for delivery in one week. He concluded his call by saying, 'I am comfortable with this aircraft. With the modification, I am sure it will reach Mach 1.5. That will give us the one thousand miles per hour asked for in the original requirement. Nobody should feel we have come all this way and failed just because of an accident. We both know the risks of testing. I shall get the second machine to the maximum design speed to vindicate the Miles people and to boost the morale of the whole team. Lastly I shall do it for Alex's sake and for his parents.'

Two months later, the M.52R hit one thousand miles per hour in level flight. Peter survived the programme. He went on to take part in a number of test projects only to die as the victim of a silly road traffic accident a few years later.

TAILPIECE

The Miles M.52 was indeed cancelled in February 1946 and the project was never resuscitated. Britain may have lost a valuable lead but its industrial might was not on a par with that of the United States which quickly caught up on aeronautical technology. Douglas DC-4s and Lockheed Constellations flooded the fleets of the world's airlines. The Lockheed P-80 and the North American F-86 soon were to conquer military markets. Chuck Yeager went supersonic in the Bell X-1 rocket research aircraft in October 1947. How much British research had been incorporated into that design, I do not know.

The hoped-for glut of new aircraft orders after the war never materialised. There were enough war-surplus aircraft around to fulfil all immediate needs. Miles Aircraft was bought out by Handley Page in 1947 and the Woodley facility did not survive for more than a few years after that. What was Woodley airfield is now covered by a housing estate.

Apart from the references to Sir Ben Lockspeiser, Captain Eric 'Winkle' Brown R. N. is the only real-life character depicted in this story. He was the pilot originally selected to fly the M.52. At the time of writing he is still alive. He deserves a very special place in the history of flight testing. He almost certainly tested more types of aircraft in his career than any other pilot did. He certainly carried out more deck landings than any other pilot in history.

The cancellation of the M.52 project is generally attributed to the views of Sir Ben Lockspeiser.

The famous airfield of Farnborough in Hampshire is on the site of the first powered flight in the United Kingdom in 1908 and in the same year H.M. Balloon Factory was established there. Military flight testing was centred there until 2003 when the Royal Aircraft Establishment moved out. Today the Farnborough facility is a business aviation airport serving the London area.

Machrihanish did not receive its magnificent new runway until the beginning of the 1960s which was well after the date which I have used in my story but that runway is still there to this day and it may well have been used for some highly secret operations within the last thirty years.

Finally, after the cancellation of the M.52 programme, some 30% scale models were made of the aircraft and these were powered by small rocket motors. They were air-launched from a de Havilland Mosquito and in October 1948, one of the models was recorded as reaching a speed of Mach 1.38. This would be some small consolation to the Miles design team which had produced such a brilliant concept.

KIA, VIETNAM, 15TH MAY 1972

This short story is dedicated to all those who served with the United States military in the Vietnam War and who are recorded as being Killed in Action (KIA) or Missing in Action (MIA).

Captain Rick Gaines was wide awake. The previous day's rescue operation kept running through his mind and would not go away. It was now the early hours of the morning but sleep would not come. Yesterday, for the first time on a rescue mission, and this was his second tour as a rescue helicopter pilot in the war zone, he had broken off a rescue attempt when his machine had started to take hits. He had been under fire on most of his rescue missions and sometimes he had wondered just how he and his crew had managed to survive. He served with the United States Air Force's Aerospace Rescue and Recovery Service. Its task was to rescue downed airmen. Its credo was based on that old army expression of solidarity, 'Leave no man behind'.

They had to fly frequently into North Vietnam where, it appeared, every single man, woman and child had a weapon of some sort and the fire from the ground was always intense. There were more anti-aircraft guns deployed in North Vietnam than there had been in Hitler's Europe in the Second World War. There were also batteries of ground-to-air missiles all over the place. Gaines and his fellow pilots were on constant readiness to fly into that hell to pluck downed pilots from the dense jungle or from the coastal waters before they were captured by the enemy. Those who were captured might be tortured to death or imprisoned in small bamboo cages if they fell into the wrong hands. Those who were more fortunate would end up in a prison camp like the infamous one at Hoa Lo, known to the Americans as 'The Hanoi Hilton'.

Pilots whose aircraft had been hit over North Vietnam would try to stay with their stricken machines until they had crossed the coast before they ejected. They knew that their chances of being rescued were considerably greater if they came down in the sea. Even there, if they were close to the coast, there was still a good chance of being captured by the enemy. All types of small boats would head towards them with their crews intent on earning a bounty for the capture and there were many shore batteries which would direct withering fire against any rescue attempt.

The previous day's rescue attempt had been made offshore a few miles from the port of Haiphong. A crippled Navy Intruder attack aircraft had just called 'feet wet' before the pilot and his systems operator had had to eject. The usual rescue package was sent out. This comprised two big Sikorsky HH-53 helicopters. The leading helicopter was Gaines's aircraft. He was the 'low Jolly' and he would attempt to rescue the two men from the water. If he failed, the second helicopter, the 'high Jolly' would go in. Their escort was the standard flight of four propeller-driven Douglas A-1 ground attack aircraft. This design was a throw-back to the Second World War but it was highly effective at suppressing ground fire. It could carry more ordnance and spend more time strafing at low level than any of the jet-powered modern types. Top cover was provided by four McDonnell F-4 Phantom fighters whose prime job was to deter any interference by North Vietnamese aircraft.

When Gaines and his crew had arrived on the scene, the Douglas A-1s, known as Sandys, were already shooting up the armada of small boats which was heading for the downed airmen. The shore batteries had opened up and when the Sandys had dealt with the boats, they would head for the coast to try to suppress the ground fire. Gaines homed his helicopter in on the signals from the airmen's rescue beacons. He could see where they were from the coloured patch on the sea marked by a dye carried in their rescue equipment and which was also a shark repellent. Gaines eased his helicopter into a hovering position above the two men and sent down one of his crewmen on the rescue cable to help each man in turn into the rescue harness so that they could be winched aboard.

As the crewman was on his way down, one of the shore batteries opened up on the helicopter. Some of the boats which had not been sunk or silenced by the Sandys were also firing at the big helicopter. The machine was starting to take hits. Gaines was starting to twitch. He keyed his microphone and told his crew they were pulling out. He eased up the collective lever and put the nose down to gain airspeed. He fled the area leaving his crewman in the water with the two airmen and set course for base.

After landing, the crew could count several holes in their machine. However, none of them had been hit and nothing vital in the machine's systems had been damaged. Gaines submitted his report. Nobody criticized him for breaking off the rescue attempt. The second Jolly came in when the ground fire had been mainly suppressed and picked up the two airmen and Gaines's crewman. The rescue mission had been a success but Gaines was not a happy man.

As he lay awake unable to sleep, he was angry with himself for breaking off the rescue attempt. He had failed those two men in the water and he had failed his crewman. The airmen flying those hazardous bombing and attack missions over North Vietnam were risking their lives every time they went out. They counted on the search and rescue helicopters coming to save them. Gaines had recovered several airmen in his two tours. He had had several narrow escapes. He had had a crew member wounded by ground fire. He had been decorated for bravery. He would never forget the grateful look on the faces of those he had rescued. It was worth all the risks he had to take just to see their gratitude. Now he had let three men down. Because he had developed a nervous twitch, he had just chickened out. He could not forgive himself for this.

Gaines was an articulate and intelligent man. He had completed a college degree before he had joined the Air Force. He had always wanted to fly helicopters and he was rated very highly as an officer and a pilot.

He did not agree with the Administration's policy on Vietnam. He served in the war because it was his duty to do so and he kept his own opinions to himself. Why was his country propping up a thoroughly corrupt regime in South Vietnam just because it was opposed to the advance of Communism? Why was his country so paranoid about the spread of Communism in any case? In spite of all the assurances from successive Administrations since the time of Kennedy that the United States was winning the war, it was clear to Gaines that it was not. The latest bombing campaign in the north, Operation Linebacker, was a desperate attempt by Nixon's Administration to get North Vietnam back to the peace talks. Certain targets in the north such as Hanoi and Haiphong had always been off limits for the bombing raids. The fear was that if these targets were bombed, Russia and China might intervene and the war would escalate to become a global one. Gaines's view was that if you fight a war, you fight it to win. In this situation, his country was fighting a war with one hand tied behind its back and it would never be able to win.

Recently whole North Vietnamese divisions had been infiltrating into South Vietnam. The South Vietnamese forces were not capable of putting up any real resistance. For several years the United States had been pouring huge sums of money, men and material into this war. And for what? All the latest technology had proved to be useless in trying to stop the enemy transporting guerrilla groups and material down the infamous Ho Chi Minh Trail. Gaines had tried to put some figures on paper as to what this senseless war was costing his country. It could only be a rough estimate but the cost was simple unsustainable in the long term. The same could be said of his unit's rescue operations. Launching ten aircraft and twenty-five

117

men to attempt to retrieve one downed airman was completely disproportionate, but it had to be done.

Gaines tossed and turned in his bed but he could not sleep. He kept seeing the grateful faces of the airmen he had rescued. He kept re-living the moment when he had abandoned yesterday's rescue attempt. This war was going to be lost. That was clear to him. However, until his tour of duty finished, it was his job to rescue fellow pilots and that was exactly what he would continue to do. Next time he would not flinch.

He had spent his first operational tour piloting the Sikorsky HH-3 helicopter which had become known in the military as the Jolly Green Giant after the well-known brand of canned vegetables. With the progressive addition of more and more armour, extra equipment and defensive machine-guns, the performance of this helicopter had gradually degraded. The HH-53, which Gaines now piloted, was a bigger helicopter with much better performance. It became known as the Super Jolly, but mission call-signs remained Jolly followed by an identification number. Although the HH-53 was much more capable than the HH-3 for rescue work, no aircraft was invulnerable if hit in a critical place.

Two days later, on 15th May, Gaines and his crew were off the ground at first light. Their helicopter had been repaired and was fully serviceable. They were designated as the 'low Jolly' again. The crew numbered five; Gaines and his co-pilot, two gunners to man the swivelling Gatling guns, and a flight mechanic. Gaines had flown several times with his co-pilot, Dave Roberts, but the identity of the other members of the crew was variable Some had flown with Gaines and some had not but they were all highly trained and each man knew exactly what he had to do whatever the circumstances were.

They were at readiness, orbiting just south of the border with North Vietnam. At 8am they had hooked up to a C-130 airborne tanker and taken on more fuel. The ability to refuel in flight gave the big helicopter much more range and endurance. This morning all was quiet until just before 9am when the call came in that an F-105 Thunderchief strike aircraft had gone down in the jungle some 100 nautical miles north of the border between the two Vietnams. Two other Thuds in the unit had seen the pilot eject and had been able to make contact with the downed pilot. He had identified himself correctly (the North Vietnamese had become very proficient at transmitting spoof messages to lure rescuers away from the real target of the rescue), had reported that he was uninjured and was heading for a clearing indicated by his fellow pilots aloft. Smokey 51 was the call sign of the downed pilot and he had enough devices to enable the rescue mission to be able to home in on his position. The two Thuds would remain on station as long as their fuel state would allow to fend off any enemy units looking for the downed pilot but their circling would also give the enemy clues as to where the man was likely to be. The usual flight of Sandys was about to depart to 'sanitize' the area around the clearing to keep any enemy fire away from the rescue helicopters and the top cover of four Phantoms was ready to go. Gaines took up the heading for the rescue site and was followed by the second Jolly.

The flight out to the rescue site was uneventful. Gaines was monitoring the chatter on the rescue frequency. Smokey 51 had successfully reached the clearing. The Sandys were flying in a race-track pattern around the pick-up spot looking for trouble. So far, they had seen no ground fire but this was not necessarily a good sign. Enemy troops might be lying in wait ready to open fire when the helicopter came within range.

As Gaines started to slow the helicopter down and begin his descent towards the clearing, all hell broke loose. There was small arms fire from all sides. The Sandys started to sanitize the area but it was clear that there was a considerable number of enemy troops close by. Gaines did not want to land in the clearing. If his helicopter was motionless for just a few seconds, it could be knocked out. He called to his flight mechanic to lower the hoist as they approached the clearing. It would be an

119

act of good judgement and piloting skill for the downed airman, to get himself into the hoist and for the helicopter to climb away all in one fluid movement.

The flight mechanic, looking downwards, called out instructions to his pilot to get the hoist into the right position for the pick-up. Gaines was becoming twitchy again but he slowed his rate of breathing and concentrated on what he had to do. His gunners were shooting at every muzzle flash which they could see. The Sandys were doing sterling work and were clearly taking out a lot of the enemy.

Suddenly one of the Sandys was hit, almost certainly by a shoulder–launched ground to air missile. This missile was new to the North Vietnamese armoury and it was deadly. The Sandy's right wing folded and the plane crashed into the trees, exploding into a fireball. The pilot had no chance of avoiding an instant death. Gaines was judging his approach to the pick-up with great precision. The dangling hoist reached the clearing. The downed pilot made it and secured himself in the hoist. The flight mechanic started to reel him in. Gaines started to add collective and some forward speed. Everything was working to plan. He started to relax a little. He had conquered his fear and saved another life. As the helicopter climbed away a second missile came streaking towards it. It slammed into the engines and exploded. All the armour plating which had been fitted was no defence against such an impact. The helicopter went down like a stone, and, like the Sandy before it, exploded in a ball of fire.

Six men had died in an effort to save one airman who had also lost his life. The pilot of the second Jolly was informed of the disaster and he and the remaining Sandys departed the rescue zone to return to their base. The bureaucratic machine would now crank into gear and produce missing in action notices for the next of kin of the departed. The status would only be upgraded to killed in action when there was positive confirmation of the men's deaths.

TAILPIECE

From 1961 when American forces first became engaged in Vietnam until their final withdrawal in 1973, the United States military lost a staggering 8,300 aircraft of all types in the war zone. This total included 5,000 helicopters. The rescue services managed to retrieve around 1,000 airmen but at a heavy cost. 100 rescue aircraft were lost resulting in the death of some 90 crewmen.

The total killed in action figure for American military personnel was just under 41,000 and the missing in action figure was just over 1,700. The total wounded figure was over 153,000.

Many individuals' lives had been changed forever by this conflict and what had been achieved? Nothing.

THE ICEMAN COMETH

(With apologies to Eugene O'Neill)

Chuck Ryan opened his eyes to see Professor Lazzard standing next to his bed.

'How do you feel, Chuck?' the Professor asked.

Chuck was still feeling pretty woozy from the anaesthetic and he could not put his thoughts into order very quickly. 'I'm OK,' he finally replied but he promptly fell asleep again.

The following day he had got over the worst of the post-operational effects and he felt much better but his right knee was still painful as were his ribs. Professor Lazzard appeared again.

'How long will I be here?' Chuck asked.

'About ten days,' the Professor replied. 'You will be able to start some physiotherapy tomorrow and that will continue after you have been released. The cracked ribs will heal fairly quickly but I'm afraid that your knee injury will prevent you from playing top level football again. You will be able to function fairly normally and your limp will be hardly noticeable when you walk but you won't be able to streak down the pitch as you used to do. Sorry to have to tell you this so bluntly, but it is best that you face up to this now and not build up false hopes.'

The blow was a hard one but it could have been harder as Chuck was prepared for it. The opposition had gone for him in the big match. They knew he was the danger man and when they hit him, they did not hold back. He lost consciousness and only came round in the clinic.

His team's coach made sure that he got the best possible treatment. Chuck Ryan was the rising star and most of the top professional teams were already after him for the next season. The big match against the nearest rivals of his college was the highpoint of his last season as a college undergraduate. All of his team counted on him winning it for them. Chuck was indestructible, or so they thought. Now his dreams had been shattered.

On his release from the clinic, those whom he thought had been his best buddies in the college team quickly dropped him, as if he had a contagious disease. All of the groupie girls who were queuing up for a date suddenly vanished. He got back to his studies, which he had neglected in preference to his football, and now he was determined to graduate honourably.

Meeting challenges was not new to him. His father was a former Navy fighter pilot who had ended his service days flying the F-14 Tomcat. He had turned to drink and had left the Navy under a cloud. His wife had then left him. Chuck had grown up spending part of his time with his father and part of his time with his mother. It had never been easy but it had taught him to be independent at an early age.

One thing which his father had done for Chuck was to teach him to fly. Flying had remained very much in the background until the football injury. Now flying had become an important element in his life. He had managed to graduate with a degree. He did not wish to become a military pilot and probably he would have been rejected because of his knee. He now had all of his civilian ratings and he had financed the cost of this himself by doing all sorts of menial jobs. He had started building his hours by instructing but the last recession had effectively stopped recruitment for the airlines. Chuck had now set his heart on becoming an airline pilot. He knew that the economy would pick up again sooner or later and that he would be accepted one day but in the meantime he had to make his own way.

Just three months previously he had been interviewed by Glen White, Chief Pilot of the local hub of the big mail and parcels operator in his area. Flying parcels in all weathers on one's own in a single-engined Cessna Super Cargomaster did not appeal to many people, particularly as the hours were not very sociable but Chuck was not put off by this and he seemed to have impressed Glen. He was accepted and after the mandatory course and type rating at Flight Safety, he started his duties.

The Super Cargomaster was developed as a freighter version of the Caravan which had carved a niche for itself as a tough go-anywhere transport ideally suited to primitive conditions. Federal Express had bought the freighter version in huge numbers and other parcel carriers had followed suit. The aircraft which Chuck was now flying had no cabin windows and had the additional belly freight pack. It was well equipped and was flown from the left seat as it was usually flown on single-pilot operations for the sake of economy. Chuck particularly appreciated the Garmin G1000 integrated panel which had been fitted and which provided him with more information than he would ever need. The only negative point for him was that the single PT-6 turboprop had not been uprated for the extra weight which the Super Cargomaster could carry, so performance when fully loaded could be sluggish, particularly in the climb. There was a rumour that the fleet was to be re-engined but it was a question of wait and see.

His rota was not always the same and he was gradually becoming familiar with several of the airports served by the local hub. As a bachelor without any strings, he made sure that he was always available and he was readily accepted as a serious and safe pilot. He had struck up a good friendship with Pete McKeever who also flew for the company. Pete was several years older and had vast experience of the aircraft and the operation. Chuck always turned to Pete for his opinion and his advice.

Winter had arrived. The first snows had fallen and the start and end of each flight was no fun as the aircraft sat on the ramp between flights and only enjoyed the relative warmth of the hangar for maintenance work. Chuck had to dress warmly for his pre-flight inspection of the aircraft and during the initial part of each flight he would still feel cold until the cabin heater made a difference.

One afternoon in mid-January, he and the other pilots who were to be flying that evening were sitting around waiting for their respective aircraft to be loaded. One of the company's big Boeing 767 freighters had come in and offloaded all the parcels to be distributed that evening from the hub. Chuck was scheduled to fly to Block City. He had already flown there on several occasions. There, when his aircraft had been unloaded, he would have a short break in the warmth of the crew room whilst a batch of parcels would be loaded for the return journey back to the hub. The flight each way would take around ninety minutes. Allowing for about an hour on the ground, Chuck would be back at the hub some four hours after departing from there. He was expecting to be going off duty shortly after midnight.

Those flying had checked the weather and their flight plans. The aircraft on the ramp all had fresh snow removed from their upper surfaces and would be sprayed with de-icing fluid before the pilots started their engines.

After reviewing the weather, Pete had rubbed his chin thoughtfully, and turning to Chuck he said, 'There is a possibility of icing up there tonight. The trouble is that it is almost impossible to predict if and when a plane will pick up ice in these conditions.'

'Have you ever picked up ice?' Chuck asked.

'Yes, just once a couple of years ago and it scared the hell out of me even though it was fairly light icing. If you are ever caught out by ice, try to climb above the icing layer. If you are concerned about letting down through dangerous conditions and you have not collected much ice, do not hesitate to turn around and head back to your departure point, particularly if the first part of the flight was clear of icing conditions. Finally, if you are in the clouds and the outside temperature is near to or just below zero, be prepared for icing. Remember that you have an on-board icing warning. If it goes off, do something about it.'

Chuck nodded. 'Sure thing.'

Pete continued, 'Many years ago, a fellow pilot gave me the best advice I have ever had about flying on instruments in the clouds. He said that the controller on the ground might ask you to do this or that and you might not be happy about it. Remember that the worst that can happen to him is to fall off his chair which will only hurt his pride. You, on the other hand, are thousands of feet off the ground and if anything goes wrong you have to find your own salvation. If in doubt, you call the shots, not the controller.'

Chuck mused on all of this. He was not particularly alarmed but he decided he would have a game plan ready based on Pete's good advice. He remembered what he had read about icing when he was preparing for the instrument rating knowledge test. The manual had stated that if ice forms on a wing in flight and only reaches the thickness of rough sandpaper, the lift generated by the wing would be reduced by 30% and the drag would increase by 40%. That was hardly comforting. It meant that the stalling speed of the plane would increase considerably and much more than cruise power would be needed to maintain level flight. The Super Cargomaster had its share of anti-icing equipment. The propeller, the windscreen, the engine air-intake and the pitot tube could all be heated to prevent ice accretion but the wings and tailplane only had rubber de-icing boots which would prevent slight to moderate icing forming on the leading edges of those surfaces but would not be capable of dealing with the build-up of moderate to severe icing further back on those surfaces. It was possible to fit TKS which would 'weep' de-icing fluid over the wing and tailplane and which was much more effective if the icing got bad but this was an expensive extra and carrying a tank full of de-icing fluid which would weigh as much as an extra passenger did not make economic sense to many operators.

Chuck put all of this to the back of his mind when he went to dispatch and checked the weight and balance form to make sure that his aircraft was inside the acceptable limits. Then he went outside into the cold to pre-flight his plane. After checking that everything was in order externally and that the load of parcels was securely stowed inside, he entered the cockpit and ran through his pre-engine start list. Then he fired up the PT-6 turbine. It might be a little short of power for the cargo version of the Caravan but it was a wonderfully reliable engine and it was simple to operate.

Soon, with the flight call-sign of 'Pigeon six-niner', Chuck was on his way. His flight plan called for a cruise altitude of 6,000 feet. Most of the ground he would be flying over was about 1,000 feet above sea level, so he would be 5,000 feet above the ground. In no time at all, or so it seemed, the autopilot levelled him out at 6,000 and he was established in the cruise at 180 knots indicated. There was no other traffic being handled by his controller which was not surprising as Chuck was flying at night in the depths of winter over a sparsely inhabited part of the country. His navigation screen was set up to show his waypoints and all Chuck had to do was to monitor his instruments.

The plane had reached and passed its half-way point when the ice detector warning came on. Traces of frost were appearing on the windscreen. Chuck had had pitot heat on all the time and now he activated his other anti-icing devices.

'Plains Center from Pigeon six-niner,' Chuck called, 'I'm starting to pick up icing, can you get me above this stuff?'

'Roger, Pigeon six-niner,' Control came back. 'You are cleared to ten thousand. We think that this will put you in the clear.'

'Pigeon six-niner departing six thousand for ten thousand,' Chuck acknowledged. He punched in 10,000 on the autopilot and went to full power. His climb rate did not look very good and he was not hitting his normal climb speed.

'Pigeon six-niner, please expedite your climb to ten thousand,' the controller reminded him. The plane was struggling to reach eight thousand and the speed was decaying. 'Pigeon six-niner, unable,' replied Chuck. 'Levelling at eight thousand'.

Even in level flight, the speed was decaying in spite of the engine being at full power. Chuck started to become concerned. When the speed approached 100 knots, a shudder ran through the plane and the stall warning sounded. He was flying 30 knots faster than the normal stall which meant he had already accumulated a lot of ice. He uncoupled the autopilot. If the plane stalled on him now, he would never be able to recover it. He had to initiate a descent to keep at 100 knots at the very least.

'Pigeon six-niner, I am icing up badly and am going down. Now out of eight thousand.'

Control came back immediately. 'Pigeon six-niner, are you declaring an emergency?'

'Affirmative,' replied Chuck. 'I have got to get on the ground quickly. Vectors for the nearest airport, please.'

There was a pause whilst Control looked for a solution. 'Pigeon six-niner, nearest is Charlesboro, 25 nautical miles. Steer two two zero. Field altitude is twelve hundred. Unicom frequency is one three two point niner. Seven clicks to activate the lighting.'

'Two two zero on the heading, Unicom one three two point niner,' Chuck replied. He needed the local airport frequency to be able to turn on the airport lights by clicking his transmit button seven times. Clearly the airport was closed to normal traffic.

Whilst he was handling all of this, Chuck had dialled in a direct route to Charlesboro Airport on his navigation screen. A bold red line ran from the symbol of his plane to the airport. All he had to do was to follow that line. He was now going down at 500 feet per minute and his speed was up to 110 knots. The figures raced through his brain. Fifteen miles to run. Get there in seven minutes per GPS. Four thousand feet above ground. Will hit the deck in about eight minutes. 'Pigeon six-niner am passing five thousand. Have the airport on my nav display but am descending five hundred per minute. It's not looking good.'

'Roger six-niner. I'll stay with you until we lose contact. Good luck.'

Chuck knew that he would not be able to manoeuvre to line up with the single runway. He would have to land across it if he got that far and he would be travelling very fast. He decided that just before reaching the airport boundary, he would select full flap. If the flaps worked, he would gain a bit of initial lift and would immediately slow down. He would hit the ground hard but at reduced speed and he might get away with it. He made sure that his straps were as tight as possible.

'Plains Center from Pigeon six-niner, passing three thousand, ten miles to run'. He was going down faster. Ground in four minutes, airport in five minutes.

'Roger, Pigeon six-niner. You are fading and will shortly be below radar cover. Emergency services are activated. Good luck.'

At 2,500 feet on the altimeter, the plane broke out of the cloud base. It was pitch dark below. Chuck's mind was quite clear. He had to get to that airport even though logic told him it was not possible. Suddenly he could hear banging noises against the rear of the aircraft. Ice was breaking off! 'Come on, Baby, I need a miracle now,' Chuck muttered.

His rate of descent was slowing but he was getting perilously close to the ground. He could not risk raising the nose even a fraction as the plane would stall and crash immediately. If he got to the airport he had to trust to luck that there were no obstructions in his path.

Chuck clicked his transmit button seven times on the airport frequency. This was simply a gesture. Even if the runway lights had come on, he would hardly be able to see them. He was now down to 1,500 feet, only 300 above the ground and GPS indicated a mile to run. Ahead everything was pitch black. He turned on his landing lights but they illuminated nothing. Then they picked out some pale white shapes ahead. Trees! He could not get over them or round them. There was nothing he could do. He just closed his eyes and braced himself.

The plane exploded in a ball of fire. When the emergency services were able to start combing the crash scene at first light a few charred pieces of metal were all they were able to find. Chuck had done all that he could but the odds had been too heavily loaded against him.

A TYPE TOO MANY

The show was on at Oberpfaffenhofen Flugplatz outside Munich. Charlie Treadwell was pitting his Spitfire 12 against the Fw 190 flown by Hans Kellermann. They had flown this dogfight routine several times and they knew the choreography inside-out. As they were performing over Germany this time, it was Hans's turn to win. At the end of the encounter, Charlie let Hans get on his tail and then switched on his smoke canister before diving for the ground. He pulled out low on the far side of the airfield away from the crowd. Pyrotechnics were exploded on the ground to signal the crash of the Spitfire. Charlie levelled at 100 feet behind a belt of trees, let his speed bleed off and turned to line up with the grass strip for his landing whilst Hans flew low and fast down the main runway to celebrate his victory before pulling up to enter a downwind leg in preparation for his landing. As usual they had put on a nice display and it had been appreciated by the large crowd.

Charlie was pleased with life. He had been a fast jet pilot in the Royal Air Force, had flown operationally in 'Desert Storm' against the Iraqi forces, had graduated at the Empire Test Pilot's School at Boscombe Down and had flown both Spitfire and Hurricane in the Battle of Britain Memorial Flight. He had then left the Service because he was increasingly in demand as a warbird display pilot. He had flown most of the warbirds on the international circuit in Britain, France, Germany, the USA and in various other countries. His performances were a yardstick for others to follow. He never pushed the limits and was always safety conscious, yet he appeared to get more out of the aircraft he was flying than anybody else on the circuit. He knew all of the other display pilots and they knew him. They formed a happy club and he had struck up a few very good friendships.

He had now flown well over a hundred different types of aircraft and he had never put a scratch on any of them even though he had had his share of emergencies.

Back in the pilots' tent, Charlie and Hans ran through their debriefing, enjoying a cool beer at the same time. They had both been sweating profusely because of their exertions and as they would not be flying again that day and ground transport was laid on for them, what was wrong in downing a couple of beers?

As they were relaxing and watching the other display items, Kurt, the show manager came in and addressed himself to Charlie. Kurt, like most Germans in aviation, had excellent English. In his younger days he had flown the Lockheed F-104 in the German Air Force. When it came to languages, Charlie was no slouch himself. He had read French and German at university before joining the Air Force and he also spoke passable Spanish and Italian.

'Sorry to bother you, Charlie,' said Kurt, 'but I have just been talking to somebody who would like to meet you and who has a proposal which he thinks will interest you. It so happens that he is staying at the same hotel as you although I didn't give him that information. Here is his card. He says that if you would like to meet with him either this evening or tomorrow evening, just give him a call at your convenience. You will see that he has written his hotel name and room number on the card.'

Charlie took the card and read: 'Dott. Paolo Castoldi' followed by an address in Milan. He was sure that he had heard the name Castoldi before but he couldn't remember where. There would, in any case, be no harm in meeting the man and hearing what he had to propose.

Back at the hotel, Charlie called Dr Castoldi's room number and got an immediate answer. He decided he would use his Italian but Dr Castoldi answered in good English. They agreed to meet in the bar half an hour later. Castoldi told Charlie to look out for the man with the black and pink striped tie. They met as arranged and settled down at a corner table. Charlie stuck to his beer and Castoldi ordered a Campari and soda.

'Now, Mr Treadwell,' said Castoldi, 'you are no doubt wondering what this is all about so I shall not beat about the bush, as you English say. My name probably means nothing to you but my paternal grandfather was Mario Castoldi, who designed the series of racing floatplanes for the Macchi company in the late 1920s and early 1930s. Maybe you have heard of them?'

Charlie thought for a minute. 'Weren't those the floatplanes designed for the Schneider Trophy races, and didn't one of them win the Trophy one year?'

'You are right,' replied Castoldi. 'That was the M 39 which lifted the Trophy in 1926. The final model was the MC 72, with the letter C standing for Castoldi. The surviving example of this aircraft is on display at our Air Force Museum at Vigna di Valle outside Rome. This machine was specifically developed for the 1931 Schneider Trophy contest but it was not ready in time. As you may recall, your Royal Air Force High Speed Flight team won the competition that year for the third time in succession, there being no opposing teams, thus winning the Trophy outright and there were no more floatplane races after that. However, the MC 72 went on to break the world's airspeed record twice and on the second occasion, in 1934, it set the first world record over 700 kilometres per hour, a record which was to last until 1939. No propeller-driven seaplane has ever flown faster than that to this day.'

Interesting, Charlie thought. Wonder what all this is leading up to.

Castoldi was still talking. 'Now, I am a wealthy Italian industrialist. I have specialised in electrical and electronic goods for many years. I play an active role in my businesses but I am working on other projects. I do fly a little as a private pilot - purely for fun. A couple of years ago I was introduced to a relative of Francesco Agello, the man who set the 1934 speed record. Poor Agello died in 1942 testing a new fighter aircraft but his name is remembered with great pride in Italian aviation circles.'

After taking a sip of his drink, Castoldi continued, 'I thought to myself: now why don't I build a flying replica of this famous aircraft? We have hardly any airworthy historic aircraft in Italy and we are completely put to shame by what you British, Americans, Germans and French have. I started looking around. I obtained a full set of plans from the Macchi archives. I got together a team of first-class craftsmen and engineers. We are now rebuilding this aircraft in great secrecy. Nobody outside the team knows about it – except for yourself. Now, we want you to fly it!'

Charlie could hardly believe what he was being told. 'But I have never flown a seaplane in my life!' he exclaimed.

'We would make sure that you get the training for that,' replied Castoldi. 'What we need is a first-rate test pilot with plenty of experience and you are the obvious choice. Although we have modernised the design internally, we know that like all floatplanes it will be very tricky to fly and therefore dangerous. The original two Italian Air Force pilots died testing it before Agello took over and showed what it could do. We are prepared to pay you to cover the next five years of your flying activity. You can work out what that figure will be and we shall accept it. Our aircraft will be ready next spring. We expect to do one year of fairly intensive flying and after that, it will only be flown on special occasions. Apart from when we need you, you will be free to continue your warbird activities. Oh, and in addition we shall take out an insurance policy on your life with you as beneficiary for death or permanent disability resulting from the project for the sum of ten million pounds.'

Charlie was just gobsmacked by what he had heard. 'I need to sleep on this,' he said. 'Can I give you an answer after the show tomorrow?'

'Take your time,' said Castoldi. 'We know that this will be a risky project. If you turn us down, we shall have to look elsewhere but you are our preferred choice, particularly as you speak Italian. One last thing. If you do decline, please do not mention this conversation to anybody. We intend our project to remain secret until we make the first flight.'

Charlie did sleep on it and when he woke the next morning, he had made his decision. He would do it. It wasn't for the financial rewards. The project was just too interesting to turn down. He then put it out of his mind as he had some catching up to do on his forthcoming assignments and then it was out to the airfield to prepare for his duel with Hans. He was too much of a professional to let the thought of the MC 72 project distract him in his afternoon's flight and as usual he and Hans brought out the best in each other in their mock dogfight. Kurt was happy, the sponsors were happy and the crowd was happy. That was how it should be.

Back at the hotel, Charlie called Dr Castoldi and gave him his acceptance. He was now a key member of the project team.

In mid-autumn Charlie paid his first visit to Milan to become acquainted with the project. He met all of the team. He was given a full briefing on the current status. His opinion was sought on various points. He was also taken to Lake Como to be given some initial floatplane training in a float-equipped Cessna 206.

Charlie was amazed at what an advanced aircraft the MC 72 was for its time. The big problem with handling those racing seaplanes on the water was that the huge amount of torque generated by their extremely powerful engines made one float dig into the water so initially the floatplane wanted to turn in a circle. These aircraft started their take-off run on the water at right-angles to their take-off path so that by the time they were starting to accelerate on the water, they had swung round enough to be correctly lined up and the rudder had sufficient 'bite' in the airflow to keep the aircraft heading straight. Castoldi had solved this problem in the MC 72 by having contra-rotating propellers fitted.

Fiat supplied two AS 5 engines for the original aircraft and these were mated one behind the other with each driving its own propeller in opposite directions. Such engines were no longer available but the team had been able to acquire Rolls-Royce Merlin engines instead which had been suitably modified. The original fixed-pitch two-bladed propellers were to be replaced by three-bladed constant speed ones. Dissipating the heat produced by the engines operating in such a confined, streamlined space had been a major problem for the original designer. Water was used in large quantities to cool the engines. In turn the water was cooled by radiators covering most of the wing surfaces, the struts connecting the fuselage to the floats and the front part of the floats themselves. The entire water capacity would evaporate very quickly so flights would always be limited to just a few minutes. There were additional radiators in the floats to cool the engine lubricating oil. The fuel tanks were also located in the floats.

Other concessions had been made to modern times. Composite materials were being used where possible for extra strength and to save weight. A radar altimeter was to be fitted in the cockpit. A small video screen would be installed to give the pilot some forward vision, which had been completely lacking in the original aircraft. It had been decided that the pilot would be on oxygen all the time to avoid any nausea or hypoxia caused by engine fumes. Charlie would be wearing a modern helmet with built-in microphone and earphones. The team had even thought of installing an ejection seat but there was no model which would fit into the narrow confines of the fuselage and the extra weight was not desirable.

Stefano was the chief engineer on the project. He was extremely capable but his English was limited. Charlie was able to use his Italian with him and the other members of the team. Stefano explained all the technical niceties, how they managed to mate the two Merlins one behind the other, just as Fiat had done with their engines, how they had managed to increase the compression, how they had designed and installed a supercharger, and how they had managed to have a special fuel refined for them which would be similar to what had been used on the original MC 72. This fuel consisted of a mixture of benzole and gasoline and which had been pioneered by the British for their final Supermarine S.6 floatplanes, which had won the Schneider Trophy outright. The engine unit had been bench run and had achieved a staggering 4,000 horse-power.

Charlie spent much of his spare time studying the aircraft he was going to fly, as well as reading up as much as he could on how those tricky floatplanes needed to be handled. He was also a frequent visitor to the Aero Club Como to continue his hands-on floatplane training. When he was asked at the Club why he had chosen to honour them with his presence and why he wanted to fly floatplanes, he simply replied that it was something he had always wanted to do.

Spring arrived and the replica MC 72 had been completed. Charlie went down to Milan to examine it and to try out the cockpit. The aircraft looked absolutely stunning in the finish which it had sported in 1934. The only instant give-away that this was not an original aircraft was the twin three-bladed propellers. Below the leading edge of the tailplane 'MC 72 182' had been stencilled on the red paintwork in white. Charlie recalled that Agello's record-breaking aircraft had been N° 181.

Paolo and Stefano took him out to dinner one evening. A table had been reserved in a quiet corner of a restaurant where they would not be overheard.

'Now, Charlie,' Paolo began, 'next week the aircraft will be transported to Como. You already know the facilities at the Club there and the part of the lake which the Club uses. It was a deliberate choice to send you there. It has also worked wonders for your Italian! The original aircraft was based at Lake Garda but there are no suitable facilities for us there and, in any case, Como is closer to Milan. We have acquired a hangar from the Club. The President knows that we have a project but he does not know what it is.'

'Doesn't he wonder what I'm doing there?' Charlie asked.

'Of course he is curious about your presence and he has probably linked you with the project, but no matter. Our aircraft will be moved in under wraps and will be re-assembled inside the hangar. Stefano and his team will make final preparations. At all times the hangar will be guarded by a security firm. Only team members with ID will have access. You have already sent me your schedule for this year. I see that you are free in this period of ten days in April.' He showed Charlie the dates on a piece of paper. 'We shall start flight testing in that period. The aircraft will be presented to the Italian media on the planned date for its first outing whether conditions are right or not. It will be up to you to decide if it will be safe to start trials that day. In any case, during the ten day period there should be one day when the media will be able to film the aircraft in flight. As you can imagine, this project is very expensive and we do not want to let our sponsors down.'

The day of the planned first outing was grey and overcast and the lake surface was a little choppy but Charlie decided that conditions were good enough for some initial taxying on the water and maybe for one or two runs to a speed sufficient to get the floats 'on to the step' to see what lateral stability was like.

Paolo's PR agency had done its work well. There were television crews and presenters from state as well as from private companies. All the leading newspapers and magazines were represented. They had been told that something very special was to happen and since they knew that Dottore Castoldi was behind this, they realised that this was an event not to be missed.

At 10 a.m. the hangar doors were opened and the MC 72 was wheeled out sitting on its launching trolley. The sight of it drew gasps of admiration. Paolo, standing in front of the aircraft started a media briefing, explaining how the project had come about and why this machine was so iconic. He then introduced his team, ending up with Charlie, who, of course, was well known to the Italian aeronautical press. After this came a time for questions and answers. Charlie was much in demand here and he delighted everybody with his knowledge of Italian.

Just before 11 a.m., Charlie boarded the aircraft by means of a ladder and the aircraft on its trolley was slowly man-handled down the slipway and into the water. The handling crew all wore wetsuits as they would be in the water to attach the aircraft to a motor launch for it to be towed away from the shore and they would be back in the water to make sure the aircraft was securely on its trolley before pulling it out of the water at the end of the test. Club flying had been cancelled for the day. The area of the lake used by the Club for take-offs and landings had been checked by two motor launches for any floating debris which might create a hazard. Two handlers remained on the floats whilst the aircraft was being towed out. They would assist with the engine start and would then cast off from the towing launch before swimming to the launch to be taken aboard. A generator on the launch would supply the electric power needed to start the mighty Double-Merlin engine.

With the floatplane in position, Charlie ran through his pre-engine start checklist and then primed the engine. He indicated to his two swimmers that the magnetos were switched on and then he pressed the start button. The two propellers kicked slowly through a couple of revolutions and then the engines came to life. The cable from the generator was disconnected and the tow lines to the launch were disconnected from the attachment rings on the front of the floats.

With the launch out of the way, Charlie put on his helmet and contacted the Club's traffic controller on a special frequency. 'Mike Charlie One Eight Two ready to taxi,' he said.

Back came the reply 'One Eight Two cleared to taxi.'

Charlie ran through his next checks, going to a higher power setting and cycling his propellers. He then started to taxi slowly, waiting for the needles on his engine gauges to get into the green arc. There were no water rudders on this aircraft since they would have created unnecessary drag and added extra weight, but, as expected, Charlie found that by applying full deflection of the flight rudder and using bursts of power, the aircraft turned easily enough. By now there were helicopters with camera crews flying around.

Charlie contacted the controller again. 'One Eight Two request high-speed step taxi.' Clearance was given. Charlie advanced the throttle. With all the resistance caused by the movement of the floats through the water it took time to get moving but thirty seconds later the aircraft was on the step of the floats, poised to take off. Not yet, thought Charlie, bringing back the power, let's try a couple more of these in crosswind conditions to see how she tracks.

After about half an hour, Charlie was through with his initial tests. He had made a few notes on his kneepad and was back in the vicinity of the launch. Before cutting his engine, he made one last call to the controller. 'One Eight Two to control. Please let Paolo know that if the post-flight inspection is OK, we can try for a first flight today at 1600 hours local time. Out.'

Back at the hangar, Charlie debriefed and pointed out a couple of minor issues to the team. The word was out to the media that probably they would see the first flight that afternoon. The team was fussing over the aircraft checking out everything. Charlie felt the need for some lunch. All he wanted to check with Stefano were two things. Unstick speed had been estimated at 100 knots and final approach speed at 120 knots. These were very high speeds for an aircraft of that time but it was designed for speed and there were no concessions made to low-speed handling. No flaps were fitted. The stall performance was unknown. Charlie would have to find out later how the machine would behave at the stall.

At 4 p.m. Charlie was back in the cockpit and the MC 72 was back on the water. Charlie fired up the engines again and the swimmers disconnected the aircraft from the launch. This time,

Charlie got the machine 'on the step' and went to maximum power. The roar of the Merlins reverberated across the lake. Charlie eased back on the stick and the floatplane was airborne.

The helicopter pilots were jostling each other to get the best position for their cameramen. They were told to keep out of each other's way and out of the way of the MC 72.

Charlie flew a couple of patterns, trying out the controls and various engine and propeller settings. When he was happy with the low speed handling, he came in and landed. Everybody was ecstatic. Another media conference was held and then the red floatplane was put away for the night.

During the next few days Charlie worked up progressively to 300 knots (345 miles per hour or 555 kilometres per hour). He also investigated the stall which was extremely vicious with a sharp wing drop and a big loss of altitude. It occurred power-off at 90 knots so the speeds they were using for take-off and final approach were quite safe.

Towards the end of the initial testing, Paolo took Charlie aside. 'Charlie, they desperately want us at Oshkosh at the end of July. It will clash with some of your other events. Can you get out of them?'

'Anything has to give way to Oshkosh,' Charlie said. 'I haven't flown there before and I don't want to miss this opportunity.'

So, the MC 72 was air-freighted to Wisconsin and the whole team travelled across to the USA. The impact which the floatplane made was enormous. Most of the American pilots had never heard of this design. Each afternoon it was given a special slot in the flying programme and Charlie had to give interview after interview.

After Oshkosh, Charlie had two months on the warbird circuit in Europe and then he had his next assignment in Como. The Italian public had taken this project to their hearts. It had helped to restore national pride.

Paolo had called Charlie at one of his shows. 'Charlie, you

just cannot believe what is happening here. After years of mismanagement and government corruption, people are pulling together because of our project. A film is being shot about my grandfather's achievements. Much of the work will be done when you are here for the next tests. There are no hotel rooms to be had in Como or in the surrounding area. Thank goodness that we have our arrangements in place. There is a whole media mobile home site which has been established just outside of Como. It is being called Cinecittà Castoldi!'

When Charlie returned to Como in mid-October, he could hardly recognize the place. It was teeming with cinema and media people and with the curious who just wanted to see the big names. Charlie was introduced to the actor who was playing the part of Agello. He had to teach him how to get into and out of the cockpit of the MC 72 without damaging anything. There was a series of balloons on cables strung out at various points on the lake. Paolo told Charlie that these marked the course for the record attempt of 1934 and it was all set up for the film.

Charlie had dinner with Paolo and Stefano that evening. Paolo seemed somewhat nervous as if he was holding something back. When they had finished the meal, Paolo cleared his throat and spoke up. 'Look, Charlie, I have told you about the course laid out on the lake. What I have not told you is that we would like you to have a crack at beating Agello's record which, as you know, still stands for seaplanes powered by a piston engine. This will undoubtedly be risky. We do not know what the limits of our aircraft are. I also have to remind you that two pilots were killed flying the original MC 72. We do not want to influence you or put any pressure on you. The decision is yours. If you consider the risk to be too great, a few passes along the course at 300 knots will suit the film people. We hold you in the highest esteem and we want you to come back when needed to continue to display our aircraft in its true element.'

'Don't feel embarrassed about asking me, Paolo,' Charlie replied. 'I was thinking of proposing a record attempt myself but I didn't want to put you and Stefano in an awkward position. I would not be the pilot that I am without having lived with danger. Flying is always a potentially risky business. A simple engine failure in a little putt-putt light aircraft can lead to a fatal accident. Now, I have been looking at some figures and I think we can do it. Agello's record is 709 kilometres per hour. We work in knots, so that translates as 383 knots. We have already achieved 300 knots quite comfortably without pushing anything. We need to exceed Agello's speed by one percent to set a new official record. I believe we have to do more than that. I think we can reach 405 knots which will give us 750 kilometres per hour. I would not like to push beyond that. The absolute speed record for a piston-engined aircraft is 850 kilometres per hour and that was set by a much more modern aircraft which had been extensively modified. We could not hope to get anywhere near that speed. However, it would be nice to have a new record for floatplanes.'

Paolo and Stefano were both smiling. They raised their glasses to Charlie. Paolo added, 'As we had to have the course laid out for the film, I invited along official observers from the Fédération Aéronautique Internationale just in case we decided to go for a record. As I pay their expenses, they are having a nice holiday as well.'

Not only Paolo and Stefano had been looking at the official rules for a record attempt but Charlie had been doing his homework as well. The course had already been laid out and verified as being exactly three kilometres long. At each end, there was an overrun which had to be at least one kilometre long. In this overrun, the aircraft would have to turn around and line up for the next run. Given the speeds involved, the overrun had been set at an additional three kilometres at each end. At no time in any of the established area could the aircraft exceed 100 meters above the lake surface. A minimum of four runs was required, two in each direction, and the average speed of the four runs would be taken as the final result. If the MC 72 managed to reach 750 kilometres per hour, it would be through the timed course in just over 14 seconds on each pass. The official recording equipment obviously had to be extremely precise.

The team had a period of ten days in which to try for the record. Charlie started working up the speed in increments of 20 knots and in doing so, he became absolutely familiar with the course. There were two days on which flying was not possible but they were not wasted as maintenance work could be carried out. Finally Charlie hit 400 knots in practice. He was a bit concerned about the high cylinder head temperatures showing on the gauges and about the risk of having all of the cooling water evaporating, but if the worst came to the worst, he could pull back the power, climb up and establish himself for a power-off landing on the lake.

The great day arrived. The weather was overcast at five thousand feet but this was not an issue. The visibility could have been better but was acceptable. There was hardly any wind. As the forecast was indicating a deterioration in the conditions with the possibility of rain later in the afternoon, it looked like a case of now or never.

The start of the attempt was scheduled for 9 a.m. local time. The officials were all in position an hour before that. The MC 72 was out on the water. In the cockpit was a sealed barograph which would reveal after the attempt if the aircraft had remained within the altitude restriction. Charlie had opted to stay at 200 feet above the lake surface. He was thankful that he had the radar altimeter which had its bug set on that height.

Before he started the engine, Charlie could hear the noise of helicopters taking up their stations. He was outwardly calm as usual but he was feeling somewhat nervous because of the responsibility weighing on his shoulders. As soon as the floatplane started to taxi, the nervousness left him. He was fully concentrated on what he had to do.

The next few minutes passed in a blur. His airspeed indicator was reading 410 knots on his first run. The awkward part was turning round at the end of each run and lining up for the next one. He needed to turn as tightly as possible, pulling a lot of 'g' and at very low level. Whatever speed he lost in the turn had to be made up very quickly. He hit 412 knots on the second run and the aircraft was absolutely flat-out. He had nothing left in reserve. On the third run he was back to 410 knots and he noticed that the cylinder head temperatures were getting dangerously high. Back he came for the final run. He was down to 408 knots but that was good enough. As soon as he crossed the finish line, he pulled up and eased back on the throttle to spare the engine but the temperature gauge needle was now well in the red zone.

Suddenly there was an enormous shudder and the engine seized. Charlie switched off immediately. He needed height to set up for a forced landing so he zoomed upwards letting the speed decay to 120 knots and then he established the aircraft in a glide. His approach pattern was already worked out in his mind. He reached down and tried to turn off the fuel cock but it wouldn't budge. He could smell burning coming from in front of him when he ripped off his oxygen mask and then, without any warning, the aircraft exploded.

Shortly afterwards, Paolo and Stefano were sitting in Paolo's temporary office. There was complete silence. Nothing but a few small fragments had been recovered from the surface of the lake and as part of the investigation, the lake bed would be trawled looking for further wreckage as soon as possible. Both men knew that unofficially the record was theirs but they had lost Charlie and they both felt guilty about it.

There was a knock at the door and the Club President entered. Without saying anything, he handed each man an envelope and left the office. Both men opened their envelopes. Paolo cleared his throat and read aloud.

'If you read these words, you will know that I am gone. Do not feel guilty about it. I made it quite clear that I wanted the record as much as you did. I have gone at the pinnacle of my career. In a few more years I would have been too old for my kind of flying. I would have found it difficult to adapt to a 'normal' existence after that.

'I shall never know if we got the record. I hope that we did. Please do not give up because of what has happened. You have another set of engines and the skill and enthusiasm of the team to build N° 183. Do this not only for me but to keep the spirit alive.

'On the attached sheet you will find the contact details of Paul Randolph in the USA and Philip Mitchell in the UK. I met them at Oshkosh. Both were inspired by what you have done. Paul is heading a project to build a flying replica of the Curtiss R3C-2 in which Jimmy Doolittle won the Schneider Trophy for the USA in 1925. Philip is heading a project to build a flying replica of the Supermarine S.6B which won the final Schneider Trophy race for Britain in 1931. We all agreed that it would be just great to have the three aircraft flying in formation at Oshkosh. Please build N° 183 for them as well. Get it to Oshkosh next year if possible for a unique fly-past.

'Finally, I have appreciated working with both of you. You have paid me more than enough for my services. As you know, I never married. My mother is still alive and I have a married sister. I have provided for them adequately in my will. I have no other immediate family. During the last few years I have accumulated a lot of money. I don't even know how much I have. For all of my assignments I received not only a large fee but I had all my expenses paid as well. I was hardly ever at home in my small apartment so I left all my affairs in the hands of my lawyer and the accountant who works with him. You will find the contact details of my lawyer on the second sheet.

'I made a revised will just before I came out here at the beginning of last week. My estate has suddenly grown by ten million pounds because of the insurance policy. The will sets out clearly what all the bequests are and my lawyer will take care of everything. Now it is time to give back. I am bequeathing three million pounds to the N°183 project and two million pounds each to the Curtiss and Supermarine projects. Those bequests are already included in the revised will.

'Keep up the good work and look to the future.'

'The text of my letter is exactly the same,' said Stefano. 'I was following it as you read yours. You may have noticed that it was written on the day when he started pushing the speed beyond 300 knots. I am sure that he gave these letters to the President himself with instructions on what to do with them.'

Paolo pulled himself together. 'Stefano, get back to your team. Keep them busy. This evening we shall go out and get ourselves drunk and tomorrow we shall start work on N° 183.'

TAILPIECE

Everything relating to the historic Schneider Trophy racing floatplanes in this story is factual, the rest is pure invention except for the conditions laid down for an absolute speed record, and the Aero Club Como which genuinely offers seaplane training. The last low-level speed record was set in the mid-1950s and thereafter runs could be made at high altitude because supersonic aircraft could perform better higher up where the air is less dense.

It is true that Agello's record set in October 1934 for a piston-engined seaplane still stands today 77 years later. The absolute speed record for a piston-engined aircraft as, mentioned in the story, was established in 1989 by 'Rare Bear' a specially modified racing version of a former Grumman Bearcat US Navy fighter.

In conclusion, I should make some mention of Jacques Schneider, son of the wealthy owner of the Schneider armament works in France. Jacques obtained his French pilot's licence and his balloonist's licence in 1911. He suffered a serious injury in a power-boat race in 1910 which prevented him from flying but in 1913 he set a French balloon record of just over 33,000 feet – this was before the First World War! He launched the Schneider Trophy in 1912 to further the development of seaplanes. The first competition had to wait until 1919 when the war was over. There were twelve competitions between then and the final one in 1931. Schneider died in 1928 at the early age of 49. The rules about permanent possession of the Trophy have often been incorrectly misinterpreted as I have in my story. It was not three consecutive victories which were required for permanent possession but three victories within five years.

GOODBYE, POP BUEHLE

The door to the pilots' lounge opened and in came Pop's student followed by Pop himself.

'Let's go into the classroom and de-brief, Ricky,' said Pop. They crossed the lounge with Pop leading the way. Pop was impressively tall and slim but his stoop had become more pronounced in recent years. He was a legend at the airport. He had just turned 96 and was still instructing every day. He might well have been the oldest active flight instructor anywhere on the planet.

It was hard to believe that this man was born in 1914, the year the Great War started in Europe. Pop was born and raised in this little township in the Middle West. He had attended High School here. When he was fifteen, in 1929, Wall Street had crashed bringing the 'Roaring Twenties' to a sudden halt. The Great Depression set in. In some ways Pop had been very lucky. His father did not lose his job. Pop, or rather Jimmy as he was known then, was already hanging around the airport in his spare time as he was fascinated by flying. This was the same little airport where he was instructing today but in those days it was no more than a grass pasture. He had seen Lindbergh land here in the 'Spirit of St. Louis' on his triumphal tour following his flight from New York to Paris in 1927. Three years later Pop was lucky enough to catch the attention of one prominent local citizen who kept his biplane there.

One Sunday this notable saw Pop hanging about, having already seen him a few other times. 'Hey, Sonny,' he called out, 'want to come for a ride?'

Pop could not believe his ears. He went up in a Travel Air biplane and loved every second of it. He was even allowed to handle the controls. Back at the airfield, this magnificent gentleman introduced the gawky youth to the 'fixed base operator', the man who ran the little airport. The latter had also seen Pop hanging around.

'Now Don,' said the benefactor, 'let me introduce you to young Jimmy here. This boy has got what it takes to become a pilot. I am going to take him up a few times but as you know, I am not an instructor. If he does some work for you at the weekends without pay, would you let him have some lessons with Bob?'

Pop could not believe his ears – even less when Don replied: 'Well, Mr Renshaw, since this is coming from you and you're a true gentleman, I'll do that. I have noticed this boy around here and if he is as keen as he looks, he deserves a chance in these difficult times.'

Mr Renshaw drove the boy home. He asked to meet his parents. He told them what was planned. 'Now folks,' he said, 'you don't need me to tell you that we are living in hard times. I like the look of young Jimmy here and I want to see him get a good start in life. Don't feel that I am trying to interfere and don't feel that you will have any obligation towards me.'

His parents were not too happy about accepting all this 'charity' but after a long talk with Jimmy, they agreed.

Jimmy was introduced to Bob and started proper flying lessons. In return he spent most of his weekends out at the airport doing everything he had to do but he loved every minute of it. Bob sent him solo after five hours.

'That boy is a complete natural,' Bob informed Don and Mr Renshaw. 'Trouble is he can't take his ticket until he is 17 next year but in the meantime I can teach him a lot more.'

Jimmy got his ticket on his 17th birthday. The next year he graduated from High School. It was now time for decisions. He had a younger brother who was still at school. He knew that his parents could not afford to send him to college and he also knew that as much as they liked Mr Renshaw, they did not want any more 'assistance' from him.

Jimmy decided to have a conversation with Mr Renshaw out at the airfield.

'Son, I know exactly what the situation is,' Mr Renshaw said, 'I've been thinking about it myself. If I were to give you a job it would make your parents feel more indebted to me. Also, any job I could offer you would not be connected with flying. The Army Air Corps needs pilots. You might find the discipline hard and it would be some months before you even got near an airplane but you would be looked after and getting some pay on top of that. If I were you, I would enlist.'

Jimmy talked his parents into it. They could see that it would reduce their financial burden. Jimmy put on his one and only suit and, accompanied by his parents, went along to the nearest Army recruitment office.

The next several weeks would have broken him if he had not had a clear goal before him. This was 'boot camp' stuff where he and all the other trainees were thoroughly humiliated. They were picked up on every little thing and were always contemptuously referred to as 'Mister'. All they were allowed to reply was: 'Sir, yes Sir'.

Pop came through all of this and after initial training was posted to Texas. For him, this was like going to the other side of the world.

On arrival, the base commandant had addressed his batch of trainees, 'So, Gentlemen, you all want to be pilots. This is where you have to prove that you have what it takes. You start off as aircraft mechanics. You will have to know everything about the airplanes you have to service. You will get no rest. Your hands will be cut and bloody and ingrained with grease. You will be going nowhere until you are passed as being a competent mechanic.'

Pop did this drudgery for six months. He never complained. He was learning all the time. One day he was summoned to report to the Commanding Officer. He entered his office and stood to attention. 'Mr Buehle, you have done well. You are

151

being transferred to flight training. You will be trained here. You are herewith promoted to the rank of corporal. You will report to Lieutenant Fane in the offices of A Hangar tomorrow morning at 09:00. That is all. Good luck.'

Pop could have wept with joy but his excitement was to be short-lived. He was not impressed when he met Lieutenant Fane the following morning.

'So, you have nearly 200 hours flight time. That counts for nothing here, Mister. Those civilians don't know what flying is all about. You start from scratch with me. Get over to Stores and draw your equipment. We go flying at 11:00.'

The first thing that Pop noticed about Fane in the air was that in spite of all his barking, he was essentially nervous and that he was trying to cover it up by being aggressive. He flew with Fane for two months. He was allowed to fly solo but at the end of that time he noticed that he had only covered about half of what was on the syllabus.

At the end of these two months Fane snarled at him, 'All right, Buehle. You will never be a pilot. You have had every chance but you don't have it. Tomorrow Captain Wilson will check you out at 09:00. He will fail you, of course.'

The next morning Pop went up with Captain Wilson. Wilson said nothing before the flight. They flew for more than an hour. Pop was asked to do plenty of manoeuvres which he had never flown with Fane. Because of what he had learned back home, he did everything with ease. After the flight Wilson shook his hand. 'Buehle, you are a natural. You start advanced training tomorrow. Report to E Hangar at 09:00.'

When Wilson got back to his office, he summoned Fane and made him stand to attention. 'Mr Fane, you are busted. You are posted to a desk job in San Antonio. Here are your orders. Make sure you are on your way this afternoon.'

Suddenly military life changed for Pop. With a glowing report from Captain Wilson, he now had the best instruction available. He sailed through advanced training like a breeze. At the end of his course he was promoted to Lieutenant and was posted to fly pursuit fighters. He was ordered to report to the First Pursuit Group flying the Boeing P-26 at Selfridge Field, Michigan. He had been in the Army Air Corps for just two years and he was starting to go places.

After two years of flying the P-26 Pop was transferred to do flight testing at Wright Field, Dayton. As a pilot, he had made it to the top. His flying skills were a benchmark to all other Army pilots but also he had acquired a solid engineering background and he was a first rate trouble-shooter.

Then the war clouds had gathered over Europe. It was now mid-1939. In spite of the isolationists in the United States, Pop, like many others, could see his country being caught up in a global war. He was content with his test work but there was now a little something nagging away at the back of his mind. When he learnt to fly, he had been given excellent tuition. In the military, he had seen too many examples of lousy tuition. Lieutenant Fane had been a case in point. Deep down, Pop felt that he could give something back. He could surely help to get fledgling pilots trained properly. The first few hours were the critical ones. After that, it was hard to undo bad habits.

When the situation with Japan became tense in 1941, Pop went to see his CO. 'Sir', he said, 'I wish to request a transfer.'

His CO was dumbfounded. 'For Heaven's sake, why, Buehle? You are irreplaceable here.'

Pop explained his point of view.

His CO sighed. 'Buehle, if that is what you want, I shall not stand in your way but you will get no promotion and no thanks for what you want to do. All I can do is to wish you well.'

A few days later Pop was on his way back to Texas to join a sprawling training base. His new CO could not understand how one of the highest rated pilots in the Service wanted to come here to instruct absolute beginners. It took the CO only a few weeks to realise what an asset he had acquired.

Pop was to instruct on the Stearman PT-17. He joined a team

of instructors whose competence ranged from good to pathetic. Within a month the CO knew that all the pupils wanted to fly with Pop.

The CO sent for him. 'Buehle,' he began, 'why is it that everybody wants instruction from you? If this were to happen, more than half of my instructors would be out of jobs.'

'Sir,' replied Pop, 'instructing is an art. It cannot be done by numbers. Each pupil is different. Those boys have to be encouraged, not chewed out by some martinet.'

'All right, Buehle, you have some kind of magic wand. We need good pilots badly. You cannot train them all. This is what you are going to do. You will not only train your quota of pilots but you will check out all my instructors as well. I have already issued the order. You have my authority to weed out any instructors who cannot do it your way. I may be seriously overloading you. If it becomes too much, just let me know.'

Pop was now in his element. Throughout the war years he just flew and flew but he never tired of it. He gave thousands of pupils their basic training and he straightened out hundreds of instructors. By now the Air Corps had become the Army Air Forces operating all over the globe. In many places pilots would be flung together for a few days, a few weeks or a few months. The talk was always about flying. Pop would have been embarrassed to learn how many pilots all over the world said with some pride that their first instructor had been Lieutenant Buehle.

And then in 1945 the war was over. Servicemen were demobbed. Bases were closed. Pop had taken no leave in those years. He had had no promotion. It was time to move on. His CO (was it the fifth or sixth he had served under at that base?) had tried to persuade him to stay.

'Buehle, we need men like you. I can certainly get you promoted to captain.'

'No thanks, Sir,' Pop replied. 'The Air Force is going to get rid of all of those wonderful taildraggers. I don't want to be associated with these new things with a nose wheel and an enclosed cockpit.'

The CO tried all he knew but Pop's mind was made up. He was given a wonderful send-off and that was the end of his Service life.

Pop surfaced in his home town early in 1946. He was still comparatively young. He had lost his younger brother in the war on a bombing mission over Germany. He moved back in with his parents. One couldn't say he was wealthy but on the other hand he wasn't poor. It looked as if the Air Force had given him a good deal. He had purchased a war surplus Stearman PT-17 and he parked it at the local airport where he had learnt to fly. The place had changed. It had been used for bombardier training in the war and had acquired two hard runways and some decent hangars. The flying school was about to open again and Pop offered his services.

For Pop it was not a case of the return of the local war hero. He had never been in the newspapers and he had never been awarded any medals for gallantry. This did not bother him. He had remained in contact with Mr Renshaw and the two got together frequently.

The new flying school did not have the same personnel as it had before the war. The present owner had been in the military but he had never come across Pop. The anticipated boom in peace-time private flying did not happen. For a long time Pop was the only instructor and the only aircraft available was the PT-17.

One day, an Air Force general landed and taxied up to the FBO. He asked if a Mr Buehle was working there. On being told that this was so and that Pop was up with a pupil, the general said that he would wait.

When Pop came into the lounge, the general got to his feet. 'Lieutenant Buehle, do you remember me?'

Pop saluted, scratched his head and said, 'Could you be Endacott?'

The general smiled. 'I knew you wouldn't forget me,' he said. 'If you are free, let me buy you lunch.'

The photo of the two of them was hung in the lounge. A couple more generals and some majors also visited. Their photos were added to the collection. The local newspaper got hold of the story. Then there were senators and congressmen who called in to see their old instructor. This was good for business and soon the owner of the flight school was able to add a couple of training aircraft and two instructors.

Now another 64 years had gone by. The owner of the school had changed several times. Instructors had come and gone. Pop's parents and Mr Renshaw had passed away a long time ago. Even the oldest of the 'airport bums' had not been around when Pop had returned from the war. Nobody could remember who first decided to call him 'Pop'.

The school now boasted a fleet of seven aircraft and four instructors in addition to Pop. Individual hangars had been constructed at the airport and Pop rented one of these for his Stearman. The control tower had been demolished after the war. No commercial services operated into the airport and it was now a typical non-towered airport where each pilot had to make his own calls. It was a good place to learn to fly and the school was doing nicely.

Pop always had more pupils on his hands than the other instructors. Those whom he had taught spread the word. 'If you want a good instructor, ask to fly with Pop Buehle.' There was more to it than that. Pop was a long-serving member of the local EAA branch. Every 'Young Eagles' Day, Pop's Stearman was out on the ramp and all the youngsters wanted to be taken up in it. He had acquired many pupils that way. Pop had modernised his aircraft so that he could cover everything in the FAA's Private Pilot syllabus. He had a radio and a transponder fitted but he refused to take pupils for their mock check-ride. 'There is no FAA examiner around here who is qualified to check candidates out in a Stearman,' he would tell them. 'I will do the whole syllabus with you, ground and practical, but you will have to do a few hours at the end with one of my colleagues in one of them there spam cans.' By this he meant the Cessna 152s and Piper Warriors which the school operated. 'You can't fly properly if you can't handle a taildragger,' he would add.

In addition Pop taught his pupils how to recover from all types of stall and how to recover from spins. For good measure, if his pupil wished, he would throw in some basic aerobatics. 'The FAA doesn't like this stalling and spinning business. They are wrong. As a pilot you need to know how to handle these things. I have known too many instructors and examiners who are afraid of stalls. That can't be right. Your aircraft tries to talk to you. You have to learn how to listen to it.'

Pop also insisted that all of his pupils studied properly for the knowledge test. 'If you can't score 90% on a mock run with me, I am not signing you off to take the knowledge test. Flying is fun but it is also a serious business. You have to work hard at it.'

Only very rarely did a pupil ask for a different instructor after a few flights with Pop. It was then discovered that these pupils could not get on with anybody else either. They were too full of themselves and they did not stay around long.

There were no longer former pupils from the war years who came to see Pop but now there was a stream of former pupils who had lived locally and who had been taught by Pop here. There were senior captains of the major airlines and military pilots of all ranks. Pop was never at a loss to remember who they were and the collection of photographs on the walls of the lounge grew and grew.

He had been asked several times why he had never married and had children or if he was not lonely living all alone. 'Not a bit of it,' Pop would reply. 'This is my family here at the airport and as for my children, I have thousands of them – they are all the pupils I taught to fly.'

Pop was particularly fond of young Danny Morrissey who was the youngest of the instructors. Pop had taught Danny to fly. Danny now had all his ratings but instead of wanting to be an airline pilot or a military pilot, all he wanted to do was to instruct. Pop had infected him. On quiet days he would go flying with Pop in the Stearman. He helped Pop to service and maintain his aircraft.

Not so long ago when Danny and several other local pilots were sitting in the lounge waiting for the weather to lift, one of them had said: 'I wonder how many hours Pop actually has. I did ask him but he told me he didn't keep a record. I just didn't believe that.'

That remark started off some typical 'hangar flying'. 'Well, there's a guy down in Alabama who flies power line patrols and who claims over 62,000 hours,' said another.

'What about airline pilots?' somebody asked.

'I don't think they should be counted,' said a fourth. 'They certainly build up the hours but they are not handling the aircraft for most of the time.'

Then Danny chimed in: 'You know, Pop started flying in 1930 – that's 80 years ago. Suppose that he has flown on average three hours a day. His average is probably higher than that but there will have been days when he did not fly because of weather or other issues, so let's stick with three hours per day. That gives a total of 1,095 hours in a year. Multiply that by 80 and you get 87,600 hours. I am sure that Pop has more than 80,000 hours and probably more than 90,000.'

Now on this early spring day, Pop came back into the lounge with Ricky after de-briefing him. 'OK young Ricky, you have your homework assignment. We are flying again on Saturday at ten. See you then.' Pop stretched his frame and looked out of the window. 'I think I have time to fly over to Cutt's Corner and do some grass landings there. Should take me about an hour and a half. Do you want to come, Danny?'

'I would love to but I'm waiting for my next pupil,' said Danny. 'Well I'll be back around five-thirty. If you're around at six maybe you can help me put the Stearman into the hangar.'

'Glad to, Pop,' replied Danny.

Five minutes later the throaty roar of Pop's Stearman could be heard. Pop did his landings at Cutt's Corner and was now on his way back. He was at 2,000 feet and admiring the countryside. Like all good pilots he always had a suitable field in view in case he had engine failure. And then it happened. The engine died. Pop had had several engine failures in his time. He quickly checked everything but could not find an answer. Probably the fuel line is blocked, he thought. He was already set up downwind for a big meadow off to his left. He put out a Mayday call on the Flight Center frequency but could not depend on them receiving it as he was already very low. He pulled off a beautiful landing. He climbed out of the cockpit and looked to see if there was anything he could fix there and then. He tried to pull the propeller through but it would not move at all. Either a rod had broken or a piston had jammed. There was nothing he could do here. On the descent he had not seen any habitation near at hand so he decided it would be best to stay with his aircraft. If he had had his mobile phone with him, he could have called base but he had left it in his locker as he so seldom used it. Oh, well, no fool like an old fool, he thought. If he had thought further, he could have manually activated his emergency locator transmitter. He was obliged to have one of these in his aircraft as he was using it for training. If he had thought of switching it on it would transmit a signal on the international distress frequency for 48 hours. This signal would be captured by navigational satellites and his position would be known immediately.

Pop knew that it was going to be a long, cold night. He got back in the cockpit and tried to make himself as warm as possible.

Back at the airport, Danny was looking at the clock and was becoming concerned. At six, Mavis, the front desk lady was to go off duty. At seven, the front door would be locked. Danny told Mavis to go. He was the only one left there. He waited until 18:30 when the light was starting to fade and then he called the Flight Center. They had not picked up anything in particular apart from a faint voice message an hour previously which they could not identify. Danny gave the details of the missing aircraft and its likely route and told Center that he would wait there by the phone for the next two hours. Center responded that now night had fallen, it would be difficult to start a search and that no emergency locator transmitter signals had been picked up. Danny finally went home at eight having left his mobile number with the Center.

He was out at the airport at daybreak the next morning. There had been no news during the night. As the other instructors rolled in he appraised them of the situation and told them to cancel their lessons. They were all going to search for Pop's Stearman. They drew up a plan of action, marking out on the charts a sector for each aircraft. Danny called Flight Center to let them know what they were doing. Center was putting other aircraft in the air and it was agreed they would all use one discreet frequency so as not to interfere with other traffic.

A whole morning's searching produced no results. This was not surprising. Looking for a downed aircraft can be like looking for a needle in a haystack. The Stearman was dark blue in colour and could easily merge with the terrain – if it was still in one piece.

Finally one of the Sheriff's Department helicopters found the aircraft in the middle of the afternoon. It landed next to it and the helicopter crew found Pop dead in the cockpit.

As it was clear that the engine of the Stearman could not be fixed there, Center arranged for a Bell Big Lifter helicopter to come in and hoist the Stearman back to the airport. In the meantime Pop's body was taken away for an autopsy.

The mood in the airport lounge was gloomy. Pop was indestructible. He was part of the airport itself. How could he have gone like that? Danny felt particularly bad about it. He should have been there. He could have made the difference. So far the media had not got hold of the story but when a large helicopter emerged with a Stearman slung underneath it, somebody would be bound to blab to them and then there would be no peace.

Dr Frazer carried out the autopsy at the local morgue. He deduced that Pop had died from hypothermia but as the man was 96, he thought it kinder to all to enter the reason for death as 'natural causes'.

A week went by and things started to return to normal. Danny couldn't get Pop out of his mind. Was anybody looking after his place? Had the old man even left a will?

Well, it was back to the routine. Danny entered the lounge one morning after flying with one of his students. Jenny was on front desk and said. 'Danny, when you have a minute, can you call this number? He called you half an hour ago.'

'John R. Erdman, Attorney at Law,' read Danny. 'I wonder what he wants.'

Half an hour later Danny made the call. He was immediately put through. 'Mr Morrissey, is it possible for you to come and see me this afternoon? I have something of importance to discuss with you.' Danny agreed that he could be there at four.

At the appointed time he was ushered into Mr Erdman's office. They shook hands.

'Mr Morrissey,' began Mr Erdman, 'I am glad you were able to come so quickly. You must be wondering what this is all about. First, however, would you please show me some ID so that I can verify that you are the person you claim to be?'

Danny offered up his driving licence. Erdman took a photocopy and then turned to his visitor.

'Mr Morrissey, I understand that you knew the late Mr James Buehle well.'

'That's true,' replied Danny.

'Mr Buehle left a will,' continued Mr Erdman. 'He left it with me. He also named me as the executor. The police contacted me after his demise last week when they entered his house and found a piece of paper on his desk which referred them to me. Mr Buehle was always very meticulous.'

Danny was puzzled. 'How do I come into this?'

'Now you may find this hard to believe but Mr Buehle has made you his sole and universal legatee. Put into simple English, this means that he has left everything which he owns and possesses to you.'

Danny gasped and stared at the attorney.

'Mr Buehle had no family. Just to be sure I have made some investigations but I had no reason to doubt what he told me. The estate is not small. There is the house, his airplane, his car and quite a lot of bonds and deposits and cash at the bank. I have to agree with the IRS whether there is any tax outstanding but from what I have seen, this is not likely to be the case. I would think that in about ten days' time everything will be wrapped up. You will be required to sign certain transfer documents and all of this can be done in my office. In the meantime I am giving you this envelope. I would just like you to sign for receipt here. My secretary will take you to one of our empty offices where you can read the contents before you leave.'

Danny was in a daze. The secretary put him in another office. Danny examined the envelope. It was addressed to him in Pop's well-known neat hand-writing. Danny slit the envelope open and took out a single sheet of paper.

'Dear Danny,' it began, 'when you read this I shall be gone forever. As you know I never had children. I have viewed you as a son although with our age difference, you would really be a great grandson. You are a good pilot and I am so pleased that you are carrying on my tradition. It is right and proper that you should receive all I have. I know that you will put everything to good use. It is time you had a place of your own and now you have it. Mr Erdman will do all that is necessary.' It was signed 'James Buehle'.

It was only two weeks later that Danny really entered into his inheritance. The Stearman was up and running again but Danny had to get used to his new property. He was amazed at the amount of money which Pop had accumulated. He started slowly going through the papers in the little study. There was a large envelope on the desk which was addressed to him. He opened it.

The top sheet read '87,236.4 hours as at 31 December 2009'. Below this there were about forty sheets in Pop's handwriting. It was his own account of his life. Underneath this, Danny found two letters. The first was from the General Hap Arnold, Chief of the Army Air Forces, dated early 1946, thanking Pop for all he had done for the Air Force and declaring that he was to receive a special pension for life which would be indexed linked and never subject to federal taxes. The other one was from President Truman, written a short time later, thanking Pop for his exceptional services and awarding him the Presidential Medal of Freedom.

All Pop's log books from the very beginning were there. There were photo albums with each photograph carefully annotated. It would take Danny many months to sift through all of this. He leaned back in the chair and gazed at the ceiling.

'Well, Pop, I am going to do have to do some writing so that the whole world can know what an exceptional aviator and person you were,' he said out loud.

NON-FICTION

THE ORTEIG TROPHY AND THE OISEAU BLANC

In May 1919, wealthy French-born New York hotel owner, Raymond Orteig, put up a prize of US$25,000 for the first aviator, or aviators to fly non-stop between New York and Paris, or vice-versa, in a heavier-than-air machine. This was quite a sum of money in those days, being worth between US$300,000 and US$1,000,000 today, depending on the criteria used. Even so, the amount of the prize was symbolic. Any attempt would cost more than the amount to be awarded. There was no equipment capable of making such a flight at the time, and seven years were to pass before serious competitors started to emerge. Alcock and Brown had crossed the Atlantic in a heavier-than-air machine in 1919 thus winning the Daily Mail award and becoming national heroes in Britain but their flight from Newfoundland to the west coast of Ireland covered only just over 50% of the distance between New York and Paris, which stands at 3,610 statute miles or 5,810 kilometres. Considering that the aircraft capable of such a distance in 1927 would be cruising at around 100 miles per hour in still air, an endurance of at least 36 hours would be needed, and, to be on the safe side, it would be rash to consider attempting the flight between the two cities without having an endurance of more than 40 hours.

The first candidate to be ready to try for the Orteig Prize was René Fonck. Fonck had been not only the highest scoring French pilot in the 1914-1918 War but also, with his 75 confirmed victories, had been the highest scoring pilot of any of the allied nations. Fonck ordered a three-engined aircraft from Sikorsky for his attempt. He was keen to try for the prize before bad weather set in at the end of September 1926. Sikorsky felt that his aircraft was not ready but Fonck would not wait. On 20th September 1926, the heavily laden aircraft failed to become airborne and ran down an incline at the end of the runway at Roosevelt Field, New York. Fonck and his co-pilot escaped from the blazing wreck but his radio operator and mechanic died in the inferno.

When the spring of 1927 came, other candidates were making their final preparations. The American Richard Byrd with his Fokker trimotor was the favourite. He had already claimed to have overflown the North Pole in such an aircraft (doubt has since been cast on his claims). His pilot was Floyd Bennett. The Fokker crashed on take-off, injuring Bennett, and this put them out of the running. Another American, Clarence Chamberlin, with his Bellanca was ready for his attempt but an injunction against him kept him on the ground. His fellow-countrymen Noel Davis and Stanton Wooster never even got to the starting line as they were killed when their Keystone 'Pathfinder' crashed during testing in April. This left only two candidates who had any chance of claiming the prize before the end of May. These were the Frenchmen Charles Nungesser and François Coli, and the unknown Charles Lindbergh.

Nungesser and Coli were perhaps an unlikely pair. The former had finished the Great War as France's third ranking ace in aerial combat with 45 confirmed victories. He loved life in the fast lane and living dangerously. Apart from flying on the edge, he devoted his time to drink, women and fast cars. The result of his numerous flying and driving crack-ups had been fractures to many of his bones and it is said that in 1918 he had to be carried to his aircraft before each flight. He had been a darling of the French public but, in 1927, he had turned 35 and was largely forgotten, as is often the case with war heroes who have lost their youth. Coli appears to have been quite different in temperament. He was ten years older than his firebrand pilot. He had also served as a French aviator in the Great War but his skill was as a navigator, not a pilot. He did not have the frequent accidents which had plagued Nungesser but he had lost an eye. After the war whilst Nungesser was barnstorming in the States and appearing in films as a stunt pilot, Coli was serving as navigator to some French pilots on long distance record flights.

Of the pair, it was Coli who was first tempted by the Orteig Prize. He wanted to have a crack at it using the services of Paul Tarascon as pilot but the latter was badly injured in a flying accident in 1926. Coli had to look for a replacement pilot and this is where Nungesser came in.

The two of them approached Pierre Levasseur's aircraft manufacturing company for a suitable aircraft for the attempt. Levasseur was not one of the major manufacturers in France but he agreed to modify one of his aircraft and put it at the disposal of Nungesser and Coli. The result of this modification was the Levasseur PL.8. This was a stocky single-engined biplane of a design which belonged to the past. It had plenty of what one would term as 'a built-in headwind'. In other words, it created a lot of drag which would degrade its performance. The heavy water-cooled Lorraine-Dietrich engine of 450hp was a generation behind the light Wright Whirlwind air-cooled engine which most of the American contestants had decided to use. The one innovative feature of this design was that after take-off, the landing gear would be jettisoned, reducing the amount of drag, and the landing at the destination would be on the water.

Looking at the pictures which I have of the aircraft, its hydrodynamic qualities would not appear to be good and I would have expected it to flip over into an inverted position on a water landing. Pilot and navigator sat side by side in an open cockpit well behind the wings. On the ground, the view forward would have been non-existent and in flight it would not have been much better either. The aircraft's weight fully loaded for take-off was a staggering 11,000 pounds or 5,000 kilos. It is interesting to compare this with Lindbergh's Ryan NYP aircraft.

His *Spirit of St Louis* weighed 5,410 pounds (2,450 kilos) at take-off – less than half the weight of the French challenger. Lindbergh had the highly reliable light-weight Wright Whirlwind engine and his aircraft was beautifully streamlined to cut down on unnecessary drag.

A further factor was against the French aviators from the start. All other competitors had decided to depart from New York. Most of the pilots were American in any case and it was natural for them to start from American soil. Of considerable importance was that under normal circumstances those starting from New York would be able to benefit from the usual westerly winds over the North Atlantic. This wind, however slight, would help them on their way and reduce the fuel burn. Nungesser and Coli, however, were to depart from Paris and would in all probability have headwinds for much of the time, which would reduce their speed over the water and eat into their precious fuel reserves. Why was this illogical decision taken? Was it forced on them by the French authorities? The answer may be lost in the mists of time but I think it was a major factor in their failure. My own guess is that the cost in time and money of dismantling the aircraft, shipping it to the States, re-erecting it and testing it was prohibitive. If they did this, somebody else would snatch the prize from them before they were ready.

Finally their aircraft was ready for the attempt. It was christened *Oiseau Blanc* because of its overall white finish which would make it more easily visible to rescuers if it was forced down. Nungesser, in a throw-back to his Great War gaudily decorated aircraft, had his personal macabre design emblazoned on the fuselage sides. It consisted of a heart shape painted black, inside which were depicted in white a coffin flanked by two candles above a skull and crossbones. This symbol may have brought him luck in the past but it hardly belonged to a peace-time record attempt.

The heavily laden aircraft departed from Le Bourget Airport, Paris, at first light on the morning of May 8th 1927. This was the airport at which Charles Lindbergh would land less than two weeks later and thus claim the Orteig Prize. When they left, Nungesser and Coli probably thought that, barring an accident, the prize was theirs.

The undercarriage was duly dropped after take-off. As far as the French coast, which they crossed at Etretat, they were accompanied by some French military aircraft and then they were on their own. They were later positively identified crossing the west coast of Ireland and heading out over the Atlantic.

Crowds were already gathering at Battery Park in New York to witness the water landing which was planned by the Statue of Liberty. Rumours circulated that they had been sighted over Canada and then over Maine. The crowd waited and waited but the *Oiseau Blanc* never arrived.

Ever since the disappearance of the *Oiseau Blanc* there has been speculation as to what happened. Only a few days prior to penning these words in February 2012, nearly 85 years after the disappearance, the news has been released in France that it is certain that the aircraft came down near St Pierre-et-Miquelon, off the south coast of Newfoundland. There is, however, still no tangible evidence. The general public thrives on unexplained mysteries. This disappearance sparked off the usual crop of far-fetched theories. In the distant past, boats would disappear at sea. With the advent of long-distance flying, aircraft started disappearing. The world may seem very small to us today but two thirds of it is covered by water and is thus relatively unknown. Several well-known long-distance aviators disappeared whilst attempting to break records. The names of Charles Kingsford-Smith of Australia, Amelia Earhart of the United States and Jean Mermoz of France readily come to mind. Even a non-pilot like band leader Glenn Miller has had whole legends built around his disappearance on a short flight from England to Paris just after its liberation in August 1944.

In spite of all the high tech equipment available today, searching for missing aviators can be like looking for the proverbial needle in a haystack. I can give no better example of this than the disappearance of multi record breaker Steve Fossett in September 2007. Fossett had taken off on a local flight in a light aircraft in the Nevada Desert area. When he failed to show up, a huge search was organised which became the biggest search for a downed pilot ever undertaken in the USA. The search was finally called off because of the enormous cost. When the crash site was found quite by chance over one year later, and the remains were identified, it was discovered that the aircraft had gone down only 65 miles from its departure point. It had apparently been caught in a violent down draught which forced it into the ground. If it takes so long to find a missing aviator in the most technically advanced country in the world in our new century, is it any wonder that so many aviators have disappeared for ever over the vast tracts of the world's oceans?

The flawed attempt by Nungesser and Coli in the *Oiseau Blanc* to win the Orteig Prize is neatly put into perspective by Charles Lindbergh, who, less than two weeks after the departure of the French aviators, landed safely at Le Bourget after dark to win the Prize and to cause one of the biggest media events of the 20th Century. He had planned meticulously, had flown alone, and had made sure that he had the best possible equipment available for his attempt.

If the *Oiseau Blanc* did come down off the south coast of Newfoundland, it would have constituted the first crossing of the Atlantic by French aviators in a heavier-than-air machine but they would still have had about a third of the route to New York before them. In my view, with obsolete equipment and the winds against them, the pair had done well to fly that far. Only one contestant can win a prize for being first. The others are quickly forgotten. Lindbergh was to suffer from huge media attention for years. His name was known to millions all over the globe. Poor Chamberlin, who had been grounded by a legal injunction, was finally able to take off from New York on June 4th. He took a passenger with him. He smashed Lindbergh's distance record by a good margin and landed just 45 miles (72 kilometres) short of Berlin. However, there was no great adulation for him. Lindbergh had already taken all the glory. Media interest in the Orteig Prize was clearly a classic case of 'no time for losers'.

AMY, WONDERFUL AMY

Amy, wonderful Amy,
How can you blame me
For loving you?
So began a catchy little song of 1930.

Well, who was Amy and why was she so wonderful? The answer to the first part of the question is: Amy Johnson, and the answer to the second part is: she had just become the first woman to fly solo from England to Australia and had covered the distance in under three weeks.

With one or two exceptions, women had not been very prominent in the world of aviation from its beginning until Amy arrived on the scene. Those women who did make it into a virtually exclusively male club came from families with financial means. In spite of the fact that Amy's father was a fishmonger and that she spoke with an accent which was decidedly not upper class, her family was well-to-do. Without money behind her she would not, in the late 1920s, have had the university education she received, nor would she have been able to afford flying lessons.

Once Amy had been bitten by the flying bug it was clear that she had the quiet determination to know where she was going. After receiving her pilot's licence in 1929 she became the first female ground engineer to be licensed by the British Air Ministry.

Her dream was to fly solo from England to Australia and to break the record held by Australian pilot Bert Hinkler, which stood at fifteen and a half days. In spite of family money, she needed more financial support for this venture and much of it came from Lord Wakefield, owner of the Castrol Oil Company. A second-hand de Havilland Gipsy Moth biplane was purchased for her jointly by her father and Lord Wakefield. The Moth series of biplanes was proving to be very popular with sporting pilots. The last of the line, the famous Tiger Moth, was to teach thousands of Royal Air Force pilots the basics of flying and it served with distinction until the 1950s.

Amy departed from Croydon Airport on 5th May 1930 with precious few flight hours recorded in her log book. The attempt which she was about to make was a good story for the media. She had 11,000 miles to cover in an open-cockpit biplane which could cruise at 85 miles per hour in still air. Instrumentation was rudimentary. She had no radio and would have to fly by dead reckoning, identifying features on the ground from her maps, correcting for the wind and estimating her time to each prominent landmark ahead. The longest leg of her route would need a flight of about ten hours. In a cold cockpit, exposed to the elements and with the continual roar of the engine in her ears, she would at times be struggling to keep her concentration.

Her route would take her from London, across Europe to Istanbul and from there over territory which was mostly part of the British Empire. There were parts of her route where the maps of the time were sketchy and of no great help. She would have to deal with tropical weather systems which could tear her frail aircraft apart. The last leg would be over the shark-infested Timor Sea. In all, she had fourteen intermediate stops on her route where fuel and services would be available.

Her progress was followed with great interest. After the Wall Street Crash of the previous year, a story like this would cheer people up. In particular it would make the British even more proud to be British. Amy's chances of breaking the record were dashed by damage caused in landings at Jhansi and Rangoon. The Gipsy Moth was easy enough to repair but it took valuable time. Amy finally arrived at Darwin nineteen days after leaving London. She was given a rapturous reception. What mattered was that a young woman had flown solo from England to Australia. The time taken was of no consequence.

Amy flew on, aiming to reach Sydney but a more serious landing accident at Brisbane put her aircraft out of commission. In Sydney she met Scottish pilot Jim Mollison whom she was later to marry. She then returned to England as a passenger and even though this was some time after her solo flight, she was given a welcome which few can have had. An estimated one million people lined the route from the airport to central London. Who would get that adulation today? She received award upon award just for this one flight.

Amy married Jim Mollison in 1932. It was a disastrous marriage. Jim was by all accounts a philanderer and an alcoholic. He rated himself more highly than any other pilot and he seemed to have contempt for the rest. That same year Amy set a solo record between London and Cape Town. In the following year, she and Jim attempted to fly from Wales to New York against the prevailing winds. They crash landed just short of their goal and their aircraft was wrecked.

In 1934 the McRobertson Trophy air race from London to Melbourne attracted huge interest. It was destined to be the last great pre-war race. De Havilland had produced the sleek Comet racer specifically for this race. Of the five examples built, three were entered. One was to be piloted by Amy and Jim. Jim was determined to win this race and he did most of the piloting although, apparently, he could not land the aircraft as well as Amy did.

The couple was in the lead as far as Karachi and had broken the London to Karachi record but Jim had been pushing the engines too much at low altitude and they were faltering when they reached the next landing site. The damage done was not repairable and the Mollisons were out of the race. In the cockpit next to Jim's seat three empty whisky bottles were found. Their marriage was on the rocks and Amy decided she would travel back to England alone. The divorce was not official until 1938 and then Amy resumed her maiden name.

The progress in aviation had been considerable since 1930.

The winning Comet in the McRobertson Trophy race had covered the distance from London to Darwin in just over two days and four hours compared with Amy's 1930 time of nineteen days.

In spite of her fame, Amy was unable to find a steady job as a pilot, no doubt because of the prejudice against her sex. She set some more solo flight records but with the war clouds gathering in Europe air races and record setting were no longer newsworthy.

When the war came in 1939 it changed many people's lives for ever and, of course, it put an end to millions of lives. In Britain it was soon realised that all pilots of any competence who, for reasons of sex, age or disabilities, could not serve with the Air Force or the Navy, would be able to play a useful part ferrying important passengers around Britain or delivering new aircraft from the factories. The Air Transport Auxiliary (ATA) was formed in February 1940 for this very purpose.

Amy joined its ranks. This service attracted several women pilots. The names of Lettice Curtis, Joan Hughes, Ann Welch and Monique Agazarian readily come to my mind. They all came from wealthy families and after the war they each made as big a contribution to aviation as they had made during the war. These ladies ferried the latest fighters and the big four-engined bombers to the operational units.

The ATA, which was disbanded in November 1945, had a magnificent war record. It had employed nearly 1,200 male pilots and approaching 200 female pilots. It delivered over 300,000 aircraft from the factories to the operational units.

Amy found herself quite at home in this organization. She was still immensely popular. When she landed at military airfields, officers would queue up to talk to her and get her autograph. There was certainly some magic about her.

On 5th January 1941 Amy was to pilot an Airspeed Oxford from Squires Gate, Blackpool, to Kidlington, just outside Oxford. Flying in wartime Britain was not easy. There was the possibility of being mistaken for an enemy aircraft and being shot at. Radio silence was to be maintained. There were balloon barrages at all potential targets for the enemy and the risk of running into a balloon cable was not inconsiderable. However, seasoned ATA pilots could almost smell their way around the country blindfolded. How was it that Amy, with her 2,500 flight hours, could not only fail to find Kidlington, but worse still, find herself over the Thames Estuary well off course and well after her estimated arrival time? What really happened will never be known. Amy's aircraft came down in the water. Maybe it was out of fuel. A female voice was heard to cry for help. A Royal Navy officer on one of the ships in a passing convoy drowned after plunging into the freezing water in an attempt to save her. That was the end of Wonderful Amy. She did not live to grow old gracefully and maybe this is how she wanted it.

Jim Mollison also served with the ATA and he survived the war – and two more disastrous marriages. Whether he finally kicked the drink problem, I do not know, but he died in relative obscurity before his time.

Amy's lasting legacy was to have inspired so many others. Women have finally secured their own place in aviation. The captain of your airliner today may well be a woman. The opportunity of being a combat pilot in the military is now open to women, and, of course, there are women astronauts. Even now, awards are still made in Amy's name. Buildings and streets have been named after her. *Jason*, the Gipsy Moth in which she flew solo to Australia, is displayed in the Science Museum in London. Amy deserves to be remembered.

A SALUTE TO SAINT-EX

I first came across you at the age of ten when my primary school teacher told my class about a book which she had read called *Wind, Sand and Stars*. There was to be a radio programme about the writer that evening and I can recall listening to it. I was introduced to Antoine de Saint-Exupéry even before I was well and truly bitten by the aviation bug which only happened a year or so later. I was ushered in to the magical world of the Aéropostale and its air mail service which gradually extended from Toulouse all the way to Dakar and then via the South Atlantic and Brazil to Argentina and Chile in South America.

It was to be some years, when I was sixteen or seventeen, before I read one of your books. This was *Vol de Nuit* (*Night Flight*) in the Livre de Poche edition. It was one of the first works of literature which I read outside of my normal studies in the French language. It was very hard work for me as my French was still schoolboy standard. The book showed that the necessity of getting the mail delivered, whatever the cost in men and materials, was an absolute priority. Without this ruthlessness, Aéropostale would never have succeeded. Didier Daurat drove you all to the limits and made heroes of you all.

For many, many years I read no more of your works until I finally picked up *Le Petit Prince* (*The Little Prince*). This little gem of an allegory enchanted me. I have since taught French pupils to appreciate its charm and wisdom. In your short life, you truly captured the imagination of millions of people in the world, be they French or those who could only read in translation. Had you lived longer, I am sure that you would be amazed by the global success of *Le Petit Prince*. The book has appeared in 190 languages and more than 80 million copies have been sold. You were celebrated on one of the last French franc banknotes (the 50

179

franc note) before the Euro was introduced. The Little Prince and the fox are used in a current television commercial. The illustrations used even today are, of course, based on your own.

How could you imagine a scenario where your aircraft had force-landed in the desert and whilst you were trying to trace the source of the failure, a little voice behind you asked you to draw a picture of a sheep? The Little Prince came from asteroid B612. You would be even more astonished to learn that an asteroid has been officially named after you. How did you find the wisdom which the fox revealed in your book? 'On ne voit bien qu'avec le coeur. L'essentiel est invisible pour les yeux.' (You can only see properly through the heart. What is essential is invisible to the eyes).

To step back to the beginnings of the Aéropostale, the creator was one Pierre-Georges Latécoère, a talented aircraft designer in his own right. He saw the possibilities of the mail service and he told Daurat: 'I have done all the calculations. They confirm the opinion of the experts . . . our idea is impracticable . . . There is only one thing to do . . . turn it into reality.'

You were one of those intrepid pilots who turned the idea into reality. You were trained as a military pilot in 1921. You then found it difficult to find a satisfying vocation in life until you joined Aéropostale in 1926. Then it became *La Ligne* (the route) whatever the obstacles were. You were piloting war-weary Bréguet 14s and apart from carrying the all-important mail, you carried a mechanic to deal with the all too frequent forced landings as the primitive engines were relatively unreliable. You could neither communicate with him nor with the ground once you were airborne. The ground stations could communicate with each other by Morse code but weather conditions could change dramatically in a few hours, and this is still true today in spite of weather satellites covering all parts of the Earth.

You would sit there with the wind in your face trying to keep track of your progress over the ground. This was easier when there was the West African coastline to follow but that long stretch to Dakar presented its own risks. There were nomadic tribesmen on the look-out for downed pilots as there was ransom money to be made out of this. Several pilots were captured and several (including the legendary Jean Mermoz) were released but some perished in captivity.

In 1928 you were Station Manager at Cape Juby, midway between Agadir and Dakar. In complete isolation from the civilized world, you had to deal with all matters within your large jurisdiction. It was here that the inspiration for *Courrier Sud* (*Southern Mail*), your first literary success, came to you.

A year later you were posted to Argentina and there you flew the mail across the Andes. This route had been pioneered by Jean Mermoz and it was a highly dangerous one, flying in open cockpits in freezing temperatures and where weather conditions could change very quickly. The Argentina experience led to your writing *Vol de Nuit*.

In 1931 you married Consuelo, a South American lady writer who was already a widow. Your marriage was a stormy one and you had a number of affairs but she played an important role in your life. Is it true that in the *Little Prince* the single rose on the asteroid represented your wife?

You did some test-flying work but it was not really your scene. You were clearly a competent pilot but you were always prone to day-dreaming, thinking out ideas for your books, and this state of mind was hardly appropriate for the rigours of testing new aircraft and new systems.

On 30th December 1935 you left Paris accompanied by André Prévot in your Caudron Simoun 4-seater in an attempt to break the speed record from Paris to Saigon. Engine failure caused a forced landing in the dunes of the Sahara near the border between Libya and Egypt. Neither of you was injured but death by dehydration became a real issue. Fortunately a passing Bedouin saved both of you. This incident gave rise to the most highly acclaimed of your novels, *Terre des Hommes* (*Wind, Sand*

181

and Stars) and it also served as the introduction to *Le Petit Prince*.

You had your fair share of injuries due to forced landings and you were seriously injured when attempting a long-distance flight in the Americas.

When the Second World War began, you volunteered for duty as a pilot in the French Air Force in spite of your condition and age. You captained a Bloch 170 reconnaissance bomber with a crew of four and flew in combat conditions. Your experiences gave rise to the book *Pilote de Guerre* (*Flight to Arras*). With France defeated by Germany you left for the United States and remained mainly in New York but also in Canada until 1943.

What then caused you to travel to North Africa to join the Free French Air Force? You were again accepted as a pilot and trained to fly more modern aircraft. In the summer of 1944 you were with a unit flying the photo-reconnaissance version of the Lockheed Lightning from Borgo in Corsica. Officially you were not supposed to be flying missions but you managed to dodge the regulations and you did your share. Preparations for the Allied invasion of Provence were under way and your unit's aircraft were needed to monitor enemy troop movements in the area.

On 31st July 1944, just two weeks before the invasion, you took off on a reconnaissance mission over the Rhône Valley and you never returned. The writer of *The Little Prince* had vanished at the age of 44.

It would probably have been better if you had disappeared without trace forever, just like your Little Prince, but it was not to be. In 1998, fifty-four years after your disappearance, a fisherman from Marseilles found a bracelet in his nets. The bracelet was later positively identified as yours. Two years later a team of divers found parts of the wreckage of your aircraft. These parts were also positively identified.

So what happened on your last mission? There was a theory that you had committed suicide but that does not seem to be very appropriate. A former Luftwaffe pilot flying a Focke-Wulf

190 claimed to have shot you down but the Luftwaffe records do not show any claim of shooting down a Lightning on that day. There was only a claim from the previous day and the victim of that encounter has been identified.

I am glad that the mystery has not been solved and that your body was never found and identified. Like the Little Prince you slipped away as if you knew that your mission in life had been accomplished. As your Little Prince said to you after you had repaired the engine of your aircraft in the desert: 'Moi aussi, aujourd'hui, je rente chez-moi . . .' (And I am going home today as well . . .).

THE TUSKEGEE AIRMEN

Tuskegee, a small township in Alabama, achieved prominence in the long and bitter struggle for Afro-Americans to enjoy equal rights in their own country. That this process should have taken so long after the abolition of slavery in the United States is something of which successive governments should have been thoroughly ashamed.

In 1881 the Tuskegee Normal School for Coloured Teachers was founded which later became the Tuskegee Institute and finally Tuskegee University, which is a centre of excellence for Afro-American education.

In 1939, when Europe was preparing for a war which America wished to avoid, there were only twenty-five licensed Afro-American pilots in the whole of the USA and a year later there were only seven of such pilots who had a commercial rating. There was a school which trained Afro-American pilots from 1938 onwards and this was the Coffey School of Aeronautics in Chicago. It trained 1,500 pupils between 1938 and 1945. With the war clouds looming and expansion of the Army Air Forces under way, the Tuskegee Institute petitioned hard to have its own flight training school. Finally it persuaded the Army to establish the Tuskegee Army Air Field at Moton, just north of the city. This training school was regarded as an experiment and since segregation was still very much in force, all the officers appointed there were initially white. What General Arnold, Chief of the Army Air Corps, as it was still known in 1940, thought of the race issue was quite clear, 'Negro pilots cannot be used in our present Air Force since this would result in having Negro officers serving over white enlisted men. This would create an impossible social problem.' Fortunately the Afro-American training programme had such staunch supporters as the First Lady, Eleanor Roosevelt, who was taken up for a flight by one of the first black instructors at Tuskegee.

The first class graduated from the Tuskegee school early in 1942. When training stopped there in 1945, 1,000 Afro-American pilots had been trained and 450 of them were to serve in combat. An additional 14,000 men and women had been trained there for supporting trades. All the pilots who trained there and who saw combat not only had to fight the enemy but also Jim Crow. There were many senior officers in the Army Air Forces who deliberately tried to make this experiment fail. Afro-American officers were always regarded as 'trainees' whereas white officers were always 'instructors'. Most of the white officers got promotion, most of the Afro-American officers didn't. The whole credo behind the Afro-American trainees was that because they were expected to fail, they had to prove that they were better than anybody else.

Finally, an all Afro-American fighter squadron was formed out of Tuskegee trainees in April 1943, the 99th, flying the Curtiss P-40, and it was shipped off to North Africa to be used in the invasion of Sicily and then Italy. This squadron survived in spite of several attempts to discredit it and it finally became part of the 332nd Fighter Group comprising four squadrons of Afro-American pilots and formed in January 1944, equipped first with Bell P-39 Airacobras, then with Republic P-47 Thunderbolts and finally with North American P-51 Mustangs.

The 332nd Fighter Group became known as the 'Red Tails' and they created something of a legend. Their main task was to escort bomber formations of the 15th Air Force on their way to and back from targets. Flying from Ramitelli in Italy, they had to fly missions as far away as Berlin, and the oil refineries at Ploesti in Romania. Whereas it was common in other fighter groups for aircraft to forget their escort duties and to break away and attack enemy aircraft at the earliest opportunity, the 332nd pilots were instructed by their commanding officer, who by now was an Afro-American, to stick close to their charges and to protect them at all times. The word spread that the Red Tails never lost a single bomber which they were escorting. This was not true but the bomber crews always breathed more easily when the Red Tails were escorting them. Very few in the Air Force knew that all the Red Tails pilots were black or that the whole of their supporting structure was made up of Afro-Americans and other coloureds. In fact, most people didn't know that this unit existed. When the war in Europe came to an end, the Red Tails had destroyed 136 German aircraft in air combat and 237 on the ground. The Group had lost 32 pilots shot down and who became prisoners of war and 66 pilots killed in action. For years the exploits of the Red Tails were conveniently forgotten. It took a film produced in 1995 and a second one recently produced to bring some long-overdue recognition to what they had achieved.

The Tuskegee Airmen's own research experts have been very fair in analysing the results of what the 332nd actually achieved. They have debunked several of the legends themselves, including the never losing a single bomber claim. No pilot in this group ever became an 'ace', scoring five or more kills in aerial combat. There were claims that one pilot did make five but had his score reduced. There were other claims that those who had scored four kills were removed from combat duties so they could not become aces. Three pilots did score four kills but were not withdrawn from combat duties. This myth has been officially squashed.

What is less well known than the exploits of the Red Tails is the formation of the 477th Bombardment Group consisting of Tuskegee-trained personnel. This group received the North American B-25 Mitchell bomber but it never went into action before the war ended since those white officers appointed to oversee it made sure that it was put together and trained as slowly as possible. The same old Jim Crow policy was applied here, namely that white officers were instructors and black officers were just trainees.

It must have been galling to those Afro-American servicemen who had to stomach racial prejudice in some of its nastiest forms. It should not be forgotten that there were race riots in Detroit in 1943 in the middle of the war. There were racial incidents among the United States personnel serving in Britain during the war. Most of the Afro-Americans put up with the discrimination with quiet dignity but in any group there are always some hot-heads and some who will dig in their heels when pushed too far. It was bad enough not being allowed to share the same facilities as white officers and airmen. It was even more humiliating for those who saw German prisoners of war being better treated than they were. What pushed several over the edge was being told to sign agreements which were clearly racist. Those who did not sign were court-martialed or threatened with a firing-squad.

When the war was over, it was the United States Air Force, as it was now titled, to be the first of the military services to introduce desegregation. However this only happened slowly and the main reason for it was standardisation. It was just too expensive and cumbersome to have separate facilities for blacks and whites. It would be too naïve to state that racial prejudice does not exist today in the United States. It exists everywhere, of course, and will unfortunately never be eradicated completely. There was a race riot at Travis Air Force Base as late as 1971. When several of the Tuskegee airmen applied for jobs as pilots with American airlines after the war, none was accepted. Those who fared best were the ones who remained in the Air Force and worked their way up, or those of outstanding ability who became leading lawyers, doctors, academics and politicians.

Finally, and very belatedly, more than three hundred of the surviving Tuskegee Airmen received the Congressional Gold Medal of Honor in March 2007. However, regarding the 101 airmen of the 477th Group who had refused to sign acceptance of a racist order in April 1945 and who had been court-martialed as a result, the Air Force finally removed the reprimands from the records of only 15 of those men. Those who were dead did not receive posthumous pardons and some simply refused to request a pardon on principle and would not have accepted it in any case.

Before the 332nd Fighter Group was disbanded, its team won the 1949 Air Force Gunnery Meet, which was a competition between all Air Force fighter groups. For over forty years the official records showed that the 1949 winner was 'unknown'. This was only put right in 1995 when the President of Tuskegee Airmen Inc. presented the facts to the Air Force. As the President remarked when the record was amended, 'They knew who won. They just didn't want to recognize us.' The trophy which had never been presented was eventually found in the archives of the Air Force Museum.

One of the 101 airmen of the 477th Group who was reprimanded for the 1945 'mutiny' was Roy Chappell who, after the war could not find a career in flying and devoted himself to teaching. He became President of the Chicago branch of the Tuskegee Airmen. Through his efforts some 6,000 schoolchildren received free flights under the Experimental Aircraft Association's (EAA's) 'Young Eagles' programme. This programme which started in 1992 has now given 1,700,000 free flights to children between the ages of 7 and 17 in some 90 countries in an effort to promote aviation. The EAA suitably acknowledged what Roy Chappell had achieved.

Moving forward in time and moving away from the Tuskegee Airmen, I am reminded of the drive behind Project Mercury to put an American into Earth orbit. Apparently President Kennedy had decreed that there had to be one symbolic Afro-American included in the selected batch of astronauts. No such suitably qualified candidate was found. So, the dyed-in-the wool racists would have rejoiced. Obviously a n***** was never going to be up to it. They missed the point that most Afro-Americans never had the educational opportunities to be able to qualify.

Now that the efforts of the Afro-American aviators have at long been recognised, what is being done about the original inhabitants of the continent, the indigenous tribes of so-called Red Indians, who were dispossessed of their lands, herded into settlements and conveniently forgotten? They have suffered the same fate as the Aborigines in Australia. If the United States is truly the 'Land of the Free', which it claims to be, it is high time that it addressed this issue which is entirely of its own making. I do not recall having seen any mention of a 'Red Indian' pilot anywhere.

My short account is dedicated to Justin, black as the ace of spades with a smile as wide as the Golden Gate Bridge and a bone-crusher of a handshake. He was introduced to flying through the 'Young Eagles' programme. He flew with me and was a real gentleman although as a professional commercial pilot, he was in a league well above mine. If one day he reads this and remembers flying across Florida with me, he will be in no doubt as to why he is in debt to the Tuskegee Airmen.

THE SHORT LIFE OF BSAA AND ITS AVRO AIRLINERS

It was clear that when the war ended in 1945, many countries which had been deprived of airline traffic for several years would want to have old routes reopened and new ones added. There had been hardly any commercial flights in Europe for six years. Services to other parts of the world which existed in 1939 had either shut down or had been operated on a much reduced basis. One place where airline services had actually increased during the war years was the United States since its airspace had not been disturbed by hostilities.

Just before the outbreak of war in September 1939 Pan American had begun the first trans-Atlantic flying boat services for passengers. During the war hundreds of aircraft were delivered by air across the Atlantic to Europe so it was not unnatural to believe that when peace returned regular trans-Atlantic passenger flights would be feasible.

Until 1939 the only way to cross the Atlantic as a passenger had been by ship. Ocean liner operators from various countries had vied with each other to capture as much of the market as they could. The time taken for the passage had gradually been reduced. The last liner to hold the Blue Riband for the fastest crossing between two lighthouses marking the extremity of each continent had been the SS United States in 1952, which had covered the distance in three and a half days. Travelling by liner was to be popular for a few more years until jet airliners managed to fly non-stop from New York to European capitals and vice-versa. After that, sitting in a relatively comfortable seat for eight hours and flying above the weather became infinitely preferable to spending four or five days at sea.

However, in 1946 when most airlines started operating again, a flight across the North Atlantic was going to be long, uncomfortable, potentially dangerous and also expensive. If everything went smoothly, the flight might take fifteen hours at low altitude but it could take much longer and the noise level and the turbulence were not for the faint-hearted or those with delicate stomachs.

In 1945 the British Government decided that new British commercial operations were going to be state-controlled. There would be three operating companies: British Overseas Airways Corporation (BOAC), which had started operating in 1939 and which had run skeleton services during the war, was to operate all pre-war Empire routes and would also cover flights to the Far East and North America; British European Airways Corporation (BEA), newly created, would operate services within Europe; British South American Airways Corporation (BSAA), another new creation, would operate services to Central and South America. It is not clear why a separate airline was deemed necessary to cover South America and, in any case, four years later BSAA, was no more and its network was absorbed by BOAC.

BOAC already had a structure in place. BEA and BSAA had to start from scratch. The latter had the more difficult start-up as it was to be conducting long-range operations where there was little room for navigational errors. The new company must have felt it was very fortunate to have acquired the services of Air Vice Marshal Don Bennett as chief executive. Bennett was an Australian, born in 1910, who had come to Britain and who had flown with the Royal Air Force before the war. He had then left the Air Force and had joined Imperial Airways as a flying boat captain. In 1938 he had piloted the Mercury element of the Short Mayo composite. His aircraft sat on top of the big Short flying boat and was released from its parent in flight. With this aircraft Bennett had established a world long-distance record for seaplanes and he had also established his reputation as a superb navigator and pilot. When the war came, Bennett was instrumental in setting up the Atlantic Ferry Command and led the first group of aircraft to be delivered from the United States to Great Britain. He then returned to the Royal Air Force and was asked to create the Pathfinder Force, the group which marked the path for the night bomber missions to follow and which also marked the targets. He became the youngest Air Vice Marshal in the Air Force and his crews did sterling work.

Bennett had one major fault. He did not suffer fools gladly. Unfortunately, his definition of 'fools' included many who were as intelligent as he was. He was an impatient man who sliced through all forms of bureaucracy considering it all to be a complete waste of time.

BSAA started operations in January 1946. It was supposed to be based at Bournemouth. Bennett made sure that it started from the new airport at Heathrow and he himself piloted the first flight from there to South America. He recruited pilots who had served under him in the Pathfinder Force. He had no time for new civilian regulations. His boys had taken considerable risks during the war. All Bennett required from them was that they became good navigators as well. The military hierarchy prevailed even though this was a civilian operation. Bennett would get the maximum out of men and machines. His pilots would get the job done with the minimum of fuel and the minimum of red tape. The War Spirit remained. Bennett instilled what we would call today 'press-on-itis'. It seemed to be conveniently forgotten that his pilots were no longer flying bombing missions over enemy territory but were carrying fare-paying passengers who expected to arrive safely at their destination.

The aircraft available for the new airline were not of the highest quality. It was essential to use British equipment. The whole of the aircraft industry had been churning out military aircraft for the last six years. It could not suddenly switch overnight to new commercial designs. The American aircraft industry with its much greater capacity had already produced two outstanding long-range military transports during the war years and these, the Douglas DC-4 and the Lockheed Constellation, were far ahead of anything which Britain could produce at the time.

The only British companies producing four-engined long-range aircraft in 1945 were Avro and Handley Page, with the exception of Shorts, who built flying-boats. Avro, whose name came from aviation pioneer A.V. Roe, who had left the company many years previously, had produced the magnificent Lancaster night bomber. This aircraft, designed by Roy Chadwick, had got off to a disastrous start as the Manchester twin-engined bomber. It entered service but was not a success as its two powerful engines turned out to be quite unreliable. Chadwick then converted his design to take four Rolls-Royce Merlin engines, the same superb engine which powered the Hurricane and Spitfire fighters. Thus the Lancaster was born. Looking ahead, Avro could only work on derivatives of the Lancaster for post-war airlines as there was no extra capacity or resources to develop anything completely new.

Two Lancaster offshoots were produced. The Lancastrian was a minimum change aircraft where the gun turrets and bomb bay were deleted and where a simple passenger cabin to carry a maximum of thirteen passengers was installed in the fuselage. Accommodation was very restricted because the wing's main spar passed through the middle of the fuselage. In the first version, the passengers sat along one side of the fuselage facing the other side. Later, more conventional seating was installed but the fuselage was so slim that the seats almost touched each other leaving virtually no room for anybody to move about in a very narrow central aisle. The nose and tail were given streamlined fairings and place for a co-pilot was made. It may be hard to believe but the Lancaster bomber only had one pilot. The Lancastrian served with BOAC as well as with BSAA. It is difficult to imagine how passengers could have put up with conditions in a narrow, cramped cabin with no soundproofing,

193

minimal heating and no pressurization hour after hour. The Lancastrian not only crossed the South Atlantic but it flew services between Britain and Australia. The type soldiered on, carrying petrol into Berlin during the 1948-1949 Airlift, being used equally by civil airlines and the Royal Air Force. Finally it was used as a jet engine test bed and for flight refuelling experiments but by 1951 the survivors were broken up and reduced to scrap metal.

The second Lancaster offshoot looked a little more like a genuine airliner. The Lancaster wing was re-positioned on top of a box-like fuselage which created considerable drag but this model could carry up to 24 passengers. The aircraft was named York. No doubt the conflict between the royal houses of York and Lancaster in the 15th century Wars of the Roses had inspired this name. The York was also to serve with BOAC as well as with BSAA. This type survived longer than the Lancastrian. It was also used by the Royal Air Force and it made a major contribution to the Berlin Airlift. One specially equipped York named *Ascalon* was used by Winston Churchill and King George VI.

In spite of it only being an interim type, the York continued in service until 1963, fulfilling many troop transportation requirements for the British forces. From the pilot's point of view, it cannot have been easy to fly. As the wing was positioned on top of the fuselage, the control runs to the engines ran along the top of the fuselage to the flight deck. All engine controls were therefore placed in the cockpit roof. The pilot therefore had to reach up to operate them. This was standard practice in flying boats where the wing was always mounted high to avoid spray damaging propellers and engines. Nowadays there cannot be many pilots who would be comfortable with operating throttles above their heads.

Even before BSAA started its services across the South Atlantic, American Export Airlines had already begun a New York to Bournemouth service across the North Atlantic using the Douglas DC-4. The flight was scheduled to take 14 hours with intermediate stops at Gander, in Newfoundland, and at Shannon. There was, however, no competition on the South Atlantic route.

The new airline had a trouble-free period until 30th August 1946 when Lancastrian G-AGWJ named *Star Glow* swung on take-off when departing from Bathurst in Gambia. There were no fatalities but the aircraft was a write-off.

Then on 7th September York G-AHEW named *Star Leader* stalled just after take-off from Bathurst and all 24 on board lost their lives. It was a night departure and the aircraft was loaded above its maximum certified weight. Add to this a high temperature and humid conditions and the recipe for a disaster was there.

For the next few months there were no major incidents and during this period the Company had moved its African base for flights across the South Atlantic from Bathurst to Dakar in Senegal. By this time TWA had begun a New York to Paris service using the iconic Lockheed Constellation. This airliner was the first to fly the Atlantic with a pressure cabin enabling the aircraft to cruise higher and avoid the worst of the weather. BOAC just had to follow suit to remain competitive and ordered the Constellation but there was no such equipment to be ordered for lowly BSAA They were promised the Avro Tudor, Britain's first airliner with a pressure cabin but this was still some time away.

On 13th April 1947 York G-AHEZ named *Star Speed* was inbound to land at Dakar in the early hours of the morning. Another company aircraft which had departed from Dakar passed the radio message that fog was starting to form there. The incoming flight did not have sufficient fuel for a diversion, it simply had to land. Needless to say the captain could not find the runway. There were no navigation aids available and no approach lights. The aircraft impacted with the terrain and six passengers were killed. Why was the aircraft so low on fuel?

Was this another example of Bennett's desire to make a profit come what may?

Much worse was to follow. On 2nd August 1947 Lancastrian G-AGWH named *Star Dust* took off from Buenos Aires on the short flight to Santiago in Chile. The distance was not an issue but the mighty Andes mountain range was. There were peaks of more than 20,000 feet in the way. The weather was not good. There were only six passengers aboard who just outnumbered the crew of five. What actually happened will never be known. The aircraft failed to arrive at Santiago. A massive search for wreckage produced no results. Years passed and the disappearance was all but forgotten. Then in 1998 two Argentinean climbers found the remains of the aircraft near the summit of Mount Tupungato. How could it have lain undiscovered for over 50 years? Tupungato was a notoriously difficult mountain to climb but others had been there before and done it. The answer was that the Lancastrian had crashed into the mountain at high speed and had been enveloped by a glacier. Gradually the bed of the glacier had worked itself down the steep slopes of the mountain and had spewed out some of the remains at the point where the glacial ice had melted. There was tremendous media interest in this find. It did nothing for the relatives of the eleven who had perished apart from locating the final resting place of the victims. The question was: why had the Lancastrian crashed? The best hypothesis is that the winds aloft were much stronger than forecast and that when the crew thought they had reached the coastal plain of Chile they were still over the high peaks. The initial descent just took the aircraft straight into a mountainside. The on-board wireless operator had indeed indicated four minutes to land at Santiago. He could only communicate by Morse code and he ended his last transmission confirming four minutes from landing with the signal: S-T-E-N-D-E-C. This was not a recognised code word and the operator at Santiago airport asked for it to be repeated which was done twice, after which there was silence. The mysterious last message has never been satisfactorily explained. There were also rumours that the aircraft was carrying gold bullion. In short, a whole myth was created.

With hindsight, it would appear that the captain should not have attempted to cross such a high mountain range in lousy weather by a direct route. Had Bennett's 'press on regardless' attitude prevailed over better judgement? We shall never know.

Later in the same month which saw the end of *Star Dust* on the slopes of Mount Tupungato, Pan American began a non-stop Constellation service between New York and London. BSAA continued to use second-rate equipment or routes which made little economic sense.

On 5th September 1947 Lancastrian G-AGWK named *Star Trail* crashed on landing at Bermuda. Thankfully there were no fatalities but the aircraft was a write-off. Less than two months later on 22nd October Lancastrian G-AGUL named *Star Watch* ground-looped on landing at Heathrow. There were no passengers aboard and no crew member was injured but the aircraft was written off. Less than one month later on 13th November Lancastrian G-AGWG named *Star Light* had departed Bermuda for the Azores when it developed engine problems. It returned to land but the aircraft broke up on the runway. Again there were no fatalities but another aircraft had been written off.

Who really cared about BSAA? Don Bennett obviously did, passionately, but he irritated far too many people in high places. He constantly flouted regulations not only in Britain but also in South America and complaints about 'his' airline were coming in from all quarters. He was probably banking on the Avro Tudor to reverse the airline's fortunes. The Tudor was another Roy Chadwick design. Once again, Chadwick's design team had to make do with what they had. The extended span of the new Lancaster (which was to become the Lincoln) and its more powerful Merlin engines were married to a new fuselage, the first pressurized fuselage on a British aircraft. Bennett had nothing but praise for this aircraft. It was British and far superior to 'all that American rubbish'. Unfortunately it was the Tudor which was the rubbish project. The latest know-how was just not available in Britain. The aircraft had a tail wheel undercarriage which was out of date. The cabin often failed to pressurize so flying at altitude, for which it was designed, was not a practical proposition. BOAC had wanted this aircraft badly. They finally rejected it and ordered the Constellation instead. BSAA seemed to be lumbered with the beast. Was this because Bennett praised it or because nobody really cared about this airline? Be that as it may, the Tudor entered service with BSAA before the end of 1947 as the short-fuselage Mark IV.

Avro had other Tudor versions in the pipeline. The Tudor II had a longer fuselage and greater capacity but it was hardly any better. The prototype was redesigned. It took off on a test flight in August 1947 with Roy Chadwick aboard. Just after take-off it dipped a wing which impacted the ground and the aircraft crashed. All four on board were killed. The inquest established that the aileron control circuit had been fitted the wrong way round. If the pilot had wanted to pick up a wing drop on the left wing, it would only have dropped further. This seems to have been a classic example of 'Murphy's Law' which states that if anything can go wrong, it will go wrong. By extension, if something can be fitted the wrong way round, it will be fitted the wrong way round. All pilots today are taught to check that their controls operate not only freely *but also in the required manner.* If somebody had monitored the control inputs on the ground this stupid accident would surely never have happened.

On 28th January 1948 brand new Tudor IV G-AHNP named *Star Tiger* flew into the Azores on its way to Bermuda. The weather forecast ahead was not good. There was a Company Lancastrian at the airport also waiting for better forecast conditions. The next day the forecast was better and the Lancastrian departed followed by the Tudor an hour later. The Lancastrian arrived safely in the early hours of the 30th and it had been in radio contact with the following Tudor. The Tudor never arrived and no traces of it were ever found. 31 passengers and crew had gone to a watery grave.

Less than a week later York G-AHEX named *Star Venture* had an engine fire and came down at night north of Rio de Janeiro. It was a miracle that only three passengers were killed.

By now Bennett was under great pressure but he was nothing if not a fighter. When the politicians went for the kill, Bennett defended himself in an exclusive interview which he gave to the Daily Express. He thus signed his own death warrant for going public and was fired on 10th February 1948.

If the politicians and bureaucrats thought that by sacking Bennett they had solved the problem of a troubled airline, they were wrong. The airline soldiered on for more than another year which was probably a major mistake, but nobody seemed to care. Almost exactly one year after Star Tiger's demise, Tudor G-AGRE named *Star Ariel* disappeared on 17th January 1949 on a flight from Bermuda to Jamaica. 20 more lives were lost. Again, in spite of intensive searches, no wreckage was ever found. The two Tudor disappearances contributed greatly to the popular myth of the 'Bermuda Triangle'.

In July 1949 BSAA was absorbed by BOAC without any fuss. The Star fleet was no more.

Don Bennett was not quite finished as a public figure. He had stood for parliament and had been elected once but his political views were very right wing. He formed an airline which operated successfully during the Berlin Airlift of 1948 to 1949. He flew many of the missions himself. What aircraft did he operate? It was the Tudor, would you believe. As long as it flew at low level it proved to be a very good freighter.

On 12th March 1950 a Tudor V owned by Bennett's airline and named *Star Girl* was bringing a party of Welsh rugby supporters back from Dublin after an international match. It stalled on the approach to land and 80 lives were lost: the highest tally for an airliner crash anywhere in the world up to that date. The probable reason for the crash was that the centre of gravity was aft of the rear limit. In other words, it had been dangerously overloaded. Bennett's airline never flew passengers after that. He died in England in September 1986 at the age of 76. No doubt to the end he believed that he was misunderstood, refusing to admit that perhaps he was the one who had failed to understand.

In its short existence BSAA had lost ten out of its total fleet of 36 aircraft and had recorded 96 fatalities, of which 74 were passengers and 22 were crew members. Without knowing how many passengers were carried safely to their destination and how many miles were flown by the airline it is difficult to put these figures into context.

The story of the unfortunate Tudor did not end there, although its passenger-carrying days were over. Several surplus airframes were left at the Avro facility and six of these had their piston engines removed to be replaced by twin jet engines under each wing. At long last a nosewheel undercarriage was fitted and these six aircraft were purchased by the Ministry of Supply for high altitude test work. These aircraft became known as the Ashton. They performed invaluable work on testing new jet engines and other systems until they were retired in 1962.

Avro came back to the airliner market at the end of the 1950s when it designed a neat turboprop 40-seater with the type number 748. By the time the aircraft flew Avro had become part of the Hawker Siddeley group and the 748, which enjoyed much greater success than the poor Tudor, was never marketed as an Avro type.

THE FALL OF THE FLYING DUTCHMAN

KLM, which stands for Koninklijke Luchtvaart Maatschappij and known as Royal Dutch Airlines in English, is the oldest airline in the world to have operated continuously under its original name. Its first scheduled service was from Amsterdam to London in May 1920. It may surprise many that a nation as small as the Netherlands has been able to produce such a record. However it has to be remembered that the Dutch were a great seafaring nation which established many overseas colonies. When aviation became a practical mode of transport the Dutch became a leader in trying to connect their overseas territories with the motherland by air.

From the outset KLM was managed by Dr Albert Plesman until his death in 1953. He was a hard taskmaster and was renowned for his miserliness but his drive and determination made his airline into one of the best known and the most successful. In 1929 the airline began regular flights between Amsterdam and Batavia in the Dutch East Indies. For several years this was to be the longest route operated by any airline. Following independence from the Dutch, the Dutch East Indies became part of Indonesia and Batavia was renamed Jakarta.

In the late 1920s a young Dutch pilot by the name of Koene Dirk Parmentier joined the airline. Parmentier was clearly a French family name. Whether young Koene had any connection with the 'potato Parmentier' is not known to me. Plesman could obviously see the young man's potential and he sent him to the USA to learn about the latest techniques in instrument and bad weather flying. Whilst in the States, Parmentier saw the new Douglas DC-1 airliner and on his return he managed to persuade Plesman to buy its successor, the DC-2. KLM thus became the first non-US airline to operate the Douglas design.

This also marked the end of several years when the airline had only operated Dutch-built Fokker designs. Fokker had not been capable of coming up with a design which could rival the DC-2, which, when it appeared, represented a huge advance in airliner technology.

The State of Victoria in Australia was to celebrate its centenary in 1934. A decision was taken to stage an air race from London to Melbourne as long-distance records were attracting much media attention. A wealthy chocolate manufacturer in Melbourne, Sir Macpherson Robertson put up the prize money. As his chocolates were named MacRobertson Chocolates, the event became known as the MacRobertson Centennial Air Race.

The race was won by a de Havilland Comet, which was specially designed and built for the event, in just under 71 hours elapsed time.

In my mind, this achievement, magnificent though it was, was overshadowed by the performance of a standard Douglas DC-2 entered by KLM. This aircraft, named the *Uiver* (the Stork), carried three fare-paying passengers and had the regular flight crew of four. The captain was none other than K D Parmentier. His co-pilot was Johannes Moll who had frequently flown the Amsterdam – Batavia route for the Company. Whereas the Comet used only the five compulsory intermediate landing grounds, the DC-2 had eighteen intermediate stops, including one which was completely unexpected. *Uiver* completed the course in 90 hours elapsed time and won first place in the handicap section. The progress of the *Uiver* caught the imagination of the Dutch nation. The country almost came to a complete stop whilst the race was on. Parmentier and Moll became national heroes overnight. Their elapsed time would have been even better if they had not flown into bad weather at night when approaching Melbourne. Uncertain of their position because of electrical storms and in danger of running into high ground, they managed to land in the dark on the racecourse at Albury. The local mayor had got local residents to drive there and two rows of cars with their headlights on marked out a rough and ready runway. Because of heavy rain the aircraft bogged down on landing. The next morning the townsfolk turned out to haul *Uiver* out of the mud. Parmentier decided that the aircraft would only be able to get off the ground if they sacrificed all unnecessary weight. The radio operator, flight engineer, the three passengers and the mail and other non-essential equipment were left behind. Parmentier and Moll managed to get into the air and shortly thereafter crossed the finish line. To this day a strong bond between Albury and the Netherlands has been maintained.

The original *Uiver* crashed with loss of all on board on its next scheduled flight on the Amsterdam – Batavia route. The aircraft has, however, been resurrected. A team of dedicated volunteers found a surviving DC-2 several years ago and restored it as the original *Uiver*. In 1990 this aircraft retraced the 1934 epic flight. It survives to this day in airworthy condition at the Lelystad Aviodrome Museum.

In May 1940 when Germany invaded the Netherlands, several aircraft from KLM's fleet were flown to England. Parmentier flew out in one of the airline's Douglas DC-3s. The DC-3s were integrated into the war-time fleet of British Overseas Airways Corporation at its base at Whitchurch near Bristol. From there, these aircraft later flew on the perilous route between Bristol and Lisbon in neutral Portugal.

Parmentier was at the controls of the DC-3 named *Ibis* on April 19th 1943 when it was attacked by a German fighter over the Bay of Biscay. The DC-3 took hits but Parmentier managed to find refuge in a cloud bank and survived. On June 1st 1943 the same aircraft on the same route was intercepted by the Germans again. Parmentier was not on board but this time the aircraft was shot down and destroyed, taking the life, among others, of British film actor Leslie Howard. Apparently German Intelligence was under the belief that Winston Churchill was being carried as a passenger. Van Brugge, who had been

Parmentier's radio operator in the 1934 air race, also lost his life in the shooting down of the *Ibis*.

Parmentier survived the war with honours. When the European skies opened up to commercial flying again, he became KLM's chief pilot. He flew the inaugural Douglas DC-4 flight from Amsterdam to Batavia. I have seen it mentioned that he had been singled out by Dr Plesman to become his successor.

KLM had remained loyal to Douglas airliners but when all national carriers decided that they had to have a North Atlantic service, the airline selected the Lockheed Constellation, not only because it looked right and performed well but also because it featured a pressurised cabin which would enable it to cruise in the rarefied air above the worst of the weather. The Constellations, like their non-pressurised Douglas rivals, did not have the range to fly from Europe to New York non-stop. KLM's service from Amsterdam used either Prestwick in Scotland or Shannon in Ireland as refuelling stops before the Atlantic crossing. If, after making the crossing against strong headwinds, fuel became critical, Gander in Newfoundland was an optional extra stop.

When the Constellation was delivered to KLM, it bore the inscription 'The Flying Dutchman' above the cabin windows on the left-hand side and the same inscription in Dutch ('De Vliegende Hollander') on the right-hand side. The Flying Dutchman legend went back to the 18th century when a 'phantom ship' flying the Dutch flag had been observed near the Cape of Good Hope. The story evolved that this ship was condemned to sail the Seven Seas for ever. Richard Wagner made use of this legend in his 1843 opera *Der Fliegende Holländer*, bringing the story to a much wider public.

On the evening of October 21st 1948, Captain Parmentier was scheduled to fly the Company's Constellation registered PH-TEN and named *Nijmegen* on the Amsterdam – New York service. The flight was due to depart at 20:00 UTC but this was pushed back to 21:10 UTC as extra freight was taken on board for delivery in Iceland which would entail an additional stop there. The first landing was to be at Prestwick, and Shannon was designated as the alternate in case of bad weather.

The weather over the British Isles was certainly not good. There were high autumnal winds and low cloud cover. Unfortunately the on-board radio operator was not able to receive the latest local weather at Prestwick which had dropped below the acceptable minima. They were unaware that two aircraft ahead of them had found conditions to be too difficult and had diverted to an alternate.

Parmentier's aircraft was cleared for a radar controlled approach to runway 32. He decided that the cross-wind was too strong so he advised that after breaking out of the clouds and having the lights of the airport in sight, he would effect a 'circle to land' on runway 26 which would be more favourable given the westerly wind. This meant that when he broke out of the cloud base and had runway 32 in sight, he would turn east on a downwind leg for runway 26 and then, keeping the lights of runway 26 in sight, he would then fly a base leg of 350 degrees and turn to 260 degrees to line up and land.

Maybe Parmentier was not aware how much the cloud base had come down. Maybe he thought he could get away with it. In any case he broke the rules which he had established for his own pilots – if the cloud base is low, one does not attempt to land on another runway which does not have a published instrument approach. This is exactly what he tried to do.

The approach chart which they had for runway 26 indicated an obstruction on the final approach at 45 feet above sea level. The chart figure was incorrect. The figure should have read 450 feet. It had been amended on the newest charts which they did not have. Parmentier flew the circle to land approach and slipped into the clouds. At that point he should have added power, called 'missed approach' and climbed away. Was he stricken with the dreaded disease of 'get-there-itis' ? On final approach, at 23:32 UTC, his aircraft ploughed into non-illuminated high tension cables at 450 feet above sea level and, of course, the aircraft crashed and burst into flames. Parmentier and his three flight deck crew, six cabin attendants and thirty passengers lost their lives. It had been so unnecessary. When I learnt to fly, nearly fifty years ago, my very first instructor drilled into me to 'never be too proud to add power and go round again if you are not happy.'

I have searched in vain for more information about Koene Dirk but without success. I have established that he was married and had three daughters. More than that I do not know. I often wonder if I would be pleased or disappointed to meet any of my fallen heroes from the past. Certainly K D Parmentier was one of them. He was forty-four years old when he died. He made an error of judgement and it cost him his life. We all make errors of judgement but we are solidly on the ground most of our lives and we have more time to reflect before committing ourselves. The Flying Dutchman did not have that luxury.

Facts become distorted with time. As I have stated elsewhere no two people will remember any past event in the same way. The writer who best conveyed commercial flying in the 1930s and 1940s was for me undoubtedly Ernest Gann. *Fate is the Hunter* is an aviation classic. Unfortunately in this book Gann decided that KDP crashed on landing in Java and not in Scotland. So, he was wrong, but this does not detract from what either man achieved. They set standards for others to follow. That is what is important.

KDP, my Flying Dutchman, is still up there alongside Charles Lindbergh, Jimmy Doolittle, Wiley Post and a few select others. As long as I am alive, they will remain up there. I hope that thereafter there will be others to perpetuate their memory.

THE MYSTERY OF THE EXPLODING COMETS

This subject has been discussed by far more competent persons than I, but it relates to events which happened more than fifty years ago and which have to some extent vanished in the mists of time.

I was twelve years old in 1954. My interest in all things aeronautical was already there and I was fascinated by this mystery. This is a story which should not be forgotten. My aim is simply to set it out in my own words.

Even during the darkest hours of the Second World War, planning for the future of British civil aviation had begun. At the end of 1942, the Brabazon Committee was formed. Its chairman was Lord Brabazon of Tara, who held the Royal Aero Club's pilot certificate number one. The brief of this committee was to decide on the transport aircraft to operate routes throughout the British Empire when hostilities finished. There were some good decisions and some bad ones. The mighty Bristol Brabazon, which was to transport passengers across the North Atlantic, turned out to be a great white elephant. It flew only as a prototype. The Vickers Viscount, on the other hand, became an unqualified success.

One of the Committee members was Sir Geoffrey de Havilland, whose company had for many years been at the forefront of aeronautical technology. Following upon the success of the Mosquito fighter-bomber, de Havilland produced the Vampire jet fighter. This aircraft lost out to the Gloster Meteor in the race to become Britain's first operational jet fighter but what was of greater significance was that the company produced not only the aircraft but the jet engine as well. Sir Geoffrey was far ahead of his time. He proposed to produce a jet airliner which became the Committee's Type IV.

When the war came to an end, only Britain and Germany had real jet engine expertise. The Americans at this stage lagged well behind. The Type IV was a bold move into the unknown but de Havilland had a brilliant team of designers and engineers. Ronald Bishop was the chief designer. He had been with the Company since 1921 and had started from the bottom up at the age of 18. He had led the team which had designed both the Mosquito and the Vampire. After many brain-storming sessions Bishop and his team came up with a concept which was to become the DH.106 Comet, the world's first pure jet airliner.

The prototype Comet took to the skies from Hatfield in July 1949 with chief test pilot John Cunningham at the controls. Cunningham had been a night fighter 'ace' during the war and had earned many of his victories flying the de Havilland Mosquito. At de Havilland he will forever be remembered as the Comet test pilot. They could not have had a better ambassador.

The Comet looked absolutely right. It immediately made contemporary airliners appear to be old-fashioned. It had a beautifully profiled nose section, swept wings and engines buried within the wing roots. Only the tail section looked 'traditional'. Needless to say, once again the engines fitted were built by de Havilland. Wherever the Comet flew it turned heads. It could cruise at 40,000 feet at a shade under 500 miles per hour. It was nearly twice as fast in the cruise as other contemporary airliners and it could operate in much less disturbed air at greater altitudes. It could climb to altitude much faster and descend much faster. It was free of the vibration associated with piston engines and propellers. However, it did have one drawback. Its jet engines, like all contemporary units, were extremely noisy. Such engines were also very thirsty and this meant that range was fairly limited. The Comet would not be able to cross the North Atlantic non-stop.

Britain was rightly proud of its Comet. At that time, Britain's major airlines were owned by the State. British Overseas

Airways Corporation (BOAC) was responsible for long-distance routes from the UK and it was the first to order the aircraft. It took delivery of the second prototype in April 1951 and set up a unit for crew training and route proving.

In May 1952 the first production Comet 1 operated the first fare-paying jet passenger service in the world from London to Johannesburg reaching its destination in just under 24 elapsed hours. It needed five intermediate stops to do this whereas today's long-range passenger aircraft can fly much longer distances than London to Johannesburg non-stop. However, this flight has to be put into perspective as it reduced the time taken by competing airlines by half. The maximum passenger accommodation was between 36 and 44 depending on seating arrangements. In those days passengers had plenty of space and commercial flying was still a romantic adventure limited to the wealthy.

In April 1953 a service was opened between London and Tokyo. The journey which previously had taken 86 hours was now cut to 33. The future looked extremely bright. Many major airlines were playing a game of 'wait and see' but UAT and Air France already had one improved Mark 1A each in service and Canadian Pacific were taking delivery of the 1A.

The BOAC Comet flight crews were privileged and they knew it. They made all other flight crews extremely envious. They flew in a 'shirt-sleeve' environment where nobody else could go, unless it was some fighter jock, kitted out with oxygen mask and strapped onto a 'bang' seat in the cramped cockpit of an aircraft of very limited duration. A Royal Air Force Meteor 8 did manage to intercept one of the prototype Comets during testing. John Cunningham allowed the Meteor to draw alongside at 40,000 feet and then he simply went to full power leaving the fighter floundering behind. In spite of this performance the Comet was docile at low speeds and did not need long runways. It could adequately cope with the strips which already existed.

There were two take-off accidents where the aircraft refused to leave the ground and these were ascribed to the pilot raising the nose too high and not being able to accelerate above stalling speed. In the first case, a BOAC flight carrying passengers, there were no casualties, but in the second case – and this was a delivery flight to Canadian Pacific – all eleven aboard perished. Following this a rotation speed was calculated which took into account weight at take-off, temperature and air density. This was a first in aviation and has been applied to all airliners ever since.

Worse was to follow when in May 1953 a BOAC Comet broke up at about 10,000 feet when climbing out of Calcutta with all 43 on board (six crew and 37 passengers) losing their lives. The subsequent inquiry failed to reach a conclusion. There were thunderstorms and severe turbulence about at the time and such a combination can destroy any aircraft. However, in spite of the fact that the Comet had already safely carried 28,000 passengers in a year of service, it was now squarely under the spotlight. It was, after all, charting unknown territory.

At 09:34 Zulu (GMT) on the morning of January 10th 1954, BOAC Flight 781, which had originated in Singapore, took off from Rome's Ciampino Airport on the last leg of its journey to London. The Comet 1 was registered as G-ALYP, and known to the airline as Yoke Peter using the then current phonetic alphabet for the last two letters of the registration. Yoke Peter was the first production Comet 1 and had operated that first service to Johannesburg in May 1952. It had flown for 3,605 hours (although 3,681 hours has also been stated). It should be noted that the first prototype had been tested in the air and on the ground over the equivalent of 10,000 flight hours. The cabin had been tested at well above normal operating pressures – and yet the Ministry of Supply had stated early on that it could not guarantee a life of more than 1,000 hours for the Comet. BOAC needed to operate its Comet 1 fleet for ten years to recoup its investment.

On board the aircraft was the usual crew of six: pilot and co-pilot, flight engineer, radio operator and two flight attendants. There were 29 passengers. One was Chester Wilmot, the Australian journalist and author. There were six airline staff or dependants aboard and one senior captain of British European Airways. The aircraft captain was Alan Gibson who, at 31, was one of the airline's youngest captains.

Some sixteen minutes after take-off, with the aircraft still in its climb at 26,000 feet and off the Island of Elba, Captain Gibson was in radio contact with another company aircraft but his transmission was suddenly cut off. At the same time, fishermen in the waters off Elba heard an explosion and saw wreckage and bodies raining out of the sky. They were able to recover fifteen bodies before night fell. It was clear that Yoke Peter had exploded – but why? The original fleet of ten aircraft was already down to seven and one further one was damaged. The remaining aircraft were immediately grounded. The French also grounded their two Comets. The Royal Canadian Air Force was operating two Comet 1As but did not see fit to ground them.

What had caused the aircraft to explode? To those on board, death was thankfully instantaneous. The Italian pathologist noted that all the bodies recovered had ruptured lungs as a result of immediate and catastrophic cabin de-pressurisation. Broken limbs occurred as the bodies were thrown about the cabin. Many theories were put forward but everybody was groping in the dark. All the remaining aircraft were meticulously examined and many modifications, which were scheduled to be done at some future stage, were put in hand immediately.

There was enormous pressure to get the aircraft back into service for economic, political and prestige reasons, not to mention the potential of a flood of orders for the new models. The Comet 2 with Rolls-Royce Avon engines and range sufficient for South Atlantic crossings was already in production. The stretched Comet 3, which was expected to be

211

able to cross the North Atlantic, was being constructed. On March 23rd, BOAC, the Transport Minister, the Air Registration Board and the Air Safety Board announced the decision to resume Comet services. Wasn't this being rather hasty as the cause of the explosion had not been identified?

Just seventeen days later on April 8th G-ALYY (Yoke Yoke) departed from Rome's Ciampino Airport at 18:25 Zulu bound for Cairo. This aircraft which was on charter to South African Airways, although still in its BOAC colours, was operating as Flight 201. It had a crew of seven and fourteen passengers aboard. At 18:57 it had reported its position as being south of Naples and still climbing. Then there was silence. The pilots of another airliner reported seeing wreckage and bodies in the sea in the appropriate area. In fact five bodies were recovered. The Comet 1s were grounded once more and would never again carry passengers.

The surviving aircraft were put to work to establish what had happened. There were ground tests and flight tests. What the Royal Aircraft Establishment pilots thought about the possibility of becoming victims of another explosion is not known to me but this thought must have been at the back of their minds as they wrung out the aircraft to the full, performing manoeuvres outside the envelope of normal operations. One of the two RAE test pilots involved in this dangerous testing was Roger Topp who a year later was given command of 111 Squadron. Treble One Squadron flew the Hawker Hunter fighter and Topp formed the famous Black Arrows display team which was a yardstick against which all aerobatic teams throughout the world were to be judged. Topp's crowning glory with the team was in 1958 when he led a formation loop of 22 Hunters at the Farnborough display. He was to retire from the Royal Air Force as an Air Commodore.

In the meantime all the various fragments of wreckage of Yoke Peter which had been recovered from the seabed in a major search operation had been flown back to Farnborough where they were placed on a mock-up, to be thoroughly examined piece by piece. Yoke Yoke, on the other hand, had come down in waters which were too deep for any recovery operation.

The RAE committee tasked with solving the riddle was chaired by Arnold Hall who was director of the RAE at the time. His team was in uncharted waters and new evaluation techniques had to be devised, some of which were to become standard for the industry. Hall was an extremely intelligent 'boffin'. He was later to become the Technical Director of Hawker Siddeley and he was a member of the committee which oversaw the development of Concorde.

The answer to the mystery was finally revealed by Yoke Uncle (G-ALYU). This aircraft had also passed 3,500 flight hours. It was taken to Farnborough where the fuselage was placed in a water tank. The wings were re-attached to the fuselage and whilst water pressure testing was applied to the fuselage, the wings were flexed up and down to simulate flight conditions. This testing went on continuously until after 5,546 pressurisation cycles, the top of the cabin failed. As the cabin was in water, there was no explosion and it was relatively easy to determine where the failure had started. It was at one corner of the front ADF 'window' in the roof. This 'window' of non-metallic material was placed there so that the signals of the radio direction finding equipment would not be impeded. What was found was a crack caused by metal-fatigue. This phenomenon was known to engineers but it had never been thought it could occur in a pressure cabin which had been tested beyond all anticipated limits in the first place. The relevant part of Yoke Peter's cabin roof had been found and the same crack was visible. Furthermore, on the upper parts of the wings recovered from Yoke Peter traces of fuselage paint had been found. This indicated that the cabin had failed first. It had split open along the top and the sides had brushed the wings before the latter had failed. The fuselage had burst like a balloon.

This had been a remarkable investigation. At the public inquiry which was held, de Havilland were fully exonerated as they had tested their aircraft thoroughly beyond all known limits before signing off on their product. The lessons learned from the findings helped all other aircraft constructors. From now on, airliners had to be built on a 'fail-safe' system, meaning that in the event of a failure of one part, another part would take the strain and keep the structure intact.

However, this disaster sounded the death-knell of the Comet 1 and had a serious impact on the market for subsequent Comet versions. The lead had vanished. With the Comet gone from the skies, there would not be another passenger jet in service in the western world for another four years and that would be the Comet 4 which just beat the Boeing 707 into service on the prestigious London – New York route in the late summer of 1958.

TAILPIECE

When the French designed the Caravelle short to medium range jet airliner, they paid de Havilland the compliment of using the entire nose and forward fuselage section of the Comet on their design.

From the Comet 2 onwards, all versions of the type had a much thicker fuselage skin. Also all cabin windows became oval in shape, thus avoiding sharp corners which could give rise to cracks forming there, which had been the case with the Comet 1's ADF 'window'.

Although the Comet 2 never entered commercial service, it was operated very successfully by the Royal Air Force, which had a fleet of ten, between 1956 and 1967. These were the bulk of the Comet 2 production batch for which no civilian buyer could be found. Five Comet 4s were later added to the Royal Air Force fleet and these served until 1975.

In airline service the Comet 4 soldiered on until 1981, which was 32 years after the type first flew. This, however, was not the end of the story. The Royal Air Force was looking to replace its ancient fleet of Shackleton maritime reconnaissance aircraft. The British government did not want to buy United States equipment which was the only option immediately available. As a result Hawker Siddeley, which had absorbed de Havilland, proposed a maritime reconnaissance version of the Comet. This was accepted and thus the Nimrod was born. In spite of all the changes, which were considerable, the Nimrod revealed quite clearly its Comet ancestry. The same overall shape was unchanged. The British Aerospace Nimrod, as it was finally known, continued to serve until June 2011 and was then only axed for economy cuts. This meant that the Comet had effectively a 62 year flying career. Those unscrupulous journalists who tried to discredit Ronald Bishop by accusing him of covering up the Comets' failings should have been made to eat their words. Ronald, who died several years ago, proved them wrong and produced an absolute classic aircraft.

My only regret is that I never had the opportunity of flying in one.

GEORGE, WERE YOU DENIED TWICE?

Those who have seen the film *Tora! Tora! Tora!,* which depicts the Japanese raid on Pearl Harbor on 7th December 1941, may recall the sequence showing two United States Army Air Corps Curtiss P-40 fighter aircraft which did manage to get airborne during the raid and which shot down a few of the attacking force. This film tried to follow facts as closely as possible. The incident was genuine. One of the two pilots was a young Second Lieutenant by the name of George Welch.

George was originally George Schwartz and came from a well-to-do family. He came into the world in 1918, the last year of the Great War and as at the time his country had entered the war against Germany and anti-German feeling in the USA was running high, he was re-named Welch, using his mother's maiden name.

He spent three years studying mechanical engineering at Purdue University before enlisting in the US Army Air Corps. On completion of his training, he was posted to Hawaii to fly the new Curtiss P-40B fighter in February 1941.

He had been at an all-night party with friends on the night of 6th December. When the first wave of the Japanese strike force attacked early the following morning, George and Ken Taylor drove to where their dispersed aircraft were parked, rapidly took off and waded in to the enemy aircraft. George was to fly two missions in quick succession and he was officially credited with destroying four enemy aircraft. After the 'Day of Infamy', America needed a hero to counterbalance all the incompetence and complacency which had been shown in not being ready for the attack. They had that hero in George Welch who was sent back to the States to join the campaign for War Bonds. The story runs that he was put forward for the Medal of Honor, the highest US military decoration, but that his commanding officer vetoed the application because George had taken off without permission. If that story is true, George was certainly denied once. He received another medal instead but at least was presented to President Roosevelt.

After being paraded around the United States, George was finally back in action in New Guinea. The European Theatre of Operations had the highest priority for the American forces and the Pacific Theatre had to make do with what it could get. George was assigned to the Bell P-39 Airacobra, an interceptor which was so poor that the Royal Air Force had rejected it without a second thought. Certainly this aircraft looked modern – it was probably the first fighter in service with a nosewheel undercarriage – but it had no engine supercharger and performed hopelessly above 12,000 feet. The engine was placed behind the pilot and the shaft from the engine to the propeller ran in a tunnel between the pilot's legs. Furthermore, access to the cockpit, with its poor vision, was by means of a car type door which would make bailing out in an emergency almost impossible. Nevertheless George was able to add some more victories to his total whilst flying the Airacobra. If nothing else, this proved what an excellent pilot could do with poor equipment.

Finally George got the transfer which he had pleaded for. He was assigned to a unit flying the Lockheed P-38 Lightning in New Guinea. Now he had a superb combat aircraft with plenty of engine power, plenty of fire-power and plenty of range. George made the most of the Lightning's potential and he increased his score to sixteen victories.

Living in New Guinea in primitive conditions and in the middle of a brutal war was certainly no sinecure and tropical illnesses of all kinds were rampant. George had to be invalided out in 1943 with a severe bout of malaria. By then he had risen to the rank of Major and had flown 348 missions. He had more than fulfilled his duty.

In early 1944 he retired from the US Army Air Forces and was recruited by North American Aviation as a test pilot. He honed his test piloting skills on the P-51 Mustang, which was probably the best fighter of the Second World War. He performed some of the test work on North American's first jet fighter, the FJ-1 Fury for the US Navy, and was then chosen to be chief test pilot for the F-86 Sabre fighter for the US Air Force, which the US Army Air Forces had now become.

From 1942 all Air Force secret military testing had been carried out at Muroc Field, a large dry lake bed next to Rogers Dry Lake in the south of California. This site was way out in the 'boondocks' and was ideal for secret work. The only attraction for bachelor pilots on the base was Pancho Barnes's Fly Inn, which sported other names as well. Pancho was very much a larger-than-life lady who could out-drink and out-swear most men. She loved the company of her fly-boys and had a particular soft spot for Chuck Yeager.

Into this scenario came George Welch and the prototype Sabre. The Bell X-1 rocket-powered research aircraft was also transported there for testing. Chuck Yeager had been appointed as chief test pilot for the X-1 project. Both of these projects belonged to the US Air Force. The Bell X-1 was specifically produced to explore supersonic flight, which was venturing into the unknown. When it became apparent that the new Sabre fighter might be able to exceed the speed of sound in a dive, the top brass apparently made it clear that it would be debarred from even trying so that the X-1 would be able to claim the credit of being the first aircraft to break the so-called 'sound barrier'.

Muroc was to provide the backdrop for the controversy over which man was first to fly faster than the speed of sound. The official record is that it was Chuck Yeager on 14th October 1947. Any claims prior to 1947 can be discounted for lack of hard evidence. Yeager's performance was at least confirmed by instruments on the ground.

The XP-86 prototype of the Sabre was ready for its first flight at Muroc on 1st October 1947. With Welch aboard, the fighter took off but there were problems retracting the undercarriage. When the wheels finally did retract, George is reported to have climbed aloft and to have entered a maximum performance power dive. He is said to have stated that in the dive his air speed indicator suddenly stuck at one point although the aircraft was still accelerating and that then the needle suddenly jumped forward. Apparently a sonic boom was heard by people at Pancho Barnes's ranch. Did George beat the barrier and go supersonic? Many experts say that the prototype's engine was not capable of developing sufficient power for the aircraft to reach the speed of sound in a dive. North American's own records indicate that the prototype reached Mach 0.93 or 93% of the speed of sound in a power dive. However, that said, the British de Havilland 108 Swallow is recorded as achieving the speed of sound in a dive in September 1948. That aircraft had no more power than the prototype Sabre and was perhaps less aerodynamically efficient.

Fighter pilots are known for having big egos and for living on the edge. If they were not so, they would not be good at their job. However, no matter how much a macho George Welch may have been, I cannot envisage him trying to fly into the unknown on the first flight of a totally unproven aircraft, particularly as he knew that he had problems with the landing gear. New aircraft are tested in small incremental steps so that problems can be fixed at an early stage. To reinforce this point, the Bell XS-1 prototype had made 37 flights performed by the manufacturer before it was turned over to the Air Force. When Yeager finally exceeded the speed of sound on 14th October 1947, it was the aircraft's 50th flight.

It is also reported that the XP-86 went supersonic in another power dive just before Yeager's record flight on 14th October. So, was George the first or wasn't he? Welch's performance could not be measured from the ground, Yeager's could. The X-1 was a pure research aircraft and the first version finally achieved a speed of Mach 1.45 and an altitude of 69,000 feet. The Sabre was to become an outstanding fighter aircraft, capable of achieving marginal supersonic speed in a dive. It was built in thousands and served with many air forces. The prototype *officially* exceeded the speed of sound for the first time on 26th April 1948 with Welch at the controls.

When the Sabre came up against the Soviet MiG-15 fighter in the Korean War, George was sent to Korea by North America to help Air Force pilots to get the best out of their aircraft. It must be remembered that at the time he was a civilian. It is reported that he took part in some sorties and scored some victories. If he did, this was quite unofficial and there are no records to substantiate it.

On his return to the USA, George prepared for his next project which was to be flight testing the Sabre's successor, the F-100 Super Sabre. He took the prototype into the air for the first time in May 1953. This aircraft was much more potent and was the first American combat aircraft to be capable of supersonic speed in level flight.

I find it a great pity that such a prominent pilot as Bob Hoover writes so disparagingly about George Welch. Hoover, who was also a North American test pilot on the F-100 project, has recorded he told Welch that the F-100 lacked stability in the yawing and rolling planes and tried to dissuade him from pushing the aircraft to its limits. Chuck Yeager, who also flew the early F-100, stated much the same thing. To him, George was simply 'Wheaties Welch' because he featured in a commercial for that well-known breakfast cereal. Was this criticism just a matter of hindsight, or was George not one to take advice? Like any new aircraft the F-100 had its teething troubles.

On 12th October 1954 George took up an F-100 and dived it to Mach 1.55. When he attempted to recover, the aircraft started to roll and yaw and went unstable. George ejected successfully but because of the high airspeed his parachute shredded when it opened and he did not survive the ensuing impact with the ground. George was gone, taking one or two secrets with him.

The F-100s stability problem was cured with the design of a larger tail fin and some changes to the wing. The Super Sabre then went on to enjoy a long and successful service career both with the US Air Force and a handful of other air forces.

Today, more than fifty years after his death, there are various individuals campaigning for a posthumous Medal of Honor for George and there are various individuals campaigning for recognition that George was the first pilot to exceed the speed of sound. I cannot see either of these claims being successful. George was well decorated and well rewarded for his work as a military pilot. There is no hard evidence to show conclusively that he exceeded the speed of sound before Yeager did. Also, if George did succeed in shooting down a few MIG-15s over Korea and made sure that other pilots got the credit, good for him. It is better to let matters rest as they are.

ALAS POOR YURI, TOO SOON YOU FELL

(with apologies to William Shakespeare – 'Hamlet', Act V, Scene I)

1957 was named as World Geophysical Year. The United States had announced its intention of putting the first man-made satellite into orbit around the Earth in that year. The 'Cold War' between the United States and Western Europe on the one side and the Soviet Bloc on the other side had been running for twelve years. In the ideological and propaganda war, the Soviets were determined to show that technologically they were ahead.

The Western World did not have a clue what the Soviets were up to. That part of the world was behind a closed door. It became a severe embarrassment to the USA when on October 4th 1957 the Soviets put Sputnik 1 into Earth orbit. Whereas the Americans had told the world what they were going to do, the Russians had been working away in great secrecy. They had sacrificed a larger, better instrumented satellite in the race to be first. Sputnik 1 weighed about the same as an average US adult male today. Its scientific research equipment had been reduced to the minimum. Its 'beep –beep' radio signal could be picked up by any radio 'ham' near to its orbit path. Sputnik 1 transmitted for 22 days and after three months burned up as it re-entered the atmosphere. However it had achieved its main objective which was a propaganda coup. The USA was deeply humiliated. The Vanguard rocket which was supposed to launch the world's first man-made satellite was a miserable failure. Not only was it behind schedule but it blew up on the launch pad with the world watching. 'US Sputnik goes Phutnik' ran the headline in Britain's most popular newspaper, the *Daily Mirror*.

The Russians then aimed at putting a dog into orbit. Laika, a three-year-old stray, was sent up on board Sputnik 2 in

November 1957. This was hastily done. The poor dog died on the fourth orbit because of overheating in the capsule. The Russians did not reveal the truth until 2002. Then one of the mission scientists admitted that it had been wrong to try such an experiment. As is widely known today, the USSR did not only risk the lives of animals but they destroyed the lives of human beings as well in the search for global superiority. The Americans used rhesus monkeys in the Mercury programme but these animals were always brought back alive.

The Americans did not get a satellite into orbit until the end of January 1958, using a Jupiter rocket instead of Vanguard. In spite of the fact that Explorer 1 had much better instrumentation for space research and that it stayed in orbit for much longer, it had been completely eclipsed by Sputnik 1. However the space race between the two 'Super Powers' was well and truly launched. The next target was to put a man into orbit.

The U.S. Air Force launched the 'Man in Space Soonest' programme in an effort to beat the Soviets. One of the zany ideas was to use the North American X-15 rocket aircraft, which had already exceeded an altitude of 300,000 feet, and attach it to a rocket to launch it into orbit. Neil Armstrong, the first man to walk on the Moon in 1969, was one of the selected candidates for the programme. This programme was scrapped in 1958 and replaced by NASA's 'Mercury' programme. With all the testing and development work attached to the 'Mercury' programme, it did not manage to put an American into Earth orbit until February 1962 when John Glenn completed three orbits. It was too late as the Soviets had once again achieved a major propaganda coup.

'The first man/person to . . .' is an over-used expression. In several cases the title has been conferred upon the wrong person. It is not always known with certainty who was first in a particular field. Who was the first person to use fire in a controlled fashion? Who was the first person to imagine the use of the wheel? Who was the first person to develop some sort of common language or of writing? The answers to these questions have been lost forever. In more recent times it has become easier to bestow accolades of this sort with a greater feeling of certitude but very little can be 100% proven. For instance, was Orville Wright really the first man to fly a powered aircraft in December 1903? There were witnesses and there was photographic evidence, but was this conclusive? Other claimants did not have such strong evidence, but does this rule them out? We have also to remember that Galileo was imprisoned for daring to suggest that the Earth rotated around the Sun, whereas the Pope, who knew better than anybody else, maintained that the Sun rotated around the Earth. Even today there is such a thing as the Flat Earth Society, but I digress.

United States confidence was once more completely shattered when on 12th April 1961 the USSR put a man into Earth orbit and successfully brought him back. I was in my last year of school at the time, having just secured a place at university and I can clearly remember the pictures on television of Yuri Gagarin being triumphantly paraded through Moscow. The Americans had been humiliated yet again.

There is no disputing who was the first human to 'slip the surly bonds of Earth'. It was Yuri Gagarin.

He was only 26 years old at the time. He completed one orbit of the Earth and then landed successfully. At no stage did he have any control over what was happening. He was riding a cannon ball – but unlike Baron Münchhausen he was inside it. The Russians claimed that he had secret instructions to follow if anything went wrong. Can you imagine an astronaut tearing open sealed instructions and then having to interpret them in just a few minutes? This is just laughable. Everything was pre-programmed but this should take nothing away from his achievement. He lived to tell the tale (although we do not know for certain if there had been any previous failures, either unmanned or manned). His single orbit took 108 minutes. Shakespeare was proved wrong. His Puck in a *Midsummer*

Night's Dream claimed that he would 'put a girdle round about the Earth in forty minutes'. The real thing took somewhat longer.

For me what comes out of Yuri Gagarin's story is his apparent extraordinary modesty. From being an unknown pilot, he became a world super-star overnight. That he seemed to survive the spot-lights and remain normal was, to my mind, a great achievement. This is the version which we are given. He was under very close escort all the time he was performing his goodwill tours outside the Soviet Union.

Yuri came from a peasant background. When the Germans invaded Russia he was only seven. His family was forced out of its home and had to live in a mud hut. His brother and sister were deported to labour camps in Poland. Yuri had a great sense of fun but worked hard and managed to become a fighter pilot. In 1960 he was among twenty candidates selected for the space programme. He was then chosen for that first historic space flight. Most of his peers thought he was the best candidate. His small stature, 5ft 2 (1.57 metres) probably helped as space in the Vostok capsule was very limited.

The Soviet authorities made a wise choice since afterwards he was expected to be the perfect ambassador for the USSR. Yuri never let his masters down even though it would have been very easy for him to defect or to become an alcoholic wreck because of the pressures on him. He toured the world and flashed his winning smile everywhere and was loved for it. The story which I like best, and I have no cause to doubt its authenticity, was when Yuri visited Manchester. It was typical Manchester weather with the rain pouring down. Yuri was scheduled to drive through the city centre where large crowds were assembled. He decided that since all those who had come to see him would be thoroughly soaked, he would not be any different and he rode through the streets in an open-topped car with no protection.

After all the world touring and the razz-matazz, the Soviet leaders decided that Yuri was too big an asset to lose and he was removed from the space programme. What happened thereafter is not very clear and my bet is that the whole truth will never be known. On March 27th 1968 it was reported that Yuri had died in a crash during a training mission. I well remember that the initial reaction of the Western press was to state that this was a cover-up for suicide, just as the Nazis had tried to cover up Ernst Udet's suicide. However it was later agreed by all and sundry that Yuri had died when his MiG-15UTI trainer had crashed, claiming the life of his 'instructor' as well. The Soviets stated that they would thoroughly examine the accident to establish the cause. None of the arguments put forward convinces me. Why was Yuri flying in such an obsolete trainer in the first place? He was apparently a very competent pilot. I strongly suspect that there has been some cover-up.

Yuri left this world but a few days after his 34th birthday. All he had to his credit in the eyes of the world was just one orbit of the Earth in space. However, what a trip that had been! He had scored one big first in the history of man and he will always be remembered for that. I hope that the Soviets looked after his family in an appropriate manner. This was the least they could do for their hero.

A FRENCH NINE ELEVEN

Nine Eleven has left an indelible mark on the calendar in the United States. The terrorist atrocities committed in New York and Washington, DC, will be remembered by most of us for the rest of our lives. France also had its 'Nine Eleven' which saw the destruction of an airliner and the death of all those on board. However, the French incident occurred many years before on September 11th 1968 and outside of the south-east corner of France it never seems to have attracted much interest. On the other hand, locally this accident is still very much a live issue as the real cause has never been confirmed.

After the British had produced the world's first commercial jet airliner in the shape of the de Havilland Comet, the French produced the second, the Sud Caravelle. The intervening Soviet aircraft, the Tupolev TU-104, can be discounted because it was simply a development of a bomber aircraft. Although the Boeing 707 was to enter passenger service before the Caravelle, it first flew a long time after the maiden flight of the Caravelle.

Air France put the Caravelle into service in May 1959 and this aircraft quickly became the backbone of the French fleet, operating domestic, European and slightly longer routes. It was a good, solid design which enjoyed an excellent safety record. The final number of airframes built was 282 and the type continued to operate commercially until 2004.

The Caravelles in Air France's fleet were initially Mark Is but these were upgraded to become Mark IIIs. The majority of the fleet was delivered new as Mark IIIs. It is perhaps surprising that all of the fleet retained Rolls-Royce Avon turbojets since more fuel-efficient turbofan engines were available and were fitted to the Caravelles of several airlines, including those of Air France's domestic subsidiary, Air Inter. The aircraft involved in the September 11th 1968 incident was number 244 off the production line and had only entered service in May of that year. It was registered as F-BOHB and, like most of its sister aircraft in the Air France fleet, it bore the name of a former French province, in this case *Béarn*. At the time of its fatal accident, F-BOHB had flown a mere 1,001 hours and completed 579 take-off and landing cycles. The only incident worthy of note prior to the crash is that the right engine had been replaced on September 4th due to damage in the original engine.

F-BOHB was positioned to fly the short route between Ajaccio, on the island of Corsica, and Nice, on the mainland, in the morning of September 11th. The distance is only 140 statute miles which hardly calls for the performance of an aircraft like the Caravelle. Eighty-nine passengers boarded the aircraft, so the cabin was almost completely full. There was a crew of six. The captain had over 8,800 flight hours. The co-pilot had nearly 4,300 flight hours. The flight engineer had over 4,300 flight hours. There were three cabin attendants. The youngest had only joined the Company in April and had 139 flight hours. All of the crew had been off duty prior to the flight for more than twelve hours.

There had been the mandatory pre-flight external inspection before the passengers boarded and nothing unusual had been noted. At 10:09 local time the aircraft took off from Ajaccio's runway 21 and started its climb up to cruise altitude which, because of the short distance to fly, was only 16,000 feet. The time spent in the cruise was only about six minutes. The flight proceeded normally until 10:30 when the aircraft was descending between 9,000 and 7,000 feet. The pilots were already in contact with Marseilles Control and they reported that they were having problems (not identified) and requested a direct approach to Nice Airport. This was authorised and they were handed off to Nice Approach. At 10:31:20 the pilots informed Nice that they had problems and 25 seconds later they stated that they had an on-board fire and declared an emergency. They were given priority for a direct approach. At 10:32:28 the pilots announced: 'We are going to crash if this continues'. After that there was no further communication from the Caravelle. The blip of the aircraft disappeared from the Nice Airport radar screens just after 10:33 when the aircraft was approaching Cap d'Antibes and a mere twenty nautical miles from the airport.

One cannot imagine how those on board would have reacted in those last few fatal minutes. Certainly many of the passengers would have panicked and probably blocked the aisle. Some would have remained calm, knowing there was nothing they could do. Most would have realised that they were about to die. Nobody, either young or old, would wish to be faced with such a situation.

An airborne search was immediately activated and floating debris was spotted at 12:22. The first body was recovered at 13:06 local time. It was soon apparent, because of the small area of floating debris, that the aircraft had impacted the sea at a steep angle. This was borne out by the later searches on the sea bed. Not only had the angle been steep but the speed had been high and the impact would have killed all on board.

The local weather at the time of the accident was not good as a cold front was passing through and there were low banks of cloud about. Nevertheless, one of the last transmissions from the pilots had been that they had the coast in sight.

The sea bed of the Mediterranean drops very quickly from the coast in this area. Although the Caravelle impacted the water about fifteen miles from the nearest point of land, the wreckage lay at a depth of 7,500 feet.

Four dredging operations were carried out to recover wreckage. The first began on November 12th and failed to locate where the wreckage was lying. The second took place in March 1969 and, with the assistance of an under-water camera, the remains were located. The third operation took place in November/December 1969. The fourth took place in

March/April 1971 and this produced the best results. In total more than eight tons of wreckage was recovered but as the impact had been very severe, all the pieces were small. It can be asked why these salvage operations were so far apart. This probably served to fuel the rumour, which was already spreading, of a cover-up.

The experts who studied the tape of the voice communications between the aircraft and the ground controllers were inclined to think the pilots had their oxygen masks on in the last few minutes. This could only indicate smoke in the cockpit. The flight recorder was recovered but because of long immersion in the water its information could not be interpreted.

A committee of investigation was set up in accordance with French law. The members were all civil aviation specialists. They had the powers to consult with any organisations or individuals as they deemed necessary. I do not think for one moment that this committee did not carry out a thorough job. The question is: were they given all the information which they needed?

It was not long after the accident that the rumour began to circulate that the Caravelle had been hit by a missile. Apparently French military exercises were being held between France and Corsica on that day. On the anniversary of the crash our local television channel reminds us each year of the tragedy. I have seen an interview with a former Air France pilot who stated that one day on this very route, he saw a missile pass in front of his aircraft. I have seen an interview with a former employee of the French Ministry of Defence who stated, 'It was one of our missiles'.

Relatives of some of the victims have been fighting a civil action in the French Courts for years. All they want to discover is the truth. Recent successive French Ministers of Defence have stated openly that there was no cover-up and that no missiles were fired that day.

To return to the official inquiry, the Committee submitted its final report in December 1972, more than four years after the accident. The debris which had been recovered clearly showed that there had been an on-board fire which was most intense between stations 50 and 53, the area of the toilet and the galley. As far as could be established, the fire had not spread forwards beyond station 45. The fire extinguishers in the fire zone had not been used. Did smoke prevent the cabin staff being able to use them? One perturbing discovery was the finding of empty gun cartridge cases in what had been the toilet area. It was however concluded by a ballistics expert that none of these had been fired from a gun.

One possible source of the fire was the water heater which was in an enclosed space in the toilet. There had already been one case of a water heater causing a fire aboard another Caravelle. In the present case, neither the water heater nor parts of it were recovered from the wreckage. If the fire had begun in this enclosed space, it would not have been detected before it became more general.

The Caravelle was the first jet airliner to have its engines mounted on the fuselage sides at the rear. It was in this area of the fuselage that the fire was most intense. However, none of the parts of the engines which were recovered showed any traces of fire and as the Committee quite rightly pointed out, if there had been a problem with either engine, the crew on the flight deck would have known immediately.

The Committee did examine the hypothesis of the aircraft being struck by a missile. The Minister of Defence formally wrote on November 19th that no missiles had been fired in the zone where the Caravelle was flying.

The conclusions of the final report are textually as follows (my translation).

The destruction of F-BOHB was caused by a violent impact with the surface of the sea, at considerable speed and at a great angle, an impact which followed the loss of control of the aircraft by the pilots.

This loss of control was caused by a fire which started at the rear of the aircraft in the zone of the right toilet and the galley. It has not been possible to establish the direct cause of the loss of control with any certainty: it may be linked to the physical incapacity of the pilots caused by toxic gases or be the invasion of the cockpit area by passengers. The commission has concluded that the cause of the loss of F-BOHB was a fire in the cabin, a fire whose origins could not be determined.

Now, more than forty years later, the children of some of the victims continue to pursue their civil action in the French Courts.

I am hesitant to subscribe to the missile theory. Even if a missile struck the Caravelle with an inert warhead, surely it would have caused immediate and catastrophic results. If it had been a radar-guided missile, such a collision would have broken up the aircraft immediately. If it had been a heat-seeking missile, it would have struck one of the engines and the pilots would have immediately known this and announced it over the radio. The fact that the aircraft flew for a further two minutes after the initial emergency call would seem to discount the missile theory. The theory refuses to go away, however. Two French journalists have recently published a book on the issue. *State Secret* claims that evidence was deliberately destroyed by the Ministry of Defence and that several people were told to keep their mouths shut.

Just outside the perimeter of Nice Airport there is a small public garden where the famous Promenade des Anglais begins. In that garden there is a memorial to those who perished in the crash. The memorial is almost hidden from view, as if it were an embarrassment. It was unveiled in 1998, exactly thirty years after the event. A brief ceremony of remembrance is held there each year.

Will this tragedy remain forever on the long list of unexplained disasters?

SCOTTY, YOU SHOULD HAVE STAYED ON THE GROUND
STEVE, YOU SHOULD HAVE BEEN MORE CAREFUL

Albert Scott Crossfield was born in October 1921. He served with the United States Navy in the Second World War both as an instructor and a fighter pilot although he was never to experience combat. He was more interested in the how and why of flying than in actual flying *per se* and after the war, resumed his university studies and took degrees in aeronautical engineering. In 1950 he was lucky enough to be selected as an aeronautical research pilot for the National Advisory Committee for Aeronautics (this was the NACA which preceded today's NASA). He was based at Edwards Air Force Base which until January 1950 had been known as Muroc. At that time, Edwards was *the* place to be as a test pilot as the rocket-powered research aircraft were based there. Scotty, as he was known to his friends, flew the Bell X-1 research aircraft which had officially become the first aircraft in the world to fly faster than sound back in October 1947. He also flew the Douglas Skyrocket rocket-powered research aircraft. Both of these types had very limited endurance and were carried aloft slung underneath the belly of a Boeing B-29 Superfortress bomber to be released at altitude. The rocket motor would be fired, accelerating the aircraft to incredible speeds but after just a few minutes the fuel would be exhausted and the pilot would have to glide down to land on a runway marked out on the bed of a dry lake. This was dangerous work, not only because the aircraft might become unstable at very high speeds but also because the rocket fuels in use were very volatile. Explosions had occurred killing more than one pilot. The Bell X-I was an Army project and the Douglas Skyrocket was a Navy project. Both services wanted to lead the way but eventually the Air Force, as the Army Air Force had been renamed in 1947, would prevail.

On 20th November 1953 Scotty was flying the Skyrocket and on that day became the first pilot in the world to exceed twice the speed of sound. He had pushed the Skyrocket considerably beyond its calculated never-exceed-speed. Scotty's fame was short-lived since less than a month later the legendary Chuck Yeager had exceeded 2.4 times the speed of sound in the Bell X-1A, almost losing his life in the process because of instability problems. Yeager and his 'buddy', Bob Hoover, had worked together as Army pilots on the Bell X-1 project from the start. Was there a feeling of antagonism on their part towards a Navy pilot? They did not appear to like Scotty. No doubt that Yeager and Hoover were excellent stick-and-rudder pilots but Scotty was much more of a scientist than they were. Also Scotty had experienced more flights in rocket-powered aircraft than Yeager and Hoover had.

In 1955 Scotty moved to North American Aviation to become chief engineering test pilot. He was to become involved with the X-15 rocket-powered research aircraft from the very beginning. The brilliant X-15 was to become the highest performing manned aircraft of all time. It was carried aloft under the wing of a Boeing B-52 Stratofortress and was launched at altitude. It would ultimately attain 6.7 times the speed of sound and an altitude of nearly 315,000 feet, which was credited as being a genuine flight into space. These performances were established in the mid-twentieth century and they may never be surpassed. Scotty flew the X-15 on all of its initial flights until it was delivered to the Air Force. He reached three times the speed of sound on one of his fourteen flights in the aircraft. He also performed the first flight when the aircraft was fitted with its definitive XLR99 engine.

The X-15 programme was to mark the end of Scotty's career

as a test pilot but he continued to work in aviation until his retirement in 1993. In the 1950s he had been selected as one of nine pilots with rocket-engine experience for the Air Force's Man in Space Soonest (MISS) programme but this project was cancelled in 1958 to be replaced by NASA's Project Mercury which put the first American astronauts into orbit. One of Scotty's fellow candidates in the MISS programme was Neil Armstrong who was also to fly the X-15 and who will be remembered for ever as the first human to set foot on the Moon. Scotty had probably always hoped to make it into space but he never did.

He gave of his free time generously and was always prepared to discuss anything connected with aviation.

Long after he had ceased to fly professionally he had bought a single-engined Cessna 210 light aircraft to take him from place to place. When he had acquired it, it was nearly thirty years old. On the 17th April 2006, Scotty flew it to Prattville in Alabama. He was due to give a speech to officer recruits at Maxwell Air Force Base the next day. He was now 84 years of age and although his eyesight and hearing were not what they had been, he was in good enough shape to be medically qualified to exercise his pilot's licence. On this trip he met up with an old friend, Judy Rice. He confided to her that when it was time for him to die, he didn't want to go in the bath or in his bed. He wanted to go out in his plane. These turned out to be prophetic words.

He was to fly back from Prattville in Alabama to his home town of Herndon in Virginia. When he checked out the weather, he could see that there was convective activity over Arkansas. He could have waited until later in the day but the air space on his route was going to be blocked for some time because of a Presidential flight so he chose to depart at nine in the morning. By eleven, he had reached the foothills of the Smoky Mountains and he came face to face with massive thunderstorms. There was no voice communication after that and a search the next day located the wreckage of the Cessna. It had broken up in

235

extreme turbulence and that was the end of Scotty. The resulting enquiry blamed both the pilot and the air traffic controller. The report stated that the pilot had failed to obtain updated en-route weather information and that the controller had been negligent in failing to provide adverse weather avoidance assistance.

It is ironic that a pilot who as a young man had put his life on the line so many times should be caught out in a situation which any sensible pilot would have avoided. There is an old saying about flying. 'It is better to be on the ground wishing you were flying, than to be flying and wishing you were on the ground'. Scotty had unwittingly fulfilled his death wish. It also came out in the report that technically Scotty was flying illegally as he was on instruments in the clouds without having had enough instrument practice in the recent past to remain current. I do not regard this violation as much of an issue. The currency rule is there to protect most private pilots. Scotty had thousands of hours of experience and I am sure that his instrument flying skills were unimpaired.

I was saddened to learn of Scotty's death but he had taken an unnecessary risk and was made to pay for it. At least he had lived a full life and was not cut down in his prime like several of his test pilot colleagues.

***

Scotty's passing reminded me of the demise of 'Steve' Wittman in April 1995 in similar circumstances.

Whereas most of the pilots about whom I have chosen to write were well-known to aviation enthusiasts, Steve Wittman was a lesser-known figure. He was born as Sylvester Wittman in Wisconsin in April 1904. That he ever became a pilot at all is quite amazing since a childhood illness robbed him of most of the vision in one of his eyes. He learnt to fly and built his first aircraft in 1924, just three years after the birth of Scotty. Steve was a leading pylon racing pilot from the 1930s to the 1970s. He was to compete in more pylon races than any other pilot, although his name never became as prominent as, say, Jimmy

Doolittle or Roscoe Turner. He also designed and built aircraft, both for racing and for leisure flying. He competed in his last race in 1989 at the age of 85. One of his designs, the Tailwind, has become a popular home-built aircraft and has been produced in some numbers.

In addition to his racing and building activities, 'Witt', as his friends called him (the name Steve was a journalist's error, but it stuck), operated Oshkosh Airport from 1931 to 1969. During the Second World War his flying school which was based there gave initial training to Army pilots. His name is perpetuated in his airport which became Wittman Regional Airport when he retired as the operator. This is where the huge EAA (Experimental Aircraft Association) Air Venture fly-in is held each year and Steve was instrumental in helping to bring the EAA event there in 1970 as he became one of the first members of that organisation. The fly-in at Oshkosh has to be the Mecca for any serious aviation enthusiast. There is no aeronautical gathering anywhere in the world on the same scale.

Steve's first wife had died in 1991 after fifty years of marriage. She was also a pilot and Steve had taught her to fly. The next year he re-married, to a lady whom he had also taught to fly. He already had his 91st birthday behind him when he flew with his second wife from his winter home in Florida to his summer home in Oshkosh. En route his aircraft, which had been designed and built by him and which was a development of the Tailwind, broke up in flight. The accident report concluded that the cause of the break-up was wing/aileron flutter caused by the fabric wing covering coming adrift. The report stated that the fabric had not been applied correctly. Steve should have been more careful whilst building his aircraft. He had survived many accidents in the past and had seen several other pilots plunge to their deaths in races. He was now made to pay the ultimate price for his apparent negligence.

ERRARE HUMANUM EST . . .

Since we, as human beings, are imperfect, we all make mistakes. By the process of reasoning we try to avoid making major mistakes. Minor mistakes can often be of no consequence. There are, however, activities where any error, if not quickly corrected, can be fatal and one of those is flying. Flying is, after all, an unnatural activity for man. We were not created to be able to leave the ground just as we were not created to be able to cross oceans, or any large stretches of water. Man's ingenuity has finally made certain distant dreams become reality. Being transported from one place to another by air is now taken for granted by millions of people, although that capability has been with us for less than a century.

Airliners have improved out of all recognition since the first commercial services were operated after the First World War. Flying as an airline passenger is statistically safer than many daily activities. Natural disasters, road accidents and accidents in the home kill far more people than airline accidents. The latter category hits the headlines every time because of the numbers involved.

Aircraft can be destroyed by natural phenomena or by structural failure. Such happenings are usually beyond the control of the pilots. What I am concerned with here are those accidents, fatal or otherwise, caused by human error.

As a pilot and aviation enthusiast I am fascinated by reports of aircraft accidents. This is not because of any liking for the macabre. I am interested in the 'why' behind any accident. We should be able to learn something from each accident so that there should be no repetition. The introduction of 'fail safe' structures in the 1950s following the loss of de Havilland Comet airliners through metal fatigue is a good example of this. If I had the possibility of having my time over again, I should probably like to have had a career as an aircraft accident investigator and specialist.

In the world of general aviation, meaning, basically, private flying as opposed to commercial flying, the main causes of pilot induced fatal accidents are: running out of fuel; and flying into limited visibility (for example, clouds) without having the experience or the equipment to be able to continue the flight 'on instruments' without any external references.

Commercial pilots are all instrument rated so no airliner or commercial aircraft should come to grief because of limited visibility in today's world, but it does happen as I shall show. No commercial aircraft should run out of fuel but that also occasionally happens and the aircraft becomes a rather inefficient glider which will end up by digging a big hole in the ground if there is not a convenient airport near at hand where the pilot can pull off an emergency landing without power.

Out of fuel...

It is the responsibility of an aircraft captain to ensure that there is sufficient fuel on board, not only to be able to reach the planned destination but also to be able to reach a suitable alternate airport in case of any diversion, for whatever reason. The fuel reserve also has to take into account taxi time before departure, which can be long at a busy airport if the duty runway is changed, and for any 'holding' or circling around prior to landing because of air traffic considerations. There are other factors, but these are the major ones. If the captain miscalculates, the error is down to him. If the fuel gauges are unreliable, he is just unlucky. But what if the fuel supplier delivers the wrong quantity of fuel to the aircraft? This would certainly constitute a human error and it can happen.

In July 1983 an Air Canada Boeing 767 on a domestic flight with 61 passengers on board ran out of fuel whilst in the cruise at 41,000 feet. There was nothing in the company's emergency manual about how to deal with this situation because it was considered impossible that both engines would quit. As a result of having no power, the hydraulic system was dead and therefore flaps could not be lowered and there was no guarantee that the undercarriage would lock down. The two pilots performed an amazing feat in getting the airliner down on a runway at a disused military base. Having no flaps, they had to land at a much greater speed than usual. Reverse thrust was not available to slow the aircraft down because the engines were dead. Nevertheless a safe landing was completed and there were no fatalities. The problem had arisen because of faulty fuel gauges and the company's new policy of having fuel weight expressed in metric and not in imperial units. The fuel required calculation was correctly made in kilograms but the fuel uplifted was in pounds, resulting in less than half the quantity required being supplied.

In August 2001 an Air Transat Airbus A330 with 293 passengers on board was on a flight from Toronto to Lisbon. Both engines flamed out over the Atlantic. Fortunately the aircraft had been routed close to the Azores. Once again two very skilful pilots managed to perform an engine out landing without the benefit of flaps. There were no fatalities. The cause of the problem was a fuel leak due to the fitting of an incorrect part on a fuel line. In other words, it was a maintenance error. If the Azores had not been conveniently located within gliding distance, there would almost certainly have been no survivors.

Limited visibility…

Modern airliners have the equipment to be able to land in conditions of zero visibility. Operators prefer not to use this ability for reasons of safety. What happens if the equipment fails, for example? If an airliner lands in complete zero visibility (the densest of fogs), the pilots will be able to see nothing. How will they know if they veer off the runway? How will they be able to taxi to the terminal? In general, when flying a precision instrument approach, if the pilots cannot see anything of the runway when they are at 200 feet above the ground (which is called the decision height), they execute what is called a 'missed approach' and they climb up and circle to try again, or if the weather does not improve, they head off for the alternate airport if better conditions are forecast there.

In March 2001 a chartered Gulfstream III, one of the largest of the executive jets, with a crew of three and fifteen passengers took off from Los Angeles International Airport bound for the ski-resort of Aspen in Colorado. The passengers had a dinner appointment in Aspen and one of them was not prepared to allow the pilots to divert if the weather was bad at the destination. He had already made this clear to the operator before the aircraft took off. Some of the passengers turned up late. The result was that the pilots would be pushed to reach Aspen before nightfall.

As Aspen is surrounded by mountains (the runway is at an altitude of 7,815 feet), it is illegal to land there flying an instrument approach at night. Also, because of noise abatement requirements, the aircraft would have to land before 18:58 local time. The scenario was building for a disaster. To add to this, there was no precision instrument approach available for the runway in use. The crew would have to execute what is known as a VOR/DME approach, which, being less precise, requires the runway to be identified visually much further away and at a greater altitude than on a precision approach. In this case, at three nautical miles from the touch down zone on the runway, the aircraft had to be nearly 2,600 feet above the elevation of the runway. If it descended below that altitude and the pilots could not see the runway, they were required to execute a 'missed approach'.

The weather in Aspen was not good with intermittent snow showers. The pilots could hear other pilots ahead of them

241

calling missed approaches. They were also up against the night time curfew. They should have tried the approach once and if they could not see the runway, they should have gone to the alternate. However, there was the one passenger, presumably the leader of the party, who would not accept that. The aircraft did not have a flight data recorder (the famous black box, which is actually orange in colour) since this is not mandatory on aircraft flying non-scheduled services but it did have a cockpit voice recorder. What the recorder picked up was that one passenger was installed in the stowable jump-seat behind the pilots before the approach to land. Was this the belligerent passenger who was demanding that they landed in Aspen and nowhere else?

During the approach the flight was already beyond the latest permissible landing time. The pilots went below the minimum descent altitude and then called the tower to declare that they had the runway in sight. What they picked up were the lights of a road and not the runway lights. The aircraft impacted with the ground and all aboard were instantly killed.

This accident constitutes one of the most senseless series of errors that I have read about. The pilots were clearly browbeaten by a customer because he had paid a huge fee to be in Aspen for his special dinner. Big spender paid the price and made sure that everybody died with him.

In November 2004, a Gulfstream III was on its way early in the morning from Love Field, Dallas, to William P. Hobby Airport, Houston. Apart from the two pilots, there was only a flight attendant aboard as the aircraft was flying the short distance to pick up former President of the USA, George Bush Senior.

Both pilots were highly experienced and had 19,000 flight hours each. The visibility was very poor that morning and an ILS approach to the duty runway was called for. The captain was flying the aircraft and the first officer was monitoring the situation.

The first officer failed to set the correct frequency for the ILS system. He kept informing the captain that they were above the glideslope whereas they were below it all the way down. Things did not look right to the captain but the first officer kept telling him that everything was okay. At this point, they should have abandoned the approach, sorted the matter out and gone round again. Finally the first officer saw his error and dialled in the correct frequency for the ILS transmitters. By now it was too late. The ground proximity warning sounded and the aircraft hit a light pole well short of the runway and broke up. There were no survivors.

Beware of macho pilots…

'There are old pilots and there are bold pilots but there are no old, bold pilots.' Thus runs an old aviation cliché. Bold pilots should never be let anywhere near a passenger-carrying aircraft. They may kill themselves but they should not take anybody with them. Here are two examples of what macho pilots have done.

In March 1976 a Lockheed JetStar, one of the first executive jets to enter service, had been purchased after a long lay-up in a hangar at Midway Airport, Chicago. Two pilots who were apparently qualified on the type arrived to ferry the aircraft to its new owner in California.

This JetStar was a Model 6. The pilots only had experience of the Model 8 which had more powerful engines. They did not even bother to take a test flight to check that everything was functioning normally. Midway Airport has relatively short runways and the pilots were advised to take off at a relatively light weight and to take on more fuel at an intermediate stop on the way.

The captain would have none of this. He ordered the tanks to be filled to the brims so that he could fly to the destination non-

243

stop. He then agreed to take two passengers and their baggage with him. The loaded weight of the aircraft was to be crucial. Had the captain computed the runway length needed taking into account aircraft weight and external temperature? Had he properly examined the performance figures of the Model 6?

The aircraft failed to become airborne. When it was clear to the captain that he was running out of runway, he abandoned the take-off but it was too late. The aircraft ran off the end of the runway, crossed a road and slammed into a concrete wall. Nobody survived the impact and the ensuing fireball.

In October 2004 a Bombardier CRJ-200 of Pinnacle Airlines was to be ferried from Little Rock to Minneapolis where it was to pick up passengers the next day. As the aircraft was empty and it was late in the evening, the captain decided that he would see if en route the CRJ-200 could reach its maximum operating ceiling of 41,000 feet which was well above the flight levels used for normal operations. Their flight plan had been filed with a cruise altitude of 33,000 feet. The cockpit voice recorder revealed that the two pilots were treating this as a piece of fun.

They reached 41,000 feet with the stall warner sounding and the stick pusher trying to force down the nose. The airspeed was too low and both engines flamed out. The aircraft then stalled but was recovered with a slight loss of altitude. The captain advised the controller that they had lost an engine and were trying to re-start it..

At that stage, there were six airports close enough to them to be reached in the glide. The operating manual stated that a speed of 240 knots was needed to keep the engine cores turning to facilitate a re-start. The pilots never reached this speed in the descent. Both engines became core-locked and a speed of 300 knots would be needed for a successful re-start. It was only fourteen minutes after the engines had flamed out that the pilots declared that they had lost both engines. By then it was too late and they failed to reach Jefferson City Airport which was their last option.

An expensive airliner had been lost because two pilots had decided to try things outside of what they were trained for. They paid for their stupidity. The official report mentioned their 'unprofessional behaviour' and their 'poor airmanship'. Was the captain trying to impress his first officer, who only had 760 hours of flight time?

Distractions...

The hallmark of a good flight deck crew is that it can perform efficiently when under pressure. This is where good training and good team work really pay off. When the chips are down, an airline passenger would be comforted to know that he has a Captain Chesley Sullenberger and a First Officer Jeff Skiles up front who will coolly put the airliner down in the Hudson River without any casualties instead of it ending up as a smoking piece of wreckage and with no survivors.

When the airlines realised that it was safer to have two pilots on board and two sets of controls and instruments, the captain of the aircraft became God. The poor co-pilot was tasked to do all the menial chores which were beneath the dignity of his captain. The co-pilot, if he was unlucky, would only learn by observing. Thankfully the God and his servant relationship finally changed. Co-pilots began to receive their share of the flying, the take-offs and the landings. Duties were divided between who was doing the flying and who was monitoring and checking. The captain was still the captain and carried the ultimate responsibility so he could always take command at any time. This relative democratisation of the flight deck created problems of its own. Pilot and co-pilot could become too friendly and indulge in unnecessary chatter, thus becoming distracted and missing something important.

A classic example of this occurred in August 2006 when a CRJ-100 operated by Comair came to grief at Blue Grass Airport,

Lexington, Kentucky. Of the crew of three and the 47 passengers, there was just one survivor, the co-pilot who was at the controls and who became a paraplegic for the rest of his life. The aircraft was scheduled to fly to Atlanta in Georgia. It was to be an early morning departure before sun-up. The company had two of its Regional Jets parked on the ramp and our flight crew started the day well by boarding the wrong aircraft. They were advised of this by a member of the ground crew and then went to the correct aircraft. Both pilots were experienced. The captain had 4,710 hours and the first officer had 6,564 hours. Both clearly got along well with each other and were discussing career possibilities. They were advised that the departure runway was 22 and they confirmed this. They set the heading bugs on their heading indicators correctly. When boarding was completed and the aircraft was ready to depart, the pilots repeated their clearance instructions. They only had a short taxi to the threshold of runway 22 and to get there, they had to cross the threshold of runway 26. The captain performed the taxi and during this, the two pilots continued their discussion about career prospects. The captain stopped the aircraft short of runway 26 and handed control to the first officer who was to fly this leg. Clearance for take-off was given. The first officer turned on to runway 26. Neither pilot realised that they had turned on to the wrong runway. They failed to check the runway alignment with their heading indicators and their heading bugs which would have revealed the error immediately. The first officer remarked it was strange that the runway lights were not on. This was another warning which was ignored. Full power was applied and the take-off roll began. Unfortunately runway 26 was too short for the required performance. The rotation speed needed would come after rolling 3,744 feet but the runway was only 3,500 feet long. The airliner failed to become airborne and impacted a belt of trees beyond the airport.

There was only one controller working the night shift whereas there should have been two. In consequence, the controller had to deal with all ground and tower functions and work the radar screens as well. When he had cleared this aircraft for take off, he went back to his radar watch. If he had looked out of the window, he would have seen the airliner turning on to the wrong runway. He was not at fault over this, but he could have prevented the disaster.

Back in December 1972 a very new TriStar of Eastern Airlines' fleet was about to complete an uneventful flight from New York to Miami. There was a crew of thirteen and 163 passengers aboard. In the last half hour of the day the airliner was on its final approach. When the undercarriage was lowered there was no green light on the instrument panel to indicate that the nosewheel gear was down and locked. The captain informed the tower and was authorised to break off the approach and head out west so that the problem could be examined. He was instructed to maintain 2,000 feet and at that altitude he engaged the autopilot.

The pilots and the flight engineer and an airline maintenance engineer, who happened to be on board, tried to solve the problem. It could just have been a burned out light bulb and the gear might well be down and locked. Unfortunately all of those on the flight deck concentrated on the nose gear problem and nobody was monitoring the instruments. The aircraft gradually lost altitude – apparently a certain pressure on the control column would disengage the autopilot until the pressure was released. Either the captain or the first officer was inadvertently knocking the control column whilst looking around and trying to fix the problem. Each time the aircraft lost 200 feet before the autopilot levelled it.

Eight minutes after declaring the problem, the captain sensed that something was wrong. The first officer declared that they must still be at 2,000 feet, without looking at his instruments. The aircraft then impacted the ground in the Everglades swamps. Without the swamp to soften the impact, all aboard would have died. In the event there were 75 lucky survivors.

The accident report concluded that the cause of the accident was the failure of the pilots to monitor their flight instruments.

I conclude this section with a personal confession. The highest point in my time as a pilot was to earn an instrument rating which would enable me to fly like an airline pilot in weather conditions where the ground or the horizon are not visible. I decided to take this rating just to set myself a target, knowing that I would never use it in a real situation in the future.

During my flight training, I was at times seriously overloaded. I always had an instructor with me so I was not alone. I was, however, beyond normal retirement age and it showed. What a younger person could accomplish with ease was much more difficult for me. At the start of each flight my instructor would give me a simulated clearance which informed me of what to do after taking off. I had to write this down and read it back, just as a professional pilot would have to. I had become quite proficient at flying precisely on instruments alone. This skill used up most of my brain power and I was therefore struggling with everything else. If I then had to handle radio transmissions or work out a new course in my head, I was just swamped.

A few days prior to my check ride with the examiner, I had one of the last 'dry runs' with my instructor. I copied down the clearance before we took off and read it back.

'Read back correct,' my instructor said. I took off, and knowing that the airport to which we were headed was south of us, and therefore to my right, I began a right turn.

'What on earth are you doing?' my instructor asked. 'You were asked to turn left, you copied it down and you read it back correctly.' I felt very small. I had no excuses for my stupidity.

'Do that on the check ride with the examiner, and you have failed,' I was told. Back on the ground I focussed on what I had to do to pass. If I concentrated on making sure I knew right from left, I would blot out something else. My mental salvation was to double-check at every decision point. It did not really matter if I took a few seconds longer. On the flight test, I did just that and I qualified for the rating.

What I learnt from this was how to cope with the pressure on me. I found my own solution by analysing the issue and figuring my way out of it. In the airline business, all known areas of confusion are progressively flagged until guidelines which are effective are found. To implement these guidelines takes time and, in any case, when it comes down to just a few seconds to make the correct decision, how easy is it to be right or wrong? The following example illustrates the fine line between right and wrong.

In January 1989 a newly introduced British Midland Boeing 737-400 with a crew of eight and 118 passengers was on its way from London to Belfast late in the evening. At 35,000 feet the left engine failed. The pilots acted swiftly but, because of no conclusive evidence from the engine instruments, they shut down the right engine (the wrong one) and set up for an emergency landing at East Midlands Airport. If they had been able to listen to passengers and flight attendants in the cabin, they would have been told that the problem was with the left engine. From the cabin, they could all see which engine was playing up as it was belching flames.

Having closed down the good engine, the pilots were unable to make it to East Midlands Airport and the aircraft impacted the ground after crossing a motorway within sight of the runway. 47 people lost their lives in the ensuing crash, which has become known as the Kegworth Disaster.

The Boeing 737-400 had different systems from the Boeing 737-300 which British Midland had been operating. The official report concluded that what had happened was 'outside the training or experience' of the pilots. This must mean that either Boeing and/or British Midland were to blame for poor training.

The risk of collision...

In spite of the large number of aircraft flying today and the increasing numbers of areas where there is very heavy traffic around major airports, the risk of two aircraft sharing the same minute piece of sky at the same moment is very small. This is because flying takes place in a three dimensional environment, unlike other forms of transport which operate in a two dimensional one. However, organisations like insurance companies are very conscious of the laws of possibility which can inform you of how remote your chances are of winning the jackpot on the lotto or of being struck by lightning or of two aircraft colliding in flight.

The first recorded collision of two commercial aircraft was in April 1922 when a British aircraft carrying only mail hit a French aircraft carrying three passengers. Both aircraft were on the London to Paris route. The weather was bad and both pilots, coming from opposite directions, were following the same railway line over northern France. Given the low cruising speed of the respective aircraft, it is surprising that they managed to hit each other, but they did and all seven lives were lost.

When radio became sufficiently developed for transmitters and receivers to be installed in airliners in the 1930s, ground controllers were put into place at major airports. They could advise inbound pilots of local weather conditions and could assist with arriving and departing flights. Radio beams were then utilised to assist with landings in bad weather. The instrument landing technique was already functioning in simplified form before the start of the Second World War. The next big contribution to flight safety was made by radar, whereby a ground-based observer could plot where traffic up aloft was in relation to his position.

What followed was the development of airways, or highways in the sky, and sections of airspace only open to qualifying traffic. This all took time. The USA was a leader in all of this.

In June 1956 a Douglas DC-7 of United Airlines collided with a Lockheed Super Constellation of Trans World Airlines over the Grand Canyon at 21,000 feet. The combined 117 passengers and 11 crewmembers all perished. Both aircraft had left Los Angeles International Airport within three minutes of each other. The DC-7 was headed for Chicago and the Super Constellation for Kansas City. There were no airways and no controlled airspace in that area. Both aircraft were trying to dodge towering cumulus clouds and had no idea that they were sharing the same little piece of sky. The possibility of this collision was very slight, but it happened. A collision between an airliner and a military jet the following year led to the Federal Aviation Act of 1958 which put the control of all of United States airspace in the hands of the FAA.

Today, above 18,000 feet all air traffic operates under instrument flight rules (IFR), under radar surveillance, and flying in accordance with a flight plan which has been filed with air traffic control. As the flight progresses, the pilots are handed off from one controller to another. This makes flying at altitude very safe. At least it should be so, but then we come to the language problem. English is the international language of the air. If all pilots and all controllers used it all the time, many accidents and near-misses would have been avoided. Unfortunately some countries do not enforce this. France is a glaring and unnecessary exception. I flew for a few years from Cannes Airport. I acquired a French pilot's licence which meant taking all exams in French. I used French with all local controllers *because it was expected of me*. Cannes handles a lot of international business jet traffic. The controllers there are perfectly competent in English and will switch to it for any international flight. What is the point of them doing this yet continuing to monitor local traffic in French at the same time? It is obvious that any pilot should know what other traffic is being asked to do when it is in close proximity. Too often, the local now what the jet pilot is doing or being asked to ‸rsa. To my mind this is unacceptable. On one of ‸ourses in France I got to know a pleasant young ‸ who was first officer on an Air France Airbus A340. He wou‸ scuttle away if any English speaking person approached him because he had no confidence in his ability to speak English. Just imagine what might happen if a controller gave him an instruction which was outside of the usual English phrases that he understood. I rest my case.

For me, the most glaring example of an accident where a language barrier played a part was the mid-air collision between a British Airways Trident and an Inex-Adria Douglas DC-9 over Zagreb in September 1976. The Trident was on its way from London to Istanbul and the DC-9 was climbing out of Split bound for Cologne. All 176 persons on both aircraft lost their lives. The Trident was cruising at 33,000 feet towards the Zagreb VOR beacon. The captain of the DC-9 had requested a climb to 35,000 feet which would put his flight into the zone belonging to the upper-air controller at Zagreb, who was dealing with the Trident. The upper-air controller was being seriously overworked and had no extra support, which was badly needed. The DC-9 hand-off to his zone was done without his immediate knowledge. When he became aware of what had been done, he saw two blips merging on his radar screen. He had precious little time in which to react. He called the DC-9 in the Serbo-Croat language to stop his climb immediately. I do not think that in fact the language error was much of an issue. Neither aircraft had been told to look out for other traffic. The DC-9 was already above 33,000 feet when the call came to stop the ascent. The result of ground control's frantic call was to bring it back to 33,000 feet, directly into the path of the Trident. The poor controller was found guilty and was imprisoned only to be released later. He had to decide immediately on what to do and if he had not called for the DC-9 to stop its climb, there would have been no collision.

If flights at high altitude are relatively well protecte, safety factor decreases nearer the ground. At busy maj., airports where there is heavy traffic arriving and departing all the time during the day, trying to keep aircraft out of each other's way becomes much more difficult. For this reason no aircraft may enter a so-called terminal area without being in radio contact with a controller. However, the risk of human error is always there.

Take the case of Pacific Southwest Airlines' Boeing 727 heading in to land at Lindbergh Field, San Diego, California, in September 1978. Whilst it was approaching, a small four-seater Cessna 172 was carrying out instrument approach practice on the single runway. The pilot was 'hooded' so that he could not look outside. His instructor was the only one on board able to look outside. Both aircraft were being correctly monitored by the controller in the tower. The Boeing pilots were instructed to look for the Cessna and to confirm that they had it in sight. They confirmed this. They were now expected to keep it in sight but they failed to do so. What they were being asked to do was, in fact, quite difficult. Cockpit windows are small with the result that airline pilots have a very restricted view outside. These windows are deliberately small because of the dictates of a pressure cabin. Spotting another aircraft above the horizon is quite easy if it is in the field of view but looking for an aircraft below the horizon, where it can easily merge with the ground below, is difficult.

The pilots should have informed the controller that they had lost sight of the Cessna. They reasoned that it was now behind them and out of their way. They continued their descent and collided with the small aircraft. The impact completely destroyed the Cessna but also disabled the control surfaces on one wing of the Boeing which caused it to plummet to the ground. All 135 passengers and crew on the Boeing, both airmen in the Cessna and seven people on the ground lost their lives.

ent investigation established that the cause of
as the failure of the pilots aboard the Boeing to
a in sight. However, local surveillance radar was
ime, so why were the pilots of the Boeing asked to
do som. g in addition when they had their hands full with
the approach? A controller monitoring the radar screens could
surely have kept the aircraft apart.

The concern today is not so much trying to avoid collisions in
the air, since airliners are now fitted with collision warning
systems, but rather trying to avoid collisions on the ground. The
aim is to prevent runway incursions where an aircraft taxiing on
the ground fails to respond correctly to the taxi instructions
received and then either turns on to or crosses a runway directly
in the path of a departing or arriving aircraft, which can do
almost nothing to prevent a collision.

The worst accident in aviation occurred in March 1977 not
because of a runway incursion but because one aircraft tried to
take off from a runway in very poor visibility and could not see
another aircraft taxiing towards it on the same runway. The
accident which resulted in 583 deaths took place at Tenerife
North Airport. The airport was congested because of several
flights which had been diverted there. The taxiway to the single
runway had several aircraft parked on it so departing aircraft
would have to back-track down the runway before turning
around at the end before beginning the take-off roll. The
visibility was deteriorating rapidly as a KLM Boeing 747 was
cleared to back-track down the runway. Following it, some
distance behind, was a Pan American Boeing 747. The Pan
American aircraft was instructed to take a specific turn off so
that it would be clear of the runway to enable the KLM aircraft
to depart. As the visibility worsened, the Pan American aircraft
missed its turn-off point. The KLM Boeing was now in position
to take off and the captain believed that he had a take-off
clearance. This was not so but the phraseology used by the
controller had been confusing. Naturally, the KLM captain

believed that the Pan American aircraft was now clear ᵕ runway. The extremely poor visibility meant that he could nᵕ confirm this visually.

He began his take-off roll. At the same time, the Pan American captain tried to report that he was still on the runway but he 'stepped on' a transmission from the controller to the KLM aircraft. Therefore neither transmission was audible. At the last moment the Pan American crew could see the lights of the KLM aircraft emerging from the gloom. They tried to clear the runway but had run out of time and only managed to get their aircraft broadside-on to the KLM machine. The KLM captain pulled back on the yoke early to try to vault over the other aircraft. The KLM 747 sliced into the top of the Pan American 747. The disaster was complete.

As if by a miracle, the nose section of the Pan American 747 was spared as the aircraft had turned just far enough. 61 souls aboard survived the crash.

There was no ground radar at Tenerife North at the time as it was only a regional airport. In consequence the controller in the tower could see neither aircraft, and the two aircraft could not see each other. In those circumstances all aircraft movements should have been stopped until visibility improved.

And, finally, what about landing at the wrong airport?

On average, once a year an airliner will land at the wrong destination. Often the intended arrival airport and the actual arrival airport are close together, but how can air traffic control allow this? Are they asleep, are the pilots asleep? These are incidents and not accidents as there is no loss of life and there are no detailed reports published as to what actually happened. This is wrong. Such incidents should be fully documented so that they do not happen again. Also such incidents are potentially highly dangerous.

.998 a NorthWest Airlines DC-10 from Detroit
o land at Frankfurt, Germany, with 241
board. It was handed on progressively from
ndon and then to Brussels Air Traffic Control. At
some poi... controller decided that the flight's destination was
Brussels. Nobody as far as I know has come clean on this error.
The result was that instead of the flight continuing at high
altitude over Belgian territory on its way to Germany, it was
instructed to descend to be fed into approach control at Brussels.
The pilots contacted Brussels approach and referred to it as
'Frankfurt' on more than one occasion. Brussels never
questioned this. The instrument landing runway assigned to the
flight was in the same direction as the Frankfurt runway but the
radio frequency was, of course, different. Passengers in the
cabin could see from the presentation on the overhead screens
that their destination had been switched to Brussels. The
message was not passed to the pilots who eventually landed in
Brussels. This was a hugely embarrassing incident and nobody
seems to have accepted the blame. If there had been any loss of
life, you can bet that heads would have rolled.

So, is airline flying safe?

Yes, but it could always be safer because human error can never
be eliminated. I have flown 1,600 hours as an airline passenger,
covering nearly 700,000 miles. I have never felt that I was in
danger. The worst incidents which I have experienced have
been a few cancelled departures, a couple of go-arounds at the
destination airport and two diversions to the alternate airport
because of the weather. Am I put off flying because of the
accidents which I have looked into? Not one little bit. I could be
carried off by something else tomorrow without any prior
warning. I shall continue to fly as a passenger or as a pilot as
long as I can – and I shall enjoy the experience!

EPILOGUE
When it is time to go . . .

When it is time for me to go, I do not expect to end up in that Big Hangar in the Sky as I remain unconvinced that there is any existence after death. Provided that I know when my last few minutes have arrived, I shall imagine a final approach and landing in an aircraft and at a place which are both dear to me.

I may only be a low-time pilot but I have always felt a thrill at being able to make a good final approach and then to pull off a good landing. For me, this is the ultimate piloting skill. I have honed my skills at a small airport in central Florida over the past fifteen years. Every visit there has given me a sense of fulfilment. I have not counted the number of my landings there but the total is approaching a thousand, split between landing towards the east and towards the west on opposite ends of the single 3,600 foot runway. My preferred approach is to the east, heading towards the Atlantic coast.

My small airport is full of interesting aircraft. Apart from having two flight training schools, it is a haven for private pilots, several of whom have built their own aircraft there. There are publicity-banner-towing aircraft which parade their messages up and down the beaches. There is also helicopter activity. The runway may be relatively short but it is more than ample for the small aircraft which I fly. I have on more than one occasion seen Cessna light business jets land there and, at the heavy end of the scale, I have witnessed the departure of a Douglas DC-3. The airport does not have a control tower so each pilot has to announce his intentions to other fliers in the vicinity over the radio using a common assigned frequency. There are some aircraft using the facility which are not fitted with a radio. They have to be particularly alert to other traffic.

I have landed in several different types of aircraft at this airport. Most of the time I have been either piloting a Cessna 152 or 172 or one of the Piper Cherokee family. The aircraft which I have chosen for my fantasy final approach is a Piper Warrior II, a member of the Cherokee family. I have only to close my eyes to see this particular aircraft. My Warrior was built in 1978 so it has been training pilots for well over thirty years. It is the only individual aircraft in which I have exceeded fifty hours of pilot time and in addition it helped me through my instrument rating check-ride, so it is very special to me. No type of aircraft is perfect. I do not like the long floor-mounted flap lever on the Warrior and prefer the little tab on the Cessna's instrument panel which operates the flaps electrically. I also do not like the fact that the only door in the Warrior is on the other side of the aircraft from me, which would be a hindrance in an emergency. The Cessnas have a nice big door right next to the pilot. The Warrior does, however, have a neat engine control pedestal which is much more user-friendly than the plunger controls on the Cessna. Finally, the Warrior, by virtue of its low wing, gives the pilot an excellent view looking into the turn whereas the high wing of the Cessna blots out the view which the pilot needs to have in the turn.

It is my last flight and I have been up for a local flight of about an hour. I know the local area like the back of my hand. I have kept clear of controlled airspace and have been manoeuvring around doing slow flight, stalls, steep turns and the like just to keep up my skills and now it is time to return. I took off to the east but then reversed course and have been flying in the practice area to the west of the airport. The weather is clear and the air is calm. I am anticipating landing on the easterly runway but before planning my approach, I tune in to the automated weather observation service which is transmitted from the airport. I am given the current information about the wind – still out of the east at five knots, the temperature, and the altimeter setting. I look at the Kollsman window in my

258

altimeter. The setting has not changed in the last hour. I then switch to the common traffic frequency for my airport and listen in. There is one aircraft in the pattern. He has just called left downwind for the east runway. If he continues to do patterns I shall keep my eyes open for him. In any case I continue to keep a good scan outside. There is often military traffic heading into or climbing out from the military air base close at hand and they will not be communicating on my radio frequency.

I plan in advance how I am going to join the landing pattern. As I am to the west of the airport, I could just do a long, straight, final approach, but this is not the preferred method. The American pilot's 'bible' recommends as best practice joining the downwind leg of the pattern from a position above pattern height and at an angle of 45° to the leg so as to be well clear of all aircraft in the pattern and to be able to see them clearly. It is not always easy to see small aircraft even when near to them and finding them only comes with practice.

I am at 3,000 feet and five miles west of the airport. I shall descend gradually to 2,000 feet, cross over the top of the airport at that altitude and then steer towards some blue coloured fuel tanks on the edge of the lagoon. Those tanks are regularly used as an initial reporting point for an approach to the east runway. When I have arrived there I shall have descended to 1,500 feet and shall turn to make my approach to the downwind leg. I am looking out and listening. No other aircraft has reported its position and the aircraft which was in the pattern has made its final landing. I can also see no other traffic. It looks as if I have the air space all to myself. Before starting my descent I re-set my heading indicator against the reading on the magnetic compass.

The minutes pass. I am about to fly over the blue tanks and I announce my position and my planned entry to the pattern. I can see no other traffic and nobody else is on the radio frequency. I turn on my landing light as I head for the pattern. Any extra lighting makes me more visible and is a useful deterrent against birds. My rotating beacon light on the top of the fin and my wing-tip strobe lights have been on all the time. There are plenty of big birds of prey like turkey vultures in this area and a collision with one of them could be very damaging. I adjust my descent and my heading to hit the downwind leg mid-field at exactly 1,000 feet and ninety knots and then the whole sequence of events speeds up considerably.

Whilst downwind I set the mixture control to rich, turn on the fuel pump, check that the fuel is on and that I am on the fullest tank. I decide whether to use carburettor heat or not. Here in Florida I have never needed it. I make sure that I am tracking parallel to the runway and close enough to it so that if I have an engine failure I shall be able to glide in. Abeam the threshold of the runway I retard the throttle and put down one stage of flap. When I have 75 knots indicated I start to descend and trim to keep that airspeed. By now I am almost at the bank of the river (which is in reality part of the lagoon network). It is time to make a left turn for base lag and I make my radio call.

On base leg I go for a second stage of flaps and maintain 75 knots using power to adjust my rate of descent. I am looking towards the runway and getting ready for the left turn to final before I reach an imaginary line extending the runway centre-line. Before I turn, I look right to be sure no aircraft is coming in unannounced on long final.

I make my turn and call final on the radio. I now have the four PAPI lights by the side of the runway to assist with my approach. If I have two red lights and two white lights, I am right on the correct glide path. My mind goes back to that old training jingle: 'Red over white, you're all right. White over white, you're out of sight. Red over red, you're dead.' I put down the final stage of flap. At about 200 feet I add a bit of power knowing that with the uneven heating of the sun on the ground below, there is usually some sink at this point.

I continue down to the runway threshold and everything looks good. I am on the centre-line. I start to flare at about 15 feet with the throttle at idle and progressively raise the nose. I can hear the feeble reedy note of the stall warning 'horn' and just afterwards, there it is – a little squeak as the tyres brush the runway surface and the main wheels start to spin. I keep the nose high until it descends of its own accord and then the nose wheel gently makes contact with the surface. There is plenty of runway ahead of me. I do not need to brake. The aircraft slows of its own accord and I take the next convenient taxiway. Beyond the hold short lines I make my final radio call to announce that I am clear of the runway and now all I have to do is to taxi back to the ramp, shut down and secure the aircraft.

I wonder what the 'airport bums' made of my landing? There are usually a few of the old fliers sitting on the veranda watching every approach and take-off. They have considerably more hours and experience than I shall ever achieve. I know that some of them score landings on a scale of 0 to 10. Apparently they never award a 10. I know that on occasion I have been awarded an 8 and that is good enough for me. Maybe today I would have scored a 9. And that thought marks the end of my final final. A job well finished.

info@goldenford.co.uk
www.goldenford.co.uk